Sanctuary

Ember Markussen

THE STORY PRIESTESS

For Chloe and Kyle.

May you always find sanctuary within your own hearts.

And for Richard,

who gave me sanctuary and guided me home.

Music is Magic

Prologue

Wind carves whispers into the darkness of the forest.

Shuddering leaves tap the shoulder of their neighbor,
Urging "pass it on, pass it on".
Branch by branch they carry unspoken words
Like a message in a bottle.
They run into the veins of each green finger,
Pass into the sap of the wood and slide
down
down
down
Trunks swallow it in the sweet agony of thirst.
It spills slowly through
To the roots,
Traveling towards the mycelium
Where eager mushrooms unleash their spores
To send the message further afield,
Once more on the wings of the wind.

The circle of oaks and elders sways,

West to east

Right to left

To a song only they could hear.

They stretch from the subterranean network to the wide space of the sky.

Moonlight washes over the little copse,

Turning green

To silver

To white,

A forest bathed in milk.

Inhale.

Exhale.

Inhale.

Exhale.

Pass it on, pass it on.

She is coming.

May 1, 2024

From the Law Offices of Decker and Webb

Solace Spring, Massachusetts

Dear Ms. Whit,

Following the passing of Mr. Matthew "Matty" Harrison in February of this year, we are executing his final will and testament. As he left no family behind, Matty left his remaining funds to his friends and neighbors here in Solace Spring. However, his residence and the attached four room inn, as well as the nine acres of land surrounding them — collectively known as The Sanctuary — he chose to leave to you. In his will, Matthew expressed the hope that you and your children, "his favorite guests", would become caretakers of his beloved property.

As you currently reside in Southern California, we assume you will be selling the property to a local resident or rental company here, and would be happy to assist you in turning it over and consigning the remainder of Mr. Harrison's personal possessions. We do recommend you start this process immediately. If, of course, you plan to keep the house, inn, and acreage, and use it as a full or part time residence, then we look forward to welcoming you to Solace Spring.

Sincerely,
Cooper Webb, Esquire

Summer

Chapter One

I t was raining.

It never rained in California. That was the whole point of it, the reason everyone paid a million dollars for an ugly house with no backyard, prepackaged food, and a community of bikini-clad women of indeterminate age (and the men trying to impress them). This was paradise. And it never rained in paradise.

But as Elizabeth haphazardly threw the detritus of their last night into a trash bag, she reflected on how appropriate it was. The half-hearted deluge of misty drops from weighty clouds, letting go of what was too heavy to hold onto. She could relate. Now, of course, she would have to alter her perception of precipitation. Where they were going, a little rain was...well, normal. She wondered if the weather was welcoming them to their new home. Or whether California was crying as they left.

"Cory!"

Where was he? Certainly not helping. His sister, Lily, was already folding her sleeping bag without complaint, having dressed and brushed and eaten a perfectly portioned healthy breakfast. Whether this was because she was the textbook first-born child or because she knew her mother was already on the verge of a breakdown, Elizabeth wasn't sure, but for this morning it really didn't matter. Two of the three Whits were ready to leave. Cory's bed was empty. But Elizabeth was at a loss as to where her son had gone.

Unless...

She thrust open the front door and peered through the rain to the roof over the garage. Sure enough, there was Cory, sitting on the slick terra cotta tiles on top of the house, an angry expression on his face.

His only expression these days.

Elizabeth tried to soften her voice as she swallowed her frustration. They didn't need a fight, not now, not on their last hour of their last day. She took careful steps onto the patio, stood still, and let the waves of rage from her teenage son roll past her. *Don't react*, she reminded herself. *Don't engage.* Just the proximity to his feelings was enough to raise her heart rate. Deep breathing for a count of 4...3...2...1...

"Cor, come on down and have some breakfast."

"I'm not hungry."

"It's a long flight. You should eat something."

"I'm not hungry."

"Cory -"

"NO."

She closed her mouth. That was the line, and it wasn't worth crossing it now. It rarely was. Elizabeth closed her eyes and slowed her breath again, trying to stop herself from saying something in a temper. *Just let it go*, she reminded herself. When she opened her eyes again she saw Lily in the front window, watching her for the telltale signs of a looming argument. Elizabeth gave a tight smile, and went back inside, slamming the door as she went.

"It's OK, Mom, I already packed up his sleeping bag."

"Lily, it's not your job to pick up after him."

"We don't need to push him this morning. There's enough to do." Lily turned around and began picking up more trash, as her mother had been doing. Elizabeth saw her own burdens on her daughter's sagging shoulders. Lily had been looking after Cory for as long as Elizabeth could remember, and while she had assumed this would wear off in time, it never had. One child's happiness traded for another.

But that was why they were doing this. To get a fresh start for all of them. So she left Lily to it and began her final check of the place that had been their home for the past ten years.

Lily's sky blue bedroom was immaculate, except perhaps for the sparkles caught in her baseboards. Gone were the little fairy statues she had kept lined up by her window since the age of six. Gone, too, were the photos of friends, affixed to the wall with scotch tape year after year after year. That part hurt a little. Elizabeth knew that her daughter could befriend a brick wall, but she had never done a big move and the loss of her support system would be a significant adjustment. The closet was bare of the generations of sundresses that had been Lily's chosen uniform. Who knew when they would be used again? A nail over the door remained, sticking out like a sentry, where her lucky horseshoe had been hung in a place of honor. Elizabeth silently prayed the luck would come with them on that bent bit of iron.

Cory's room was ... still dirty. Somehow, despite the medical grade cleaning she had completed, the sense of decay remained. Even at the end, his room had to be his way. Robot parts and medieval daggers intermixed with vast quantities of carefully sketched blueprints and notations. Always a maker, Cory had created nothing in the six months of his father's absence. The toolbox his grandfather had given him was gone, but the scratches he left on the floor while using it remained.

She remembered how Tyler had yelled when he found them. A dusty shadow showed the outline of his trunk, where he kept his dark clothes and his preferred variety of dragon pendants. There were no photos on his walls, for there were no friends in Cory's life. Elizabeth was seized by a desperate desire to scour the floors, the window sills, the walls. To erase every trace of wrong that had made its home in her son's world. Instead, she closed the door on this room of pain, and made her way down the hallway to her last stop.

She knew there was nothing left in her own bedroom, having checked it several times, but it seemed like she should take one last look. It was odd, how little she felt as she surveyed these walls. No memories came to her at all ... she had rarely been in the room, except to sleep. Most of her time was spent in the kitchen making meals, or driving the kids around, or taking calls from the living room as she juggled odd jobs with odd hours so she could be home doing the things that needed doing. This room ... this room had been Tyler's. Not that he was ever in it, either. He had worked long hours, and spent the rest of his time in front of the television, trying not to think about work. But he had chosen the paint, the window treatment, the art, the furniture. He wanted it to look just right. A successful man's room, with a successful man's wife to grace it. The room had been empty before he died. And empty it remained.

As she turned to leave, their mirror caught her eye. Years ago, it had reflected a slim woman with blond hair and blue eyes, excited to begin life with her family. Now, the frame contained one slumped over, middle-aged mother, flat brown hair framing a puffy face and a falling jawline. Elizabeth barely recognized herself. She had no idea if that other woman would ever return to life. But she knew that she wouldn't be back here ever again.

Time to go.

Elizabeth closed the door, and called for a car before the house swallowed her again.

***

Their first trip to The Sanctuary had been when Lily was ten years old, and fascinated with being a witch. She had wanted to see Salem, and Elizabeth, knowing nothing of Massachusetts geography, had booked a tiny bed and breakfast in Solace Spring, three hours' drive from the Atlantic Coast and one hour from anyplace that could properly be called a town. Truth be told, she was happier for the accident. She had been hungry for some time away from people. Her body ached for silence, and trees, and something she couldn't define. The concept of "home" lay buried somewhere in the mass of unnamed feelings, but she sold Tyler on visions of fall leaves and pumpkin fields, and off they all went to the Berkshires for a week in October. After a week, the pull was so strong that they cried real tears when they left. Elizabeth found herself booking return trips, again and again, for the next five years.

At The Sanctuary, her children seemed to gain new life. Sullen Cory spent hours in the woods, building shelters and mapping creeks. His sister followed streams to frog ponds and photographed salamanders emerging from their wet dens of leaves and mud. The earth beneath their fingernails buried their preteen worries and woes, and they came back contented and peaceful each evening.

For her part, Elizabeth simply...sat. Next to a tree in the forest, or in the garden by the pond. She would bring a book, which would go unread, or paints to wash watery greens and yellows over an empty page. But mostly, she sat. On their first night she would make a vast batch of soup, which she could reheat every evening thereafter.

Everyone survived on minestrone and peanut butter sandwiches, and whatever fruits they grabbed from the local farmstand on their drive in from the airport. They rarely left the premises. Elizabeth wanted The Sanctuary's magic to swallow her completely, and she found that she needed little else.

Tyler never came with them.

Matty, the owner of the inn, brought over fresh muffins and coffee every morning and sat to chat while they all ate. He taught the children how to track deer and build fires, complimenting them on their every creation. Unaccustomed to such attention and adoration, both kids became attached to the old man. They followed him around the gardens and forests, and learned how to spot beaver lodges and spider hollows, how to remove sick trees and use a sledge to drag them back for firewood. When they arrived home they would regale their California friends with their tales of triumph, but it was clear that the charm of rural living was lost on their suburban counterparts. Elizabeth realized, though the confused children did not, that The Sanctuary only appealed to a select few. Matty had explained to them once that it chose who returned, and she believed him wholeheartedly. It must have chosen him as well, for she had never met anyone happier with his home.

A widower of many years, Matty had divided the house into two — a section for his guests, and a section for himself. During his days he gardened and whittled on the back deck, overlooking his acres of chaotic wilderness, an intersection between man and nature. At night he filled his pot-bellied stove with firewood, covered himself with the afghan his late wife had made for him on their last anniversary, perhaps watched a classic movie, and often fell asleep on the couch. That was where he had taken his last breath four months ago, at the tender age of 90, with a life chronicled in flowers.

Elizabeth wouldn't have known of his passing until their next vacation, were it not for the letter she received from his attorney. As Matty had no next of kin, his will had been carefully curated to satisfy his infinite generosity. His wooden art would go to a local gallery. His collection of typewriters, a local museum. His small savings would benefit the schools that served Solace Spring. And The Sanctuary...The Sanctuary was left to the family of Elizabeth Whit.

As she read the letter, Elizabeth felt herself being pulled out of her body, and back to the forest. Warm sunlight settled on her skin, a breeze catching her hair. A faint exhale escaped her lips. Somewhere, a Fairy Godmother had waved a wand, or a portal had opened, or a timeline had shifted. This was the wish she hadn't known to make. Elizabeth knew she couldn't pay the California mortgage rates for long on odd jobs and Tyler's life insurance. And the grief that had invaded their lives felt like a weight, slowly forcing the joy out of their existence and leaving nothing but paper thin silence where a family should be.

Without putting down the letter, Elizabeth phoned the attorney. "We'll keep it," she heard herself say. "We'll take possession in six weeks."

Chapter Two

*T*own: *Solace Spring, Massachusetts*

Population: 624

Settled: 1743

Features: The Berkshire Foothills, Solace Lake, Massachusetts State Forest, The River

Home To: Eyes Up Coffeehouse, Beauty of the Berkshires Gallery, Porchlight Pizza, The Sanctuary

Marvelous how quickly a life could change. Elizabeth looked out her window, 40,000 feet in the air. It would have taken her ancestors months, maybe years, to traverse the full breadth of the country. Climbing over mountains in cracked boots, bent against the cold wind and rain, nursing sickly babies around a campfire before moving on, and on, and on. It felt more natural, somehow, than her direct flight from Los Angeles to Connecticut. Seven hours wasn't enough time to mourn the death of one life, and breathe into the spark of another. But she had a head start.

Elizabeth couldn't remember a time when she had enjoyed California. By any standard, her life there was luxurious. Yet it drained her. Where others saw glamorous beaches, she saw only glaring stretches of sand and concrete. A wasteland. The people were often wasted, too, on promise and potential and someday. They wandered through life waiting to be seen, to be valued and evaluated. It was an aquarium she swam in, trying to hide in the plastic weeds. But California was all she knew, and so she was stuck there. Or had been, until now.

Sipping her fifth cup of lukewarm astringent coffee, the enormity of the choice began to settle in her stomach. Six weeks ago, this move had seemed a destined path to the life she had been craving for decades. Now, in her too-tight plane seat, it felt idiotic. What had made her think that her perfectly tanned ass was up to driving in the snow and cleaning out rain gutters, to say nothing of keeping up acres of land? Tyler had always insisted on having landscapers, house keepers, accountants, all manner of delegated staff to serve their needs so that he wouldn't have to spend his few free hours on domestic trivialities. Elizabeth hadn't used her life skills in years. Maybe it had been sheer stupidity to say yes to this.

"Hi folks, this is your captain again. Just wanted to let you know that we'll be landing in Hartford, Connecticut in about fifteen minutes here. Local conditions are foggy-"

Elizabeth shook her head and looked over at Lily and Cory, both immersed in their endless queue of movies and looking fairly foggy themselves. It was too late now. But this move would be good. They loved it here, and there was nothing behind them that she mourned leaving. Their new life was waiting, and all she needed to do was lead them forward. They were almost home.

***

Interstate 91 was a long, tree-lined highway that carried them out of the city and north into farmlands and forests. Civilization fell away quickly past the urban outskirts, and the occasional towns were gone before Elizabeth had a chance to ponder if it was worth stopping. Sun faded from the sky and the lights from nearby houses grew fewer. In daylight, they loved this journey, watching the shifting shadows on the road and counting the cows turned out to pasture. Autumn was coming to complete the scene, with an undulating rush of color against pristine gray skies. But now it was too early in the year, and too late in the day, and they were tired. The kids didn't talk. Half a dozen boxed sandwiches and a branch of bruised bananas sat in the empty seats, but no one felt like eating. So the moonless night bled through the car windows and into their nostrils. Time stopped. Life stopped. They existed between worlds. Right up until they pulled off the highway, past the tiny main street that was Solace Spring.

Once upon a time, Matty had told her, a family of settlers had found themselves in this valley, sick with typhoid, or scarlet fever, or scurvy. Versions varied. The native inhabitants of the place had taken pity upon them, and brought them to their sacred spring of healing waters. Miraculously, the visitors were spared the grisly demise so many suffered. They recovered, and stayed, and built their home in close proximity to the miracle. Over time, they brought others to the spring, curing everything from warts to cancer. For a while, peace held between the indigenous people and the desperate invalids who coveted their treasure. But as the years passed, tensions rose, and one night, violence broke out over the trickling water. By morning, only the newcomers remained, and Solace Spring, as it had come to be known...was gone. The town remained around the missing waters, despite its lost purpose, and it was this tiny outpost of hope that

Elizabeth passed in the dark before pulling onto a smaller road. They began counting houses. One. Two. Three. Four. Five.

The Sanctuary.

"We're here."

Looming suddenly in the headlights, the house was invisible until the moment she had to turn in. Elizabeth cranked the steering wheel hard to the right, and for a moment the joyful rainbow of paint was visible before the engine died, and blackness swallowed it again. Everyone in the car paused, and stretched, then opened their doors into the dark.

Silence was noisy. Deafening after the muffled sounds of travel that had surrounded them all day. The night seemed alive, holding its breath as the little family exited the house. Not even the trees moved in the thick summer air.

"Here we go, guys," Elizabeth said in a cheery whisper, hoping to cover her uneasiness. She walked up the front steps, put the code into the keysafe, and opened the door to their new home.

The darkness was here, too. Shadows bending forward to greet them, an unfamiliar space blinking in their faces, contemplating their arrival. And then, with one quick switch, there was light.

They had never visited this side of the house before, the owner's side. Everything was heavily separated, and their usual rooms were on the opposite half of the house, with their own door and tiny side porch. The wall was covered in paintings of wide open spaces, and a big leather sofa sat before a very small, ancient television. On the other side of the entryway was an oak breakfast table, oval and golden, not unlike the one she had had in her own kitchen growing up. A crowded counter lay in the background, with a muffin pan waiting ready above the oven. Elizabeth felt her throat tighten.

"Well, shall we explore upstairs?" The kids needed rooms, needed their own space to process and make their home, and she was anxious to provide them with whatever they needed to begin.

"Sure Mom," said Lily, in the voice she always used when she was trying to make her mother feel better. Elizabeth felt both grateful and guilty as she took her daughter's hand, and offered the other one to Cory. He didn't take it.

Upstairs they traipsed, to the narrow hallways common in these old farmhouses. Elizabeth knew the house had been built sometime in the 19th century, when homes were made to maximize warmth rather than style. Everything was slightly crooked, formed by hand instead of by corporate work crew. Four doors were spread equidistant, like some sort of game show or perhaps a horror movie. Elizabeth wished they were open.

First, a bathroom. Ugly green and pink tiles and a tiny cabinet beneath the sink, but with drawers on either side and a claw foot tub. Old. Serviceable.

Next, a purple room, which smelled faintly of lilacs. It had old fashioned lace curtains in the window and crystals dangling from the light sconces on the wall. This had likely been a sewing room for Matty's wife once upon a time, and Elizabeth was pleased to hear a soft "Oh!" of longing escape Lily's mouth. Drawn forward by the prisms of light, the fifteen-year old girl spun around as though she were four again, a fairy princess in her very own castle. "Mine!" she sang.

"Done!" Elizabeth said happily. She turned to the door across the way and opened it with a smile.

The smile died quickly. Here was a large brass bedstead, with an orange afghan thrown over the foot. Worn white sheets had been haphazardly tucked into corners, with the matching pillows at odd angles. She wondered if Matty had made the bed one last time, or the attorneys had done a slipshod job. Hard pine nightstands waited on either side, with squat lamps and bare bulbs. A brown armchair, cozy looking if a little ugly, sat by the window, looking out on the land. A shadowy door marked an en suite bathroom that appeared much the same as the other.

"You can have the dead guy's room," growled Cory. It was the first time he had spoken since they had landed.

"Fair enough," she replied. "Let's see what The Sanctuary has for you."

The last door opened into a round space. Elizabeth knew there was a turret on the funny rainbow house, but had always assumed it was decorative. Now, however, she saw it was a glossy dark blue room with a series of small mullioned windows overlooking the pond out back. It looked laborious, as though every piece of rounded wood had been a long chore to cut — as it probably had, she reminded herself. The ceiling was pitched, like the tower above, giving one the feeling of being inside a witch's hat.

"Cool."

Elizabeth whipped around to find her son, amazingly...smiling. He'd never been much for smiling, even before his father's death, and it had happened precious little since then. But the whites of his teeth showed as he revolved slowly on the spot, his eyes traveling up and down in hearty approval.

"All yours, kiddo."

Running steps banged through the hall.

"DUDE! A round room? That's awesome!"

"It's MINE!"

"I don't WANT it, I was just SAYING-"

"Well you don't need to SAY anything, I called it-"

"Kids, let's go grab our things from the car so we can all get some rest."

Ten minutes later the suitcases were open on the living room floor while both kids wolfed down the mashed sandwiches. Elizabeth opened cabinets and the refrigerator (a revolting project for tomorrow), looking to see what else they had to work with.

"What will we sleep on?"

"Mmm?" she answered absentmindedly.

"What will we sleep on?" Cory repeated. "There's no beds."

"I had the attorneys remove them. Our furniture will arrive tomorrow. We may just have to sleep on the couch tonight."

"Where he DIED? I'm not sleeping where a guy died."

"Cory, he died of old age, the couch doesn't have cooties." Irritation began to boil at her youngest child's challenge.

"I'm not doing it."

"OK, sleep on the floor. We have our sleeping bags."

"Great, that'll make for a fun first night."

"Cory," Lily began to console her brother, "it'll be fun..."

Rolling her eyes behind their backs, Elizabeth opened a closet door off the living room and flicked on a light switch.

Blankets. Row upon row upon row of neatly folded blankets, in every size and color. The closet was completely full of delicate lengths of knitted yarn. She put her hand out to touch one and felt the deep, unconditional love that had been poured into it. Elizabeth withdrew her hand, and wiped away a tear.

"I think we'll manage," she called.

The three of them stood in the door, looking at the treasure trove of comfort. Lily put her arm around her mother's waist, her eyes bright. Elizabeth brought Cory's shoulders, as high as her own, over to hers, and kissed his head. Wordlessly, they each reached out and began selecting their beds.

When the lights went out, each child was snuggled up in a nest of knitting, their chests lifting and falling under the fuzzy load. Elizabeth went up to her new room, curled herself up in the brown armchair, and looked out at the night until her eyes succumbed to rest at last.

Chapter Three

S he was warm. Snuggled. Well worn leather had formed to her shape and held her tight, while an armful of knotted yarn piled over her chest and stomach. Shifting slightly in the chair, Elizabeth was dimly aware of gentle light on her face, and the weight of cozy things across her lap. And something...moving.

Her eyes flew open, and Elizabeth looked down at her feet to see a large, gray shape skittering towards the closet.

She screamed.

Standing on the squishy cushion, she let a string of curses erupt from her in an undertone. Rats. Of course there were rats. She reminded herself that the house had been disused for months, and had probably been slowly atrophying before that. Who knew what Matty had been up to repairing or keeping up. But rats. Ewwwwwww.

Unfortunately, no one was coming to save her from this rodent, and this was her first opportunity to step up - or rather, down. Carefully, she tiptoed over to the closet, noticing the scattered crumbs from her purse. Damn her emergency granola bars. For a moment she questioned the wisdom of opening this door (did she really want to know what was back there?), but then decided that it needed to be done sooner or later. One quick wrench back revealed a lot more scratching and squeaking noises, and a flash of disappearing tails. Pushing aside Matty's shirts, jeans, and serviceable jackets, she saw big gaps between the end of the wall and the floor, presumably where the rats were getting in. An easy fix.

Once she got the rats out.

Reminding herself to donate Matty's clothes, she turned towards the remainder of the room. Shades for the bedside lamps. Curtains for the window. She moved into the bathroom where there were no hooks for towels and the shower curtain had grown mold. Elizabeth splashed some water on her face in front of the hazy mirror. Her mental to-do list was growing rapidly, and she hadn't even left her room. She showered (at least the fixture was in good shape), dressed, and headed downstairs.

Belatedly, she thought of how nice it would have been to make those Sanctuary muffins for the kids, but of course she didn't have any ingredients. Or his recipe. She opened cupboards at random and found some packets of instant oatmeal and bags of darjeeling. While the kettle filled, she let her eyes wander. This side looked different now, bathed in an early morning glow. The yellow kitchen walls were hopeful instead of dirty, the living room cheerful rather than aged. Elizabeth walked to the window and looked out at the sea of green trees beyond the sculpture garden. She could feel them waving a lazy hello.

The kettle went off just as Cory trooped downstairs. Lily was a few minutes behind, though she usually rose early.

"I was meditating," she informed them immediately. "The vibes in my room are AMAZING. I feel so many good presences in this home."

"Maybe it was the rats," Elizabeth muttered.

"RATS?" Both kids looked horrified.

"It's an old house and it hasn't been cared for recently. I'm sure we'll get it fixed up quickly," Elizabeth said calmly, wishing she had kept her sarcasm to herself. "Who wants breakfast?"

As they ate, they planned for the day. The moving van wouldn't arrive until two, leaving them time to go into town and get new bedding, towels, and food. But when Elizabeth opened her phone to look for shops, she found...nothing. Some small farm stands, a coffee shop, a gallery, a mechanic, and a few other odds and ends. The closest big box stores were an hour's drive.

Exhausted, Elizabeth realized that travel was about to become a major use of her time. She had known, of course, that the place was remote. It had always been a charming factor when they visited. They'd pick up groceries at the nearest college town before heading into the woods for their break with modernity. But somehow, the reality of that long drive hit a little harder now.

"We have to get back in the car?" Lily hated car rides. She had a testy stomach, and drives were always hard on her.

"Well, let's go right after breakfast, while you're full of oatmeal, and we'll do one full trip while we have this big SUV." Her own car would be delivered next week.

"Yeah, we can fill the trunk with rat traps," said Cory. He didn't smile. Elizabeth laughed anyway.

They spent the morning at every big box store in the nearest town with an intersection. Elizabeth was careful to pick up cleaning supplies, dry goods, canned vegetables, and of course, rat traps. Lily picked out a bed set covered in mushrooms and flowers, while Cory opted for straight black. Sheets, toilet plungers, paper towels, eggs and milk, light bulbs...they filled every inch of the large cargo hold to the brim before driving the long hour back to their new home.

Pulling up in the light was a kinder experience. The rainbow colors of the house dazzled in sunlight, as the fairy weathervane danced on the roof. Jokes were tossed between siblings as they unloaded the car, and Elizabeth allowed herself a single moment of relief.

Until...

"Excuse me," came a harsh feminine voice. "If I may have a word."

Elizabeth jumped. In The Sanctuary's isolation, new voices were invasive. Turning around, she saw a thin older woman, arms crossed and eyebrows bent, walking up the drive like a tiger poised to strike.

"Oh! Hi!" She hastened forward to smooth over whatever had clearly gone wrong. Unconsciously pitching her voice an octave higher, Elizabeth smoothed her hair and grinned while batting her eyes. It was an instinct finely honed from nearly all of her adult interactions over the past two decades, and it was perfectly executed. Subtle adjustments had been made over the years to ensure that everyone found her trustworthy, charming, and friendly. It never failed. When she needed to, she could sparkle. "I'm Elizabeth Whit, I'm the new owner."

"And I am your neighbor," the woman said frostily. "Lisa Fry. Your moving van is blocking my driveway."

"Oh!" Elizabeth's eyes widened. Surely this wasn't her fault? "They must have gotten the wrong house. I'm so sorry, I'll call them now." She wondered why Lisa hadn't simply told the drivers to move one house down. Unconsciously, she stepped back towards the house.

"No point," flared the other. "They're stuck. It's taking them a good long while to back that truck out without hitting any of my trees."

"Oh," Elizabeth said again. "Yes, I can see how that would happen. Were you heading out? I'd be happy to give you a ride." The saccharine sweetness of her offer sounded feeble even to her, but she didn't have much to work with at the moment. She had rarely felt so wrong-footed. No one in California was ever openly hostile. She took another step back.

"I don't need your help," snarled Lisa. "I just wanted you to know what an inconvenience you caused. Not a very nice way to introduce yourself. We believe in manners around here, you know."

Elizabeth resisted the urge to point out the poor manners currently on display. "I'm so sorry. We arrived late last night. We were hoping to take a few days to get set up and then come around and -"

"I don't need to hear it, I'm busy. Just keep your West Coast crap off of my property." And she turned, and left.

Elizabeth stood in shock for a moment. Not even the trophy wives on the PTA had ever treated her this poorly. It looked like at least one neighbor wasn't pleased to have them. There was a good distance between their separate homes, and they weren't likely to see each other over the maple trees that ran between the two, but still...it wasn't the welcome she would have hoped for.

By three o'clock the van had found its way and the children had beds, boxes, and various other items to unload the rest of the evening. The old couch was replaced by a new one, along with a matching coffee table and armchair, but they kept the old breakfast table and well worn chairs. Elizabeth hadn't had it in her to bring the bed she had shared with Tyler, so the old brass bedstead would have to do until she decided on something new. For now, everything was boxes and bubble wrap, and they ate turkey sandwiches on the floor while they watched one of Matty's old movies (on VHS) and passed out on itchy new sheets.

In the morning, Elizabeth finally took a moment away from the chaos to survey the view from the back porch. This was the reason they had come, the scene that had called them back time and again. Sun rising over the placid pond, blushing the treetops on the other side and waking the birds from the branches. Theirs was the only sound that broke the stillness. Dots of color emerged darkly from their garden beds, sleepily shaking dew from their petals. A glorious firepit sat surrounded by a ring of standing stones, huge boulders of granite that created a Stonehenge effect in the Massachusetts woods. Rock walls meandered in serpentine patterns towards the boundless woods. Somewhere on the horizon was an unmarked border, and past it the forest rose up into gentle hills and crossed rushing rivers. It was peace. And it was hers.

Turning back to the door, Elizabeth saw something that had not been present the night before. A pillar candle rubbed with green dust stood faithfully by the doormat, waiting to be noticed. She picked it up, noticing the brittle feel of the powder in her hands and the waft of rosemary in the air. She turned it carefully and found a simple tag on the other side, handwritten but unsigned.

Welcome home.

***

The next few days were devoted to making the house come alive again. Elizabeth excused her children from the horrors of cleaning out the moldy refrigerator, a task that could only be handled with industrial strength bleach and a strong stomach. Instead they hung their artwork and argued over bathroom drawers, and made a list of the sundries that would need to be ordered from afar. Lily helped clean out kitchen cabinets, while Cory volunteered (unusually) to tackle the garage. Three hours later, Elizabeth looked out to find no progress, but a large pile of odds and ends that Cory was tinkering with under the scant light of a single bulb hanging from the ceiling. She left him to it.

As each corner of the house was emptied, dusted, and scrubbed, the list of to-dos grew ever longer. Elizabeth hadn't touched the guest side yet as she knew it to be in better repair, and had plans to tackle it after the school year began. She did begin taking long walks of the garden between chores, both noting the work to be done (weeding, replanting, adjusting irrigation) and letting herself find her old love of the place. They had been to The Sanctuary in all seasons, save winter, and while the inside of the inn was charming, she had always come for the wild freedom of the land. Even knowing the hardship that awaited her in her new home, she felt rejuvenated as she walked the winding pathways through the grounds. Several times a day she would take a cup of tea to the back porch and just look at it, clear and unwavering and calling to her in a language that she didn't understand.

She felt it, though. In the way her feet hugged the ground, the way her body seemed to pull her out of the house and into the world. As soon as her toes touched the earth, a separation occurred, as though she had shifted from one reality to another. The Sanctuary was a pocket of space that existed out of normal time. Drawn into its vast promise, Elizabeth stayed out too late, and when the dusk turned to dark she could have sworn she saw lights in the distance, asking her to come just a little bit farther.

***

One day, after the boxes had been cleared and the disinfectants copiously applied, Elizabeth got ready to make herself a cup of coffee, only to find that she hadn't purchased any (presumably because her brain was low on…well, coffee). She remembered seeing the coffee shop on Solace Spring's tiny downtown map. She'd need to go local eventually. Today was as good a day as any, and she could get a little luxury in.

An hour later, the Whit family was parked on Solace Spring's Main Street, home to a scattered handful of shops: a few small restaurants, a compact grocer, a mechanic, an upscale art gallery, a metaphysical outpost, and the town hall. A library sat at one end, the church at the other, with a post office squarely in between. Here and there were houses, mixed in with businesses which looked like houses, anyway. Only the large shingles out front denoted the difference. Behind Main Street ran the town common, an open green field that slowly turned to trees, beyond which the Solace Lake was just visible. The river, one of the innumerable tributaries of the region, meandered past the common, its body snaking up near the cemetery on the hill and disappearing into the wood.

Everything else was farmland.

Eyes Up, the sole coffeehouse for miles in any direction, was a white-washed cube of a house, with a groovy shingle painted violet and sky blue. On either side of the name was a single eye, focused upwards as three beams of light poured from above. The bottom was a deep well of black liquid. Apparently this was coffee that led to enlightenment.

They entered the shop, Lily with a rapturous expression on her face and Cory looking, as always, suspicious. Elizabeth just looked tired.

"Hi," said the woman behind the counter. She was maybe ten years older than Elizabeth, with gray hair worn in long dreadlocks adorned with purple and blue beads that exactly matched the sign outside. Her brown eyes sparkled under a wide forehead, and her grin was friendly and inviting. Well-muscled arms emerged from under her tank top, and Elizabeth could just make out what looked like psychedelic bell bottoms beneath her black apron. "Welcome to Eyes Up! What can I get for you today?"

"Well, what's the specialty of the house?" Elizabeth answered enthusiastically. Despite her patent exhaustion, the higher vocal range arrived unbidden, accompanied by the fixed smile.

"Coffee," grunted a voice behind her. She turned to see an older man, reading a copy of the *Boston Globe* next to his mug of joe, taken black.

"Ignore Mr. Grover," said the barista firmly. "He's just a sourpuss. Our maple latte is real popular, though for summer my favorite is brown sugar and peach. It's a little unorthodox, but I make the peach syrup myself and it just tastes like a good day." That broad smile again.

"That sounds great, I'll take one." Elizabeth returned the smile. "Plus whatever these two want." Lily put in a lavender tea, and Cory asked for plain black coffee. "And do you happen to sell beans by the pound?"

"Sure do! How many pounds do you want?"

Elizabeth thought it over. "Let's do two."

The barista looked her over curiously. "Nothing in your hotel room? How long are you staying for?"

"Well hopefully a good long time. I'm Elizabeth, I...inherited The Sanctuary." It was a strange thing to say, given that she wasn't family, but facts were facts. "These are my kids, Lily and Cory. We're just getting moved in."

The barista's beaming face lit the whole shop now, as she came around the till with open arms. "Elizabeth! Of course! Welcome welcome welcome! Matty told me so much about you, I should have known you right away. So nice to meet all of you. I'm Denny." Lily received her hug with enthusiasm, and Cory with surprise. "I hope you guys will feel at home here in Solace Spring. It is a wonderful community, and we are so happy to have you. Matty was the heart and soul of this town, it will be good to fill his shoes a little bit."

Her nerves frayed slightly at the concept of becoming the "heart and soul" of a town she barely knew existed. She wasn't sure that she was ready to fill shoes of any kind. She was barely handling her own feet. Overwhelmed, Elizabeth realized her hands had begun to shake, and she quickly shoved them in the back pockets of her jeans as she hoisted her perky expression up again.

"Well we have to get the inn up and running again, first. And make some repairs. I don't suppose you can recommend anyone to help with some odd jobs? Matty probably had a tough time doing it all himself." *Hence the rats' victory*, she thought to herself.

"Hmph," from behind the newspaper. "Can't even take care of her own work up there. One week and already crying for help."

"Now you stop it, Grover," Denny chided. "You know as well as I do that Matty struggled to keep up with the maintenance up there." She turned to Elizabeth. "There's a lot of seasonal help that comes through here, working at farms and sugaring houses, so you may be able to grab some of those folks between harvests. Let me give it some thought."

Jing jing jing. A bell tinkled as the shop door opened again, and a man with bronze skin and a black beard and ponytail walked in. He reached over the bar, added coffee to the travel mug in his hand, and walked back out.

Denny started laughing. "Well speak of the devil. That's Joe, and he would be perfect to help you out." Denny gave her an appraising look. "He's in high demand, good with machines, but I'll see if I can talk him into taking some time."

"He's certainly good at taking some coffee," Elizabeth remarked.

Denny chuckled.

"You're a funny one! That's good, it will serve you well while you're getting acquainted. This town is a little like high school. Everyone knows everybody else, and they can get a little defensive when new folks come in. No one wants to lose their place, see. It takes time for them to warm up. Joe," she started steaming oat milk, "is sort of the popular guy. Everybody likes him, and everybody's always willing to do him favors. He gets free coffee here on account of all the times he has fixed these damn gadgets for me." Denny gestured around. "Mr. Grover there," she said loudly, "used to be our principal. And he forgets he's not anymore. Always keeping everybody in line, whether they like it or not." She winked at him while he rolled his eyes. "Matty was sort of the student body president, and I guess I'm everybody's cheerleader." She looked sidelong at Elizabeth. "You should join the book club! It would be a great way to meet everybody. Well, all the women anyhow. The guys around here never seem to be very interested in reading." Her eyes rolled over to the grouchy retiree with a mischievous look.

"Maybe we all have something better to do," Mr. Grover said, grabbing his paper and nodding affirmatively before walking out the door. Denny rolled her eyes.

"Mom," whispered Lily, "I like it here."

***

Wind picked up that day. Elizabeth sat on the back porch, freshly brewed coffee in hand, allowing the golden sunshine to play on her face. She watched the trees sway. She wondered whether they liked her, and whether they would let her call this place home.

*E*yes closed, ears shut.

    Too long, too long, all have been gone so long

They have forgotten.

We stand ready behind a curtain that few ever lift.

So here we sit, ready and waiting, poised for the moment of incitation

—

The beginning.

Oh the anticipation thrills us, makes us quake down into our roots,
makes us reach higher for

At any moment

It

Starts.

But always there is the worry, somewhere in the darkness, that this is
the time we fail.

We have never failed before. Yet there must always be a first.

A beginning to every ending.

Every ending begins now.

Breathe.

Inhale.

Exhale.
Begin.

Chapter Four

Solace Spring was the smallest town Elizabeth had ever visited. California's suburbs were sprawling concrete jungles, with perfectly manicured lawns and carefully selected tropical plants, and a grocery store never more than five minutes away. Nothing in her 44 years on this planet had prepared her to live in "the country", where one had to watch their gas mileage carefully and bring coffee from home. As much as she loved the peace, Elizabeth had to admit that the rural lifestyle was a massive adjustment from her pampered life at the beach.

Groceries had been the priority, and Elizabeth soon found that she needed to plan far better, and purchase far more. After three consecutive days of driving forty minutes to the supermarket for things she had forgotten, she began the work of buying — and storing — in bulk. Luckily, the local farms were brimming with fruits and vegetables at this time of year, so as long as she kept proteins and staples on hand, she didn't need to go far for something fresh. A deep freezer was delivered and installed in the basement, and she managed to anchor an assortment of heavy shelves to the adjacent walls for the buckets of flour and sugar and endless rows of beans. Lily had grand visions for a vegetable garden in the future, so sealed boxes of mason jars sat on the bottom tier, waiting to be filled.

Several trips to town had also yielded more scrub brushes and cleaning supplies (desperately needed and also purchased in bulk), along with a new set of tools — Tyler had never done much work on their house, and Elizabeth had left his few broken items behind. Matty had a shed full of gardening equipment that looked several decades old, but knowing the weather would be turning soon, Elizabeth opted to save that expense for later. She was glad to see that he had, at least, invested in the latest model of snowblower. Her neighbor, Lisa, had been quick to notice each trashcan six inches over the property line, and had left three curt notes informing Elizabeth that she needed to clear the branches *her* trees had dropped on Lisa's property. She hated to think what would happen if she left a section of snow too close to their border.

While it was nice to feel increasingly settled, the lack of entertainment was taking its toll.

"I'm bored," Cory announced to the living room ceiling for the fifth day running.

"We know," growled Lily, uncharacteristically harsh. Too much time together was their recipe for disaster.

From her seat on the kitchen floor, toothbrush in one hand and bleach in the other, Elizabeth massaged the back of her neck. This was quickly becoming a daily routine, and it was one she couldn't let continue. Her grand plan of a calm and quiet home did not include her children holding screaming matches in the living room by 10am.

She ran through the usual options with them.

"We could go swimming at the lake."

"With the SNAKES?!" squealed Lily.

"There are some excellent museums-"

"No," Cory said flatly.

Elizabeth forced herself to quell the choice language she would prefer her children not hear. Instead, she chose a dark stain on the baseboard and scrubbed it with a ferocity that could have cracked the wood. It yielded. The clean white baseboard looked like a refreshingly blank page. And suddenly, a flash of brilliance.

"What about the library?"

Both Lily and Cory were voracious readers, which was always a relief to Elizabeth. No matter how bad the incessant bickering or teenage mood swings got, as long as there were books, the kids were happy. So they piled into the car for a blessedly short drive into town, and parked in front of the squat gray square that was the library.

In this way, Elizabeth thought vaguely, perhaps Massachusetts had a leg up on California. Their local library had been adequate, even nice — one of the few in the county that had been updated since 1985. But it was bright and modern, and lacked the coziness that she craved while reading. A plaque on the outside of the Solace Spring Local Library noted that the building was 200 years old, and also that it was only open twice a week.

Better than nothing.

Summer's muggy breath bogged down everything it touched, but the library was surrounded by alder trees with thick trunks and wide crowns. Weighty and full, their boughs umbrellaed each door and window, creating an almost subterranean look. It was a place protected. The library cowered in the shade, curled up upon itself, waiting for closing time so it could nap. As she reached for the brass doorknob, wind ruffled the border of leaves, and Elizabeth heard the building sigh.

Inside, yellow lamps hung from the ceiling, barely illuminating textured walls and peeling baseboards. The floorboards were uneven, as they often were in older New England homes, built when good enough was, well, good enough. The familiar stacks of tax forms and free periodicals soothed her nervous system. Libraries were the same everywhere.

Her teenagers rushed past the children's room with its colorful handwoven rugs, past the computer lab full of last decade's models, and directly into their respective rooms: "Fiction" (for Lily) and "Non-Fiction" (for Cory). Elizabeth wandered along the empty checkout desk towards the community cork board, where everything sat at perfect right angles. A small yellow note carefully positioned between neon ads indicated the local book club Denny had mentioned, and a full color page advertised the town's annual electronics recycling day, which had passed two months ago. She continued on, noticing that this library smelled lightly of Earl Grey tea, and that the walls had a network of hairline fractures that spiraled out like spiderwebs. A small alcove under a steep staircase marked "Agriculture and Archive" featured a single yellow armchair and carved wood table, set in front of a wide bay window. Outside, Solace Lake sparkled in the sun, mirroring the blue sky and the tops of the trees that lay on the far side of its shores. Beyond that, green hills rose and fell like waves, a vast uninterrupted sea of earth. This is why she had come here — to sit in a spot just like this.

Sinking into the chair, Elizabeth let the sunbeams caress her face, the silence become a heartbeat. Weight lifted from her chest. Despite the many inconveniences of her new neighborhood, she couldn't deny how much better she felt in Solace Spring. In comparison to the old frenzy of school and shopping and activities and tasks, when she sat in its open arms, there was simply time. Maybe when there was nothing to do, you could truly enjoy doing nothing.

Nothing was a rare luxury. She used to pride herself on the fact that she never sat down. This was Elizabeth's secret, the reason she had been able to secure admission to the best college, a fat ring from an ideal partner, a white picket fence and two green-eyes babies. She never stopped moving. Always working, cleaning, feeding, socializing. No breaks. Only new highs to achieve, and new records to set, in addition to maintaining everything she had already created. Each moment of her life had a to do list a mile long, and rest...rest was unfamiliar. A rare stolen moment, paid for in guilt and anxiety. Until now.

How long she sat there, she didn't know, but her stomach was rumbling when she finally roused herself to find the kids. Lily was sprawled out in front of an empty stone fireplace with a stack of darkly romantic novels. Leaving her to finish the chapter, Elizabeth veered into Non-Fiction, and found Cory hunkered down on a couch that had seen better days with a stack of books two feet high. His face lit up when she whispered his name.

"Mom!" he called, ever in combat with his "inside voice". "Look at what I found! This one—" shaking the tome in his hand—"is entirely about black holes, and this one"— he waved another from the top of the stack—"tells you how to choose the best spots to use your telescope."

Cory was the proud owner of a decent telescope, a gift from several birthdays ago, but as the light pollution had been so strong in the suburbs, he had rarely had occasion to use it. Now, however, his grin stretched from ear to ear, and Elizabeth could see his visions of grand stargazing adventures here in the hills.

"That's awesome, Cory." She was relieved to have found a place for her children to belong. "Let's get you a library card."

He waved his hand at her dismissively. "Lily and I already checked everything out."

"What? How?"

Cory rolled his eyes. "Mom, we're teenagers, I think we can figure out how to ask for a library card." He gathered up his books and marched towards the exit, where Lily was waiting with a similar load and her eyes on the children's room. "I'm hungry."

***

That night, Elizabeth went to kiss both kids goodnight, and left Cory to his pleasure reading late into the evening. Lily, however, looked less pleased. She sat on her bed, fussing with the loose threads of her blanket, eyes darting and hands flapping. Shallow breath was pushed through pressed lips, and her cheeks were damp. Her room felt dark and invasive, despite the fairies on the windowsill.

"What's wrong, sweetie?" Elizabeth asked. She was often "too busy" for her daughter's tender heart, something she was always working on, and then forgetting to work on. Mommy's little girl had always shown up perfectly in the world, able to navigate the inconsistencies of humanity and bridge the chasms that swallowed her brother. Lily was strong, strong enough to hold herself and her family upright, and be cheerful while she carried them. So she slipped through the parental cracks. Her smile lit up every day, and Elizabeth herself forgot that some of them were lies. After all, Lily had learned that smile from her.

Lily inhaled deeply. "I don't know, Mom. I love it here. I do. But..." Tide pools filled her eyes, held back only by her resolve. "I'm homesick. A little. I miss my friends. I miss the ocean." She threw her hands up and smiled a little. "I miss Target." They giggled together for a moment, and Elizabeth caught her hand as it halted its restless motion. "It's a lot to get used to, here, and I just worry…" She glanced apprehensively at her mother. "I worry we made a mistake." Lily gulped as the tears spilled over, finally admitting the horrifying fear she had tried to hide in her small body.

As Lily's shoulders broke forward, Elizabeth caught her in a hug, and held her first baby against her chest while she cried, so that she would not see her own anxiety written on her mother's face. "My sweet girl," she whispered over and over. She kissed the top of her head, and ran her hands over the golden curls. Rocking ever so slightly back and forth, Elizabeth made her voice low and soothing. "It's hard to start someplace new. You're right. And I miss Target, too." Lily chuckled between her moans. "But I know that these feelings are meant to come and go for awhile while we adjust. And then they'll grow less over time. And someday we won't really feel them at all. The sadness and nostalgia will be gone, and all we will have is peace and happiness." Again she kissed her teenage daughter with the soft touch she would give an infant. "We just have to take really good care of ourselves, and be patient for awhile. OK?" She tipped Lily's face back and watched her nod lightly. "And you can always tell me how you're feeling and get all the hugs you need. Home is wherever we are together."

They sat locked in an embrace until Lily's tears had run dry, and her body ached for rest. And Elizabeth sat still longer at the foot of the bed, back against the wall, waiting for her big girl's breath to grow slow and deep, and hoping fervently that she had not let her daughter down.

Chapter Five

The golden days of summer were moving resolutely towards fall, and despite Elizabeth's best efforts, they were all blending together. The work on the house was interminable. It was a war of neverending battles, and she was definitely losing.

Cory had found plants growing in the basement, with mildew all around and an impressive variety of bugs. Lily had been bouncing down the stairs while dancing when her foot went straight through the bottom step. Elizabeth had had a nasty surprise when she went to use the laundry for the first time, and ended up with a knot of wet clothes that took over an hour to separate before washing each item in the bathtub by hand. The garage was a graveyard of appliance bits and metal flim flam, some of which Elizabeth was sure were ending up in her son's closet.

Hardening her resolve, Elizabeth had donned her ugliest gym wear discards and begun to face the tasks that were foreign to her. But the time lapse videos she watched each morning before setting to work failed to communicate the details and downsides. She had stuffed steel wool in the rat holes, which didn't stop her from hearing them scurry around in the dead of night. Screens on the windows had holes, too, so often the house became stuffy and warm in the late afternoon, when opening windows may invite in mosquitoes (or more rodents). Both kids complained loudly of not having a real television to watch, but deliveries were slow to make their way out here, and Elizabeth was privately worried about her ability to mount and wire the monstrous widescreen she had ordered — she had never been great with electronics. Cory had eagerly volunteered his help, which was nice in theory but likely still required supervision. She wasn't sure her skills would be adequate to the task. She was already struggling with her areas of expertise, like the kitchen.

Once upon a time, when she was an adoring newlywed, Elizabeth had prided herself on her cooking, and she had hoped that being in a rural space would help her connect to her pots and pans again. But without access to her usual international groceries and daily trips for fresh ingredients, cooking felt more like drudgery than artistry. After several nights of sandwiches in a row, she decided it was time to up her game.

"OK guys," she called up the stairs, "I'm making your favorite dinner tonight!"

No response.

She trudged up the tiny staircase and found both doors open, and both kids in front of their laptops with headphones on.

"HEY!"

Four eyes looked at her in surprise.

"You don't have to shout!" Lily said, hurt.

Elizabeth exhaled, and allowed her excitement to beam. "I'm making your favorite dinner tonight! Kebob Alexander! It's about time you guys got a real meal with all of the help you've given me."

She meant it, too. There was no way she could have gotten through everything that needed doing without them, and she was grateful. They deserved to be given something, and her food was what she could offer. Kabob Alexander was their favorite, a Turkish dish of steak and pita bread smothered in a buttery tomato sauce that Elizabeth pulled out as a reward for jobs well done.

"Mom, they don't carry pita bread here." Cory had been quick to note that many of his favorite foods from Southern California were in short supply here, namely tortillas and pita bread for his mid-afternoon meal. A big kid for his age, he ate easily three times as much as the women did. Unfortunately, Elizabeth had forgotten this detail, but she recovered.

"We'll make some!" she said brightly. "We've made bread before, the basic concepts are the same."

A vague light appeared behind her son's eyes. He loved cooking with her. From across the way, Lily grinned. "Awesome, Mom. That's a great idea."

Dismissing her daughter's pandering, and feeling more confident in her mothering skills than she had in weeks, Elizabeth traipsed down the stairs again, scrolling through her phone for a pita bread recipe.

They sat around the table an hour later, taking turns kneading the shaggy mass of dough on a yellowing plastic cutting board.

"So...how are you guys liking it here, anyways?" Elizabeth asked. The house had taken so much of her attention that she had failed to check in as deeply as she wanted to. As she should have.

"Well," Lily stole a furtive glance at her brother, confirming Elizabeth's suspicions that they had been talking about it among themselves. "We love The Sanctuary, of course. It's been great being back in the forest. And cleaning up the house has kind of been a fun project. We both had a really good time decorating our rooms, and —"

"We're bored." Cory met her eyes exactly as he grabbed the dough and gave it a swift pounding. "There's nothing to do here. There's no place to go. We're stuck."

Stuck. That was how Elizabeth had felt in California. Trapped in the suburbs, with neighbors pressing in on her and noise everywhere. Every conversation was a competition, one that always ended with money. She had hated it. And had hoped that by moving, she was sparing her children from the same fate. Less than a month in, it seemed she had failed.

Elizabeth took a deep breath. "I'm really sorry, guys. I can see how you could feel that way." She really didn't know what else to say. They were stuck. They had no place else to go now. Her choice had cost them that.

Ever the empath, Lily stepped in. "It's OK, Mom. Like you told us, it takes time to get used to a new place. We haven't started school yet, and school will make a HUGE difference. We know that." She shot a warning glare at her brother, who shrugged in admission.

"That's true," he admitted, uncharacteristically. "It's hard to tell just yet." He passed the dough to his mom, and for a moment she saw him at five years old, just starting school and looking to her for reassurance. That was something that she could give.

"Well, school starts next week," she said. "And you're right, that's a big one. We'll give it some more time, yeah? But if you finish the school year and you still feel that way, I promise we'll figure out something else, OK?" After all, that was what had gotten her through the years spent where she did not belong. The knowledge that she could always leave, always start again, always backtrack. An exit strategy was critical, even though she had never had the courage to use it. Both kids smiled, and she could feel their tension diffusing. They were one step above the closet of rats. The door to this trap was open, after all.

While they waited for the dough to rise, they took iced tea with anise stars down to the pond, and sat on a log by the muddy shores. The children ended up down here most afternoons, sitting in the shade with their books or sketchpads and allowing their minds to drift. The pond was a wide oblong stretch of flat water, interrupted at regular intervals by cattails and grasses. It was home to ducks and frogs and who knew what else. No waves disrupted the surface, unless an errant duck striped the water as he landed. Light couldn't penetrate the depths. Whatever lay beneath remained a mystery, one she had no desire to solve.

By the time they came in to escape the evening descent of the mosquitoes, a bubble of dough was waiting, round and soft in the bright green bowl. She punched it down, gathered it into little balls, and rolled them flat. It felt good to use her hands for something they knew how to do. Baking was mechanical. The familiarity of repetition, the exacting geometry, the rhythmic timing of the slap, roll, toss, slap. Soon a short stack of flatbread sat next to the griddle, and another was steaming on a plate. Tomato sauce bubbled in a saucepan, and she scraped the freshly cooked slices of beef into it. The smell permeated the living room. Within minutes, the deep dishes of bread and steak were served, consumed, and relegated back to the counter empty, and the children were on their way to bed groaning of full stomachs.

As she stood at the sink, Elizabeth let the water run over her hands, warm and soft between her fingers. For a moment she closed her eyes, picturing the calm waters of the pond, and when she opened them, black water was pouring from the faucet. Terrified, she shut off the tap, but when she turned it cautiously a moment later, the stream was diamond clear. She watched it whirl around the drain and disappear. And then she looked outside.

Something by the pond seemed to be glowing. A faint white line stretched from the pond to the forest, just beyond the edges of the gardens. Maybe it was a reflection on the window? Elizabeth stepped onto the porch, her feet carefully traversing the smooth wood as she looked for the best view of the wandering walkway. No matter where she stood, stones and bushes rose in her sightline. She began to walk down the stairs, eyes focused on the distant light, until she came to the final step...and hesitated. A light breeze tickled her cheek, and for a moment she could have sworn she heard voices, whispering through the night. Her eyes flickered towards the dark shadows of the forest. Shaking her head, Elizabeth felt the sharp sting of the air in her face. A shiver ran down her spine. Suddenly the night felt less welcoming. Crossing her arms in front of her chest, she walked back up the steps, went inside, and turned out the lights.

***

"Up and at 'em!" Elizabeth's voice rang up the stairs. "First day of school!"

True to form, Lily was down in a heartbeat, wearing her favorite pink sundress and a cardigan over it. Cory slouched down a few minutes later, all in black as usual, with a pendant hung around his neck and his hair still wet.

"You guys are going to have a great day," Elizabeth intoned, serving up hot pancakes and mugs of tea and milk. "I know it's hard to go to a new school, so try not to make any judgments yet. Just give everything time to settle. It can take a little time to find the right people."

"Aren't there only three people in each grade anyway?" asked Cory with a surly look.

In California, both kids had walked down the block to the large, wealthy, and high-achieving middle and high schools. Here, they would be attending the same school, which served all upper grades and had a total enrollment equal to Lily's old freshman class. It served nine towns altogether.

"You'll be able to really know everyone," Elizabeth slanted it. "And you'll get so much more attention from your teachers. You'll love that." This was true. Having little time with his absent father meant that Cory bonded to his teachers instead, and he was always the smartest kid in his class. He loved learning. Socializing with classmates, however, had always been...difficult.

But that wasn't a problem here. Yet.

Both kids looked nervous as they departed the car, and they were shoulder and shoulder as they entered the single building that was their new school. It felt daunting, even to Elizabeth, seeing the smallness of their new world. She would have coveted this tiny space, the ability to understand each facet of her community perfectly and find a safe place to hide within it. Vividly she recalled sitting alone with her book on the grassy knoll of her high school campus, unnoticed by the giggling girls who walked the halls in lockstep. Solace Spring was supposed to save her children from that undesirable anonymity. She only hoped they found their place fast enough

Elizabeth shook her head clear as she pulled out of the parking lot. She couldn't think like that. Today, she needed to keep herself busy. Today, she was going to open up the guests' side of the house.

A good businesswoman would have opened that side first, Elizabeth thought bitterly. But she wasn't a businesswoman. She wasn't anything. Her adult life had unfolded like a bag of popcorn – every so often, something would burst open, and she'd move onto a new path. Then...well, then it started to devolve. And after a time, it seemed silly to keep trying. After all, there was so much to be done at home. The kids needed support, and her husband's job was too important for him to lend a hand. All the errands, cooking, cleaning, fixing, and parenting fell to her. Work didn't make sense. So she took contracts here and there, and otherwise, she did just what she had been doing since she got to Solace Spring — tended to the broken things and cleaned up someone else's mess.

And here was the mess.

With great trepidation, she opened the guest door. It looked clean, no doubt because professionals had handled the work after the last guests left. The ancient couch was bowed but whole, the bar containing a notebook of tourist information stood ready, and the kitchen looked clean...except for that trail of crumbs.

Elizabeth already knew what she'd find. Her shoulders slumped as she opened the guest bedroom door, and heard a flock of scurries and squeaks. For a moment the floor was a mass of movement, and Elizabeth slammed the door just in time. Nothing came through. It looked as though she had once again found the rats.

Halfheartedly she began the laborious task of going through the kitchen cabinet, which stood slightly ajar. The last visitors had left a magnum of granola bars, which were clearly gourmet rodent food. She swept out the remainder, tossed the remaining food in the shelves for good measure, and began making a list of pantry staples to replace.

With mounting frustration, she turned on the sink to wash her hands, only to find that nothing came out. Cold fury boiled inside of her as she whacked it irrationally with her hands. Nothing happened, except that her hand hurt. Furiously she wrenched on one handle, then the other, then both, to no avail. She stomped into the bathroom and snapped on the sink there, which worked too well and splashed all over her clothes. It was a nice distraction from the smell of moldy towels, waiting patiently in the hamper for the laundering that had never come. Elizabeth thought of the knot of clothes that resulted from every washload and hot tears began to build on her lids.

"Damnit!"

She sank to the floor of the wood-paneled bathroom, wet and tired with nostrils full of rat droppings and mold, and thought about her precious babies at school. What had she been thinking? Why had she done this, and in what world did she think she could succeed?

Hands shaking, tears stinging at her eyes, Elizabeth began to drown under the weight of her own panic. Desperately, she took the towels and locked the guest door. There was more to review, more to see, more to fix — but in that moment, she had to get out.

Down at the pond, Elizabeth let herself cry. She let herself scream. She took carefully placed rocks from the garden beds and slammed them into each other, breaking them into jagged pebbles next to her raw red hands. She hit them until she bled. Then she sat, shaking, heaving big, gulping breaths of the air — air she hated in that moment for its sweet pine scent. She craved air conditioning. A leisurely stroll through Target. A cute bar with a bohemian boutique next door where she could lose herself in overlarge sunglasses and $40 lotions and pretend she was fine.

Here, she could not pretend. Here, she was not fine. Here, she was a muddy reflection in the water, begging to be cleaned.

Her blood hit the earth. One drop, seeping from the open wound she had just inflicted on her own right index finger. It multiplied as it pooled. As she watched, blood trickled onto the path, rolling towards the forest edge and leaving a ruby trail in its wake. Here and there tiny rivulets branched off, as though they were forming their own veins, branches on a fast-growing tree of her flesh. On and on it went, until

Elizabeth lost sight of it completely on the dusty ground. She looked back at her finger. It was healed.

For a moment she reconsidered her own sanity, and whether it might have finally broken. But she recognized her surroundings, remembered where she was. Nothing else seemed out of place. Elizabeth closed her eyes, took a breath, and opened them again. The pattern on the ground remained. Frantically she mussed the dirt, noting its muddy texture, yet even when she removed her hands, the stain persisted. As she looked at it, the voices echoed in her mind, and in the breeze, growing louder the longer she stared at the scarlet sigil. Whatever this was, she wasn't imagining it. It was real. Something strange was happening at The Sanctuary.

Looking out at the water again, she noticed the pool of blood before her mimicked the exact shape of the pond. The whole thing resembled a treasure map, with an unknown X someplace beyond her vision. All of the sudden she didn't want to be out here anymore.

Hungry, raw, and exhausted, Elizabeth stood and marched back into the house, where she vigorously splashed water on her face and went to collect the kids.

***

"How was it?" asked a voice that was not her own, with a cheeriness she did not currently possess.

"Great!" sang Lily, resplendent with her pink cheeks pinching back her smile.

"Sucked," growled Cory, throwing his backpack upside down on the car floor and slamming the door.

Not again, please not again, prayed Elizabeth. Her eyes fought back the tears. Someone needed to be the strong one.

"Good news first."

Lily rattled off the friends she had made, how well she had done in her classes, the club she had already signed up for and how she was planning a run for student council. Elizabeth saw her son trying not to cry.

She knew he wanted to be like this. To be likable, to be easy. To be able to walk into a room and be instantly adored. In truth, he was closer than he knew. Good looking and athletic, a voracious reader who could speak humorously on any subject at all, Cory was what many men hoped to be. But he was only a boy. And he had inherited his father's distrust of...everyone. So he treated everybody like the enemy. And they, in return, saw him as theirs.

"Lily, that sounds awesome. I'm so happy for you." Her sensitive daughter was off to a good start, and the upside of a tiny school would be that she would be able to help her brother. Elizabeth hated herself for thinking it, knowing Lily had over functioned for her brother since the toddler years, but if desperate times called...

"Cory, any good news?"

"The work is easy."

"That's good! So your teachers should be pleased." That wasn't too much to ask for, right?

"Apparently I have an attitude problem."

Elizabeth's narrowed eyes met her son's in the rearview mirror. "Cory, I love you, but you admit to that one."

Grudgingly, he nodded, shifting in his seat. "Look, another kid was teasing me about my pendant and I called him a –"

"Cory, come on. You know better than that."

He punched the door of the car, then slouched. "It just wasn't a great start."

Her heart melted for her son. "I'm sorry, honey. But the first day is just that. Tomorrow is another one." He didn't look up. "Want a pet rat?"

His head snapped. "Huh?"

"Nevermind. Hey, shall we treat ourselves to some ice cream?" She had seen a sign at the farm stand this morning, fresh maple soft serve. A local treat that never lost its appeal.

That night, full of maple cream and bacon and egg sandwiches (Cory's favorite), Elizabeth called and left a message on the Eyes Up voicemail.

"Hi Denny, this is Elizabeth, over at The Sanctuary. Listen...I need help. Could you help me get in touch with that repair guy?"

Chapter Six

As she stood in front of the shadowy bathroom mirror, Elizabeth carefully traced her lips with rosebud pink stain. She had taken extra care with her appearance that morning, zipping herself into a black pencil skirt and adding a thin, sleeveless pink shell. Pearl earrings graced her lobes, and the last dollop of her high-end moisturizer was putting up a good fight against the bags beneath her eyes. The night before she had stayed up late going over the house from top to bottom, trying to make everything look presentable. Including her. This was her first visitor, after all. She didn't want to risk any harsh judgments on her home, her business...or herself. It was a small town, and first impressions mattered. She put on a pot of coffee, brushed her lank hair for a third time, and sat waiting idly on the couch, her back to the door while she listened for incoming signs of life. When the gravel growled in the drive, her hand contracted over the cushion, and her throat tightened. Why did she feel so nervous?

His footfall was surprisingly soft up the steps, and his knock was almost lazy. Elizabeth took a deep breath. Something was making her feel hazy, slow. She crossed the room in a daze, the warmth of the doorknob hot on her fingers as she pulled the door open and let the sun pour in.

Joe was almost exactly her own height, and their eyes met immediately. Two deep brown oceans stared at her, rimmed by long lashes. The black hair in his ponytail was wavy, she noticed now, and his beard meticulously trimmed. His build was slight. Somehow, she expected him to be bulky from doing repairs all day, but now she realized he likely worked more from brain than muscle. His fingers were delicate, presumably also an advantage. A faded orange flannel draped over a white tank top tucked into too-big jeans, and his work boots seemed at odds with the silence of his movements. A twig was stuck in his mouth. He didn't smile.

Something odd was happening. The edges of her vision went dark, and the silence was unnatural. Power expanded between them. It flowed from her body to his and back again, a circling that left her dizzy and weak. Elizabeth had no concept of how long they stood there. Time seemed to freeze while they stared at each other, recognition and confusion battling instinct. She could not breathe.

Eventually, she managed a weak, "Hi". He didn't answer, but he did walk in. Their eye contact broke as he surveyed his surroundings, footsteps still all but noiseless. He nodded.

"He was stubborn," Joe said. A hint of amusement ran through his husky voice. Deftly, he removed the stick from his mouth, holding it like a cigarette. "I kept telling him I could help him out, but he wouldn't take it. I respected that." He turned to look at her. "How bad is it?"

Oh. Business. Right.

"Well, I don't think there are any structural problems," Elizabeth answered in someone else's voice. She was shaking inside, but somehow her voice was steady, and borderline disinterested. In her house, or in him? "There's a sink that doesn't work, a washer that eats my clothes, a broken step, and what appear to be several strongholds of rats."

Joe's eyebrows went up. He said nothing.

"I don't expect you to take care of that," she hastened. Was that offensive? Was he as disgusted as she was? "But if we can fill their holes —"

"I can take care of it," he said with finality. "Doesn't sound too bad. Denny let me know the basics, I have some supplies in the van. You go about your day, I'll get to it."

Elizabeth felt herself being dismissed, and didn't appreciate it. Business women were supposed to show more strength. "I'm sure I can help," she said in what she hoped was a sweet but firm tone. The California smile showed up, a little late to the game but at full sunshine-power. "At least show you where—"

"No need."

She stared at him, that tension still running in the background as a new feeling emerged. Annoyance. Her grin slipped.

"I just don't want you to feel like—"

"Do you want me to fix it?"

"Well, yes—"

"Then I'll fix it. You'll pay me, problem solved. That's how this works." Joe looked at her with a furrowed brow and a look that registered somewhere between judgment and disbelief. "Are you always this controlling?"

It landed like a slap across the face. Elizabeth wasn't even sure how to respond politely to that. "I ... I guess I'm a little nervous. I'm used to doing things myself."

"Yeah, we noticed you don't come into town much." Joe shrugged. "Some people around here are like that. Just want to keep to themselves. Moved here so they can be alone. Nothing wrong with it, just wondering where you fall."

"Where do you fall?"

Joe had been heading for the door, but he stopped. He looked back over his shoulder, and put the twig back in his mouth. "Depends on who's asking."

The door closed silently behind him.

Elizabeth heard him opening the door to his van and took advantage of the opportunity to leave. Slowly she walked down to the pond and out of sight, letting the shaking strengthen as she paced back and forth. Little jumps moved through her, and she exhaled forcibly until she became lightheaded, and finally found a seat on the shore.

What the hell was that? What had happened to her? Maybe she was simply that tired, or that burnt out. That had to be the explanation. She was drained. She couldn't be ... lonely.

The word felt shameful in her thoughts. Gathering her knees to her chest, Elizabeth bent her head forward. For many years, she had focused on her children, her work, and herself, in that order. It wasn't that she never had friends, it was just that they didn't have deep conversations ... or frequent conversations ... or long periods of time together. Lots of people liked her, but she had never quite belonged. In truth, her marriage had felt much the same. Nothing bad, but nothing good either. Isolation had been her status quo, and it rarely bothered her. She didn't think about it, really. She didn't have time to think about it while she was keeping so many plates in the air. And in the few moments when she did ... well, she didn't like to admit it, but there was a longing in her. That ... perhaps, maybe ... could be called lonely.

But why had *he* set it off? Moreover, why had he noticed? Surely it wasn't normal to call someone controlling the first time you meet them. Begrudgingly, Elizabeth admitted to herself that people in Massachusetts were more brutally honest than she had expected. Maybe it was simply that. Culture shock.

But even that didn't explain what happened when she looked into those fathomless brown eyes.

Thinking of his eyes made the world go fuzzy again. She imagined falling into them, that mouth closing over her lips as she was held firmly in his arms. It was a silent, static daydream, a foreign sensation. Elizabeth studied it wonderingly. This man was a complete unknown, yet he was so familiar. Like The Sanctuary, Joe felt like a piece of her life just falling into place.

She sat by the pond, staring at the spot where her blood had sunk into the earth. The red trail had disappeared, though she thought the shadow remained if she looked hard enough. Where the initial wound had dripped, however, a new flower had sprung up. This was a surprise in itself, since most flowering plants had already moved to fruit or seed by this time of year. The bloom was fresh as a spring day, its five round white petals hugging a deep red heart. She had seen it no place else on the property, and the speed at which it had grown seemed unusual. Perplexed, and thinking to uproot some new weed, Elizabeth grabbed its dark stem and pulled. Pain shot through her thumb as tiny thorns pierced her skin, followed by a tingling sensation. She withdrew her hand but saw no puncture wound, and within seconds the strange feeling had subsided. When she looked back at the plant, a second flower had bloomed, and from the base, the same spidery red pattern had emerged on the earth, leading off into the distance. Elizabeth, distracted from her original purpose, rubbed her thumb absently against her palm, and took care not to step on the strange plant as she returned to the inn.

Metal sounds were echoing from the garage when she entered the house again, and the smell of coffee permeated the kitchen. Feeling a renewed sense of calm, Elizabeth poured it into two mugs, watching the black liquid flow, and then stop. She pushed aside the sense of déjà vu. Heavy clay steadied her hands as she balanced one cup in each hand and headed for the garage.

Joe's arm was deep inside the washer well, his back to her. The flannel had been removed, and she could see his bronze shoulders working some unknown piece. A piece of his hair had fallen into his face. She willed herself not to look at his waist, despite its demand for her gaze. Instead she cleared her throat, and he glanced over, not moving out of the washer.

"Brought you a cup of coffee," she said softly. Why couldn't she figure out which voice to use? Was she a businesswoman or a housewife?

She suddenly remembered that she was no one's wife. That looking at waistlines was, in fact, allowed.

He smiled at her.

Another wave distorting time and space sent her someplace warm and fluid. Now the shaking she had felt all morning reached her skin at last, and her fingers began to vibrate because he had smiled at her and her vision was failing again and something was falling apart and maybe it was her. He reached out and took the coffee.

"Thank you," he said. "You're welcome to stay, if you'd like."

"Sure," she answered, a little too quickly. "Maybe you can teach me something." Oh that sounded wrong. "About fixing machines!" she added hastily. "Or anything else I need to know about living here." *Deep breath, Elizabeth.* "It's been a bit overwhelming." These words had not been spoken aloud, and she felt them land in the room like an awkwardly placed elephant.

He looked back and smiled again, his lips tight. Probably pity, Elizabeth realized ruefully. She must seem like a wreck. But his response surprised her.

"Looks like you're doing fine so far. Last time I dropped in on Matty you could smell the mold in the house, and I saw bite marks missing from the food on the counter. So you've definitely made improvements."

Poor Matty. "I imagine he struggled living alone at that age."

"I imagine he did," agreed Joe to the washer basin. "But there were lots of folks who were ready to help him, if he hadn't been too proud to ask." He looked around at Elizabeth. "They'd probably help you, too, if they knew you."

"I already have the reputation of a hermit, huh?" she said quietly. The coffee was dark and cloudy in her hands, and she stared at it, the absence of reflection both a comfort and a wound.

Joe shrugged as he reached his whole arm into the washer, as though searching for a tiny sock. "California comes with a reputation, and new people come with a little suspicion. It's a rough combination. We don't know you yet."

We.

"I understand. I'm...not great at making friends, I suppose. Just never been one of my strengths. I hoped that moving here would help the kids, give them a nice tight-knit community...but maybe I didn't think that all the way through." The understatement of the century. Why was she telling him all of this?

Joe had his whole head in the washer now, and she could hear something being ratcheted in. "Just takes time," his voice echoed metallically. He pulled up, shook his ponytail out of his eyes, and met hers. "Give it a shot."

She smiled. "I will."

He laughed quietly to himself, turned the dial on the washer, and held his hand on it as the rhythm tapped perfectly. This time the world slowed down to a crawl as he paused before her, and the washer clicked with agonizing lassitude. Her breath was reluctant to leave her lungs. It disappeared entirely as he turned away, until his voice snapped her back into normality.

"What next?"

The next few hours passed companionably. Joe fixed things, she refilled coffee cups, he told her the best spots for fresh vegetables and cheap gasoline and which rivers to swim in while the weather was still warm. He spoke little of himself, and asked nothing of her. Elizabeth had never experienced a conversation this peaceful. She didn't need to keep up, or sound interesting, or make small talk. Joe was just as happy for her to sit quietly while he worked. Something about him put her at ease. Time continued to run at a variable pace as he sat with her, the sun slipping into an easy rest instead of rushing across the sky. In fact, she was alarmed to find it was nearly time to pick up the kids, and Joe still had projects to finish.

"No problem," he drawled in his low voice. "I can come back another time. Grab your kids, I'll be by again." No day was specified, and Elizabeth found herself more frustrated by that than she should have been. She was eager for another lazy morning. But all she said was "Thank you," as she walked him to the door. He stopped to look at her as he left, and that sensation of quiet stillness swam through her body. A hum began to whirr in the back of her mind, like a machine, or a chant, or a swarm. She was warm. She was too close to him.

He left without saying goodbye.

Just a little more time.

Time is inhuman, unbound by rules and regulations,
Running at his own pace in any direction he chooses
Backwards,
Forwards
In meaningless circles
Dancing around himself
A great fool with an eye for irony.
We watch him.
With enough observation even the chaos becomes
Pattern.
He has begun his spiral, like a hawk who spots a juicy morsel
Quivering beneath the golden blanket of leaves
No hurry
He can always stretch the moment
Let the salivary glands drip
Allow the wind to catch him just so.
There.
The first tip of the feather

Before he begins a slow descent
And at last
The dive.
Time is predictable.
We see the beginning.
It is time for the returning.

Chapter Seven

Denny's coffeehouse was jam-packed now that kids were back in school and tourists were back on the Mohawk Trail. It was still too early for "leaf peepers", the city folks who came up to see the fall foliage before retreating to their concrete jungles, but the apple orchards were ready. Weekends found them flooded with photographers capturing flannel-bedecked families, little girls crying because their new boots had mud on them while big brothers threw rotten apples at the ground to watch them burst. In stopping for her morning brew, Elizabeth got her first look at her prospective clientele.

She was saddened to find that she didn't much care for them. They came with expectations and requirements, a stringent idea of what they wanted and no concept of the place they were entering. She couldn't see playing maidservant for upper middle class socialites, which was, after all, what she had been trying to move away from. Having a loud family in her house, with video games going at top volume while parents spent their time on "very important calls", seemed to be against everything The Sanctuary stood for. True, she couldn't pick her guests, but she knew that the way she chose to market the spot would speak to different groups of people. When she had found The Sanctuary, she had been looking for someplace isolated, rustic, almost a separate world from the life she had been living.

So how did she find other people desperate to escape?

Her newly-purchased journal sat blank in front of her, with a bevy of colored pens at the ready, and inspiration nowhere to be found. Who wanted to escape to the cold and isolated backwoods of New England?

"Stephen King" she wrote. Strong start.

Escape.

"Moms."

Escape.

"Unhappy people."

This was getting her nowhere. She cradled her apple chai cider in her hands for a moment then held them to her forehead, letting the heat soothe the furrow she was holding between her brows. Why had she come here? Why had everyone else in town come here?

"Whatever you're writing, it looks like it hurts."

Elizabeth looked up to see Denny standing over her with a teasing smile on her face.

"What made you come here, Denny?"

Eyebrows flew up, and the smile softened. Denny pulled out the seat across from her. "Well now," she said. "It's been a long time since I came, and I was real young. Just out of high school. Knew I didn't want to stay in the South and really didn't much care where I ended up beyond that. So I came chasing a girl who was working on farms, which I thought was real cute. She moved on to the next town ... I stayed behind." Denny looked into space, apparently savoring the memory. "Just felt like home here, you know?"

Elizabeth nodded. She did know. It was the home that she wanted to share, the feeling of being back in some long forgotten childhood haven. Yet it had none of the hallmarks of childhood.

"What about the other folks in town?" Elizabeth asked, picking up a pen. "Why did they come here? Why does anyone come here?"

Denny laughed. "You're asking big questions! I think most folks come here because they're tired of being someplace else."

She remembered what Joe had said, about how many of the Solace Spring residents kept to themselves so purposefully. It was almost a community of introverts, she thought. Everyone wanting the best for each other...just as long as they didn't need to talk too much.

She thought of the silence of the pond. And then of the voices.

"What about spiritual people?"

"Lots of them, though they seem to prefer Vermont to here, or some of the bigger cities where they can get fancy crystals and such."

"We could have fancy crystals here."

"We already do," smiled Denny, her eyes moving up. "This cafe was certainly built with that vibe in mind."

"How did you choose the name?"

"I worked here when I moved, pouring crappy black coffee for working men and dried up Earl Grey sachets for the grannies. The guy who owned it got up every morning at five a.m., and made me do the same, just so we could be ready when the first logger came in at six. I hated the coffee, but I loved the people. When I turned twenty-nine, he sat me down to tell me he was planning to retire. Gave me one year to raise enough money to buy it from him. I did odd jobs, I cleaned houses, I helped with harvests, I did everything you can do in this town." Denny smiled, her elbows on the table as she leaned into her story. "I was a thousand dollars short the week of my 30th birthday. I cried all week, thinking how close I was to having my own business, my own place, the whole nine yards, and I had missed it." She leaned back. "The day I turned thirty, a big old group of folks came in and handed me a shoebox with a bow on it. A thousand dollars. They knew me so well by then that they had taken up a collection." Maybe it was Elizabeth's imagination, but it sure looked like there were tears in Denny's eyes. "I was so grateful to whatever higher beings had delivered me this home that I named it for them. Give everyone in town free coffee on my birthday every year since." Her eyes became keen again as she looked sidelong at Elizabeth. "There's a lot of power in this place," she said softly.

Time halted again, just as it had when Joe had come and gone. Whispers played around her ears, and her fingertips shook. Then the lights flared and she could hear the hustle and bustle of the coffee shop again, and Denny was gone. Elizabeth breathed deeply, her eyes unfocused, the pen limp in her hand.

A higher power.

She wrote it in the middle of a new page. Was that what everyone here was seeking? Was that why it felt like home? Maybe the trees brought people here against their will. A sort of earthy homing beacon, magnetizing seekers of magic. Of mystery.

Suddenly her cheek stung, and she looked around to see Lisa, her irate neighbor. The gaze which was fixed upon her was a complex mix of anger and curiosity. For a fleeting moment, Elizabeth wondered if she, too, held secret knowledge of these hills and streams. But a scowl settled onto the older woman's features, and she grabbed her coffee cup in a huff as she stood and all but ran out the door, practically running Mr. Grover down as she went.

"People have no manners these days," he growled, as he pushed his way through the door. "Everybody running around with their head up their own —"

"Here's your coffee, Grover," Denny said soothingly. "Do you need a cookie?"

"I'm not a child and I'll thank you not to treat me like one," he humphed. He sat in Lisa's empty seat and opened up a thin magazine, his reading glasses pinched halfway down his nose.

Well, maybe not everyone felt it, Elizabeth reflected. But she'd rather not have Mr. Grover staying in her home, anyway.

She checked her watch to see if she had time to return to The Sanctuary before school let out. Two hours left — more than enough time. Closing the journal, Elizabeth downed the last couple of sips, letting the spices burn her throat. She grabbed her purse and turned to go, just as Cory entered the front door. Dark hoodie intact, he moved straight up to the counter and ordered a coffee as she stared blankly at her truant child.

Denny looked at her. Cory followed her glance, and swore loudly.

"Young man, we do not tolerate language like that in this town!" Mr. Grover exploded. "We respect the public sense of decorum." He glared at Cory over the rims of his glasses. "Shouldn't you be in school, boy?"

It was a bad choice for Cory, whose temper was always so close to the surface. "Don't call me boy!" he yelled, standing threateningly over the elder man.

"Cory!" Elizabeth screamed. "I'm so sorry," she apologized to the crowd at large. "I'm sure Cory has had a rough time today or he wouldn't be here." She wheeled around to throw dagger-eyes at her son. "He's going to tell me all about it on the way home."

"It wasn't my fault."

"Somehow it never is," she grumbled.

"This kid pushed me!"

"Did he push you or run into you?"

"It's the same thing!"

"No, Cor, it isn't!" One hand slammed the steering wheel. "People are not out to get you! You can't keep acting like everyone passing you in the hallway is the enemy."

"They are the enemy!"

"No they're not!!!"

She knew it was stupid to shout, knew it was ruining her chance to have a rational discussion about it. They had the same fight every time, and no one ever won. It only made them both feel worse. From deep in her stomach, Elizabeth pulled out one small moment of calm. Her anger rolled out of her lips with her breath, and she felt herself steady. "How did you get all the way downtown?"

Cory's defensive posture dropped and he curled his shoulders over, moving deeper into the seat. His eyes shifted guiltily. "Hitchhiked."

Elizabeth felt her eyes widen to popping point and gagged on the punishment she longed to fling at him.

"Don't you know how dangerous that is?"

Her youngest child looked up at her with wet eyes. "I just couldn't stay, Mom." His voice cracked. For a moment she could see him as a two year old, scared and confused. "I couldn't stay one more moment."

The pain cascaded off of him, taking her temper with it. "Why didn't you call me?"

He shrugged, looked out the window. She saw the tears rolling down his cheeks.

"Let me call the school," Elizabeth said. "And then I'll make you a cup of tea."

So many calls. Calls from the school, calls to the school. Calls to kids' parents, and relatives. So many calls over the years, with the profuse apologies and assurances of good intent. She knew what they said when she hung up. She knew the damage was done, the teacher was pissed, the friend was gone. Worse, he knew. He knew that he had destroyed an opportunity — again.

Cory loved so hard. He was deeply passionate about his interests, his world, his books...and every so often, even a person. He was funny and creative and charismatic and intensely brilliant. It would be im-possible for anyone to understand all of his facets. Most people barely understood one. But his quirks made people angry, and his lack of social skills didn't help. So he attracted bullying, gave it back in spades, and was nearly always the one to end it. Usually in the principal's office.

She had hoped this time would be different.

At least the principal here was more mystified than angry, and she could have sworn she heard a chuckle when Elizabeth told him about the hitchhiking. He promised he and Cory would have a discussion the next day, which made Cory groan but Elizabeth breathe easier. He wasn't suspended. Not yet, anyway.

They drank tea on the porch, silently watching the yellowing leaves sway on the trees, growing ever more numerous and crowding out the great patches of green. Thick air seemed to weigh down the plants, bowing the stems and withering the flowers. Ducks flew overhead, some landing on the pond while others continued on, and on, to whatever warm country shores they dreamed of. They didn't speak ... until ...

"I miss Dad."

She knew it was coming but she couldn't think why. Tyler had always taken a hard line with Cory, making him feel worse with every infraction and taking his frustration out on the family as a whole. Acting appropriately was a high priority for Tyler. He expected his children to be delightful overachievers with their mother's good looks and his decisive ambition. And Cory ... just couldn't.

But a boy loves his father, and she had long ago accepted that even her best, calmest, most effusive love would never make up for Cory's dad. Dead or alive.

"I know."

Elizabeth put her arm around her little boy, and held him close to her heart.

That night, while both kids slept, Elizabeth doodled on a piece of paper. In the middle, she wrote "Sanctuary". Around the edges she carefully printed the people she wanted to shelter, identifying them by their dreams and fears, their needs. Their ghosts.

Loss

Grief

Identity

Peace

Inspiration

It was missing something. The connection. The magic. Something...vulnerable.

Community

The pen made big swishy movements in a circle, drawing everything together. Community. A place to be held while you healed.

Now *that* was magic.

As though they had heard her, voices seemed to whisper at the window. Pausing her list, Elizabeth closed her eyes and listened, trying to hear what they were saying.

A soft "*l*" shushed on the breeze. An open mouthed sigh. A swoop.

Light. Liiiiiiiiiiiiiiiiiight. Light.

She opened her eyes. There, in front of her, was the candle that had appeared on her doorstep when they first moved in. Home. Green and pungent, it seemed to look at her expectantly.

Light.

Elizabeth took the pillar in her hand, and reviewed her list again. Who needed a home here?

Me, she wrote.

She lit the candle, which perfumed the room with the smell of rosemary and lavender and something sweeter, and felt her body relax in response. Murmuring under her breath, she sang herself a lullaby, and let the candle burn until the moon had risen over the trees.

It all begins with circles.

Left to our own devices, we will all go in circles
Chasing our tails
Following our footsteps
Trying to get back to where we started.
When we arrive, the circle has always disappeared.
Yet on we travel,
Spiraling in search of
That Thing we were seeking,
Lost even from our tongues yet so clear in our hearts, and now
We know we must collect as we go.
Our helpers.
Our guides.
This acorn
That rock
The late rising sparrow.
We gather them to us, these priceless artifacts of our journey
Our solace on the lonely road.

Chapter Eight

The weekend dawned golden over The Sanctuary, heavy air finally replaced by a light breeze from up north. An indecisive earth basked in the warm sunlight and shivered in the dark patches. Stillness hung over the forest, as if it was waiting. One foot forward, one behind.

Lily and Cory had volunteered to do some work on the yard. While the garden's needs were less demonstrable than the ones inside, there was no doubt that a hefty portion remained to be done out in the waning heat. Piles of weeds to be pulled, beds in need of new soil or more water, and bushes that needed to be beaten back with a machete. In truth, Elizabeth expected that Lily had coerced her brother into it, but she wasn't about to turn it down. Some sunlight and physical labor wouldn't hurt either of them, and she knew that they were all racing against time to get the outside work done before the weather turned. It wasn't gratifying, this preparation — no pretty flowers or juicy fruit for your troubles. They were preparing the garden for death, as nobly as they could.

Cory was in a surprisingly good mood. His principal had, unexpectedly, congratulated him. He told Cory he had been impressed by his initiative in hitchhiking away from school in the middle of the day. Elizabeth's jaw had almost hit the floor when Cory told her, but as she watched his cheerful demeanor that evening, setting the table and talking about the joke he told in class, she had to admit that perhaps the man knew his stuff. The frank admiration, even paired with the detention time, was working wonders. Rather than feeling defeated, Cory felt respected, and nothing mattered more to him than respect. With the weekend before him and a clearer record than expected, he was feeling like the new school wasn't so bad after all, and had even offered a grudging apology to the kid who pushed him (or more likely, walked by at the wrong angle).

So she decided to leave the kids to it for a bit and do a little self-care for once. Promising to be back within an hour or two to pitch in, Elizabeth headed up to the road and found herself, for the first time since they arrived, wandering away from her own land.

Farmhouses rose and fell on both sides, separated by what would have been two or three blocks and a strip mall back at home. Here it was just...space. It was easy to lose track of how far she had gone, with no landmarks to mark the distance between here and there. Just an endless sea of trees that faded one into the other, differences so miniscule that she could not use them for footing. Only the occasional homestead charted her course through the wilds of the Berkshires.

She had just passed a short brown house with a field of late sunflowers and a slope-backed white horse in the pasture when she saw a road leading off to a little glen on the right. Down she followed it, running a little to catch her feet, until the path curved around and flattened out. Soon she was out of sight of the main road, traveling between maple trees and beech groves, a few yellow leaves weakly carpeting the ground at her feet.

Strange how the same forest felt so different. The deep gravitas she felt in her own backyard was tempered here. She felt softer in the liminal space beneath these branches. Cozy little dens awaited her here, tempting her to nap beneath the trees like some sort of elderly fairy. A pocket universe waiting for her to awaken it. And until then ... nothing. Nothing happened here. She couldn't say how she knew it, but the void was obvious. Nothing good. Nothing bad. Nothing. Truly empty space.

Elizabeth passed through the thicket of trees, and as the ground grew darker she could hear the river bubbling nearby. It must run narrower here, she thought. Or maybe this was one of the innumerable streams that branched from it, coming and going with the rains and snows. It sounded gentle, like the water was laughing. So she chased it.

Joyfully, she quickened her step, listening to the water's call. As she drew closer to the river, the bubbles turned to rushes ... the water must have deepened. Somewhere in the back of her mind, she heard the crash of waves on hot sand, the soundtrack of their previous summers. There had been no lakes or rivers to speak of in their near-desert habitat out west, and for Elizabeth, the ocean had always been too strong and willful for her to enjoy. But it was the thing to do, so she went, and brought her children up in the waves she avoided, wading in only as far as her children's safety required. But this river was different. Inviting. It coaxed her with a song as varied as the woods that surrounded it, moving from the light to the dark, the shallows to the depths. The river was a story that just kept going.

Golden leaves fluttered from peeling white birch trees, thicker here in the cakey mud. The sun felt warmer. It filtered through the canopy and came to rest on tiny specks of dust that hung motionless in the air, an earthy mist of light. Elizabeth was pondering the phrase "golden afternoon" when she heard music coming from nearby. She hadn't seen any signs pointing to a house, but around here that made little difference. Anxiety clutched her heart for a moment — property protection was real in this area, and most people kept guns in the house — but as she still saw nothing, she veered closer to the sound of the water and moved into a clearing, where she finally saw the sparkling water emerge from the forest. Music was indeed pouring not from a house, but from a VW van, in pristine shape and parked near the river with a camping chair and table out front.

Elizabeth assumed that guns were less likely for van-dwellers, and walked on, intending to bypass the little dwelling entirely. But a bar of music was carried on the wind, and she paused to listen to a familiar feminine voice croon lyrics assuring her that it wasn't too late for love.

One of her old favorites. Elizabeth moved closer to the sound, eagerly trying to catch each line. For a moment she forgot herself, her face in the sunshine and her feet dancing on gold, swaying slightly with eyes closed. When she opened them, Joe was standing by the camp chair, watching her.

"Sorry!" she ejected breathlessly. "I love this song." It spurted out of her unbidden, a waterfall hello. She was spilling over the ground, fighting to remain upright in his gaze. Behind him, trees shifted and waved, a dizzying field of light.

He smiled. "I can tell." Slowly, he walked towards her, in the unhurried way he did everything, each step measured and intentional. He held out his hand to her. "Would you like to dance?"

For just a moment, she took it, felt his fingers close onto her hand as he pulled her close...and then the music ended.

Silence stretched on.

"I guess that's the end," Elizabeth said nervously, a tight smile on her lips.

He dropped her body, and turned his back. "Record players are like that," he said over his shoulder.

She followed him back to the van, unsure what the protocol was for this kind of interaction.

"Do you want some coffee?"

"Sure," she replied. She saw now that the van was far more than a mode of transit. It was a castle, carefully tucked into a puzzle. One side door was open, revealing a thick mattress with a faded quilt and a blanket knitted from crushed purple velvet. The walls were lined with books — philosophy, history, motorcycle maintenance — that were secured by wooden shelves, and a solar powered lantern sat atop a small anchored nightstand. Drawers lined the back of the passenger seat, beneath a fold out counter supported by a beam on the running board. Upon it was a single burner, still smoking slightly, with a sturdy steel French press on a trivet beside it. Joe pulled two mugs from one of the drawers and filled them with dark liquid, lightening one with a few drops from his tiny pot of cream. He handed it to her.

"This is amazing," Elizabeth said, unable to take her eyes from the marvel of the van. "Did you do this all yourself?"

"Yup," he answered, sipping. She saw pride in his eyes, the master engineer who had created this all-serving machine. "It took about six months to get everything up and running the way I wanted it. Now I'm free."

A shadow passed over his face. Nothing changed in his tone or features, but the air grew chill for the briefest moment. An angry fire roared in her chest, and in the same moment, subsided. Bewildered, Elizabeth pressed on.

She looked at him. "You live here? All the time I mean?"

"Yes."

A beat of silence again, and an unspoken dare to react. An invisible door shut between them, and he stared at her defiantly through the window. He was unreachable.

"Doesn't it get cold? Doesn't the engine freeze?"

"I'm careful to keep it warm enough, and I have space heaters inside. There are solar panels on top, and I keep propane handy for the camp stove. In the winter, I find warmer places to park it, a garage or an empty barn, but for the most part I prefer it this way." He sipped again. "It's quiet."

"You can't beat the view, that's for sure." Elizabeth turned her back to the van and surveyed the pristine river, feeling a little sleepy as its melody lilted over her. "Don't you get lonely?"

Joe looked her directly in the eyes. "Do you?"

This felt like a rhetorical question, and one that she preferred not to ponder, so she ignored it. The river flowed on, an interrupted ribbon of black and silver against the bright green hills curling up behind. A murmur caught the air, and Elizabeth looked back and forth for the source of the sound.

"Did you hear something?" Joe stood just behind her, watching her search the air.

"I thought I did," she admitted, still looking around. The whispers were quieter, but still there. "It's been happening to me lately. I guess I'm just not used to silence."

He stared at her. Apparently, silence was no problem for him. In the unspeaking void, the murmuring grew louder again. She could almost catch the words on the wind, while she stood blinking slowly at his dark eyes. Pools of something else entirely.

He walked away.

Elizabeth fought the instinct to shake her hands out, as she felt her heart racing and wished she could run away from whatever it was that locked her here. But Joe was pulling another chair from the trunk of the van, smoothing out the multicolored canvas. Then he turned to the record player on the camp table, moved the needle, and dropped it gently onto the spiraling disk. A woman's deep voice slid over the trickling piano.

"Sometimes you need to ease into silence," Joe said. He gestured to the chair beside him. She sat, and sipped her coffee, and let the voices evaporate in the sunlight. Joe partnered her in the quiet, like a leaf unfurling in the sun. His cold exterior melted away. Gradually his movements became a dance, gently lifting his coffee as he looked out at the gleaming landscape, chest rising and falling in harmony with the music. Elizabeth envied his relaxed posture, his integration into this space where she still felt a stranger. She wondered how long it had taken him to become part of the forest. Her own body was going through a series of contractions and expansions, as the impulse to chatter rose and died in her throat over and over. Try as she might, she could not string together a sentence. A feverish glow emerged as she watched Joe's hands move to a rhythm she could not hear.

Perhaps this was how silence began.

Was it her heartbeat she felt, or the earth's? Or Joe's? Were they all the same? Was that the effect of this place, to synchronize the blood that traversed it? If you stayed long enough, did you become one of these towering giants, pumping nutrients from the mycelium up into the sky? Elizabeth thought of the maple houses common to this area, the sticky sweetness that cycled through that immense length as they poured their life force into the vivid leaf buds, or fell into winter's hibernation. Still. And silent. Until they were so rudely awakened, and drained.

"How do they know when it's too much?"

She spoke aloud without meaning to, but Joe didn't flinch. His gaze focused on her slowly, as though she was moving too fast for him to see clearly. "What's too much?'

"The maple trees. How do they know when it's too much?"

"They die."

Elizabeth's head whipped around to look at him. The look on her face must have amused him, because he gave her a rakish grin.

Settling back into his chair, he launched into a detailed explanation of maple husbandry, from when the season began to how to tap the trees, tracking their wellness and seeding new growth. She half-listened, letting his words wash over her as she observed his movements, now growing more expansive as he allowed himself free reign in what was clearly familiar territory. It occurred to her that perhaps he had been uncomfortable around her, too. Surely living in a van by the river meant he wasn't much for people, but she had assumed this was born of anger. Now she saw the shyness that fell from his face as he shared his knowledge, and felt her heart open to this strange neighbor. She had misjudged him.

Maple trees led to maple recipes, led to talk of Mexican food and white sand beaches he had never visited. Light subjects, nothing that told them anything about each other. That glass wall still stood between them. She let the ocean be carried away by the river until the silence returned. Side by side they sat as the record played, adding its scratchy notes to the flow. Soon the sun was behind them, and Elizabeth realized with a pang that her responsibilities awaited her. The empty coffee cup in her hand seemed to frown. Ruefully, she passed it back to her smiling host.

"I can make another pot."

An invitation. A tempting one.

"Not this time." Goodness, where had *that* come from? It was flirtatious. An invitation of its own. Feeling flushed, she turned her back on the pretense of noticing the sun's angle. "The kids will be needing me." Always. Always needing her. A weight seemed to bend her shoulders forward, and she felt guilty for wanting to stay. Just one more cup.

"You're welcome any time." Joe stood. "I don't usually talk this much, but I feel oddly comfortable with you." The wrinkle between his eyebrows deepened in confusion. A mismatched puzzle piece. Out of place. He took her cup from her hands, still warm. "You're easy to talk to." Elizabeth noticed his breath grow shallow with the confession. She allowed herself one last look up at him. Joe was standing still, waiting to meet her eyes, and she was surprised into smiling. The afternoon light illuminated her, erasing the years from her face and the worries from her body. A strong breeze picked up the yellow leaves from the ground and swirled them past her hair. Unknowingly, Elizabeth transformed, a radiant goddess in her evening bower. Joe exhaled.

"Thanks. I'll take you up on that offer." Her tongue felt heavy in her mouth, carrying too many unspoken words. But when she reached for them, she found nothing to say. She settled for his name. "Bye, Joe."

He nodded. She began her walk back to The Sanctuary, and when she looked behind her, she saw him watching her until he was lost from view.

Chapter Nine

"I've been thinking you need some company."

The announcement came from overhead while Elizabeth downed her morning coffee between the notes to self pecked onto her laptop. Denny stood over her, looking both loving and critical. A mother look. Elizabeth found herself slightly resentful to be on the receiving end.

"Aren't you company?" she said wryly. "I thought that was why I came here ... for the company."

Denny side eyed her as she poured a half cup into the nearly empty mug. "I meant *male* company," she said meaningfully. "You remember men. They're those other kind of people, kind of a pain in the ass but with some definite benefits." She waggled her eyebrows in a way that straddled the space between suggestive and silly.

"What?!?" Elizabeth laughed. "You must be kidding." She gestured to her body, clad in stained jersey workout clothes, free of makeup or indeed, a shower. "This is not attractive to a man. This isn't even attractive to me."

"There's more to love than looks!" Denny insisted.

Elizabeth hesitated. Tyler used to love showing her off, making sure she was the most attractive woman in the room. Just like the house, the kids, and of course, himself. Looks were all that mattered. As long as everything looked perfect, the fact that life was disconnected and painful was irrelevant. So that's how the relationship had stayed — beautiful, and broken.

"I'm not ready for that," she said firmly. "I'm a widow, remember? A stranger, and a widow. With two kids. And an inn full of rats. I am not in a place for a relationship."

"Well, maybe there's a relationship with a place for you." Elizabeth got the feeling that Denny was one of those women who wouldn't take no for an answer, but she was too tired to fight. Surrender it was.

"Tell you what, Denny, you find someone who's interested, and I'll give it one date to change their minds."

"Well as it happens —"

Of course. She should have known. Denny had already lined it up.

***

It had been a long time since she had gotten ready for a date. She stood before the mirror, placing gentle touches to her sagging neck, noticing the tiny folds appearing in the skin. Puffy pillows dragged her eyes down, and her face was somehow both pale and weather worn. She felt old. It had been simple enough to ignore while she was immersed in the preparations of the house, the land, the kids. Now, with nothing to look at but herself, disappointment clouded her eyes.

She used to be beautiful.

It had been important to her, being beautiful. As an ugly duckling of a child, growing into herself had been life-changing. It gave her a seat at the table, and she would dazzle everyone who joined her. Laughing and witty, with a tiny waist and hips that swayed, Elizabeth had been very popular for a few years. Then she met Tyler, and she had stayed beautiful for him. As the years went on, it got harder not because her body changed, but because her heart did. She took less pleasure in her own appearance, and since her husband had exited their lives, she had barely noticed herself at all. Now the lack of maintenance had taken its toll, possibly beyond repair. She hadn't even watched herself go.

At least, Elizabeth reasoned with herself, it would be easy to make this a first and last date. No need to go to too much trouble. She slapped some blush on her cheeks and some color on her lips, drew pencils across her lashes and brows, and nodded curtly to her reflection. It was a masculine gesture, and she turned away from it. Maybe a dress would help her find the woman she used to be.

Boxes still littered the house, and DRESSES was one she had not bothered to unpack. That morning she had unearthed it from its tomb in the basement, and dragged it up the stairs groaning. Now she sat on her bed, the open box in front of her, colorful fabrics peeking out of the top. She hated them. All of them. Memories strangled her as she pulled on spaghetti straps and sashes. Plastic smiles. False laughter. Overpriced cocktails and plates with too little food. These were souvenirs of the life she had left behind, and she neither missed nor desired it. But it had followed her here, sneaking in in this box of trophy wife paraphernalia, convincing her that that woman was all she would ever be.

"Mom?"

Lily was standing in her open door, watching her pull the dresses out one by one and throw them on the ground.

"I don't want to wear these."

It was more guttural than she had intended it to be. Usually she was so careful to keep her emotions in check around the kids, but caught unaware, her defenses were down.

Lily understood. "Then don't wear them, Mom." She crossed the room and took Elizabeth in her arms. A warning went off in her protective mother brain — *she's the kid, get a hold of yourself* — but for just a moment, Elizabeth allowed herself to breathe her daughter's flowery perfume and simply be held.

It had been a long time.

"Maybe I do need this date," she said, forcing a chuckle.

"Mom, it's OK if it goes well," Lily replied, squeezing her hand. "We want you to be happy."

Elizabeth squeezed back. "Thank you," she said, "but I don't think I'll be happy in any of these."

Lily's eyes lit up. "Wait here!" She ran out of the room, reappearing a minute later with a massive armful of clothes. "Olivia gave them to me, she's changing her style and didn't want to toss them. But I don't think they're me, either. Maybe they're you."

Intrigued by her daughter and the unknown Olivia, Elizabeth ran her hands over the raw cottons, the sober blues and earthy greens, heavy fabrics that proudly showed the imperfect spaces where human hands had touched them. Chunky sweaters and peasant blouses. Corduroy skirts and linen pants. They felt like this place. Like part of the land.

Elizabeth looked at her daughter with deep gratitude.

"Thank you."

She kicked the hated box of cocktail dresses over.

"Trade you."

***

Wind tickled bare skin as her hands moved convulsively to the fabric every few seconds. The ponderous folds donated by a local teenager felt foreign on her body, like curtains over a stage that she wasn't ready to stand on. The olive skirt drifted lazily around her ankles, with a waistband refusing to meet the short cream colored peasant blouse Lily had paired it with. Elizabeth folded her arms over the single inch of midsection that was left exposed, somehow feeling both liberated and ill at ease. Apparently discomfort was the cost of freedom.

There were no streetlights in town, so she sat on the porch of the local pizza joint trying to fade into the blackness without actually running away. Denny had told her that Mitch was a nice man, a divorcé with no children but a classy house near the Vermont border, where he had a woodworking shop and (like everyone else) a maple grove. Elizabeth vaguely remembered him on the laundry list of names Denny had pointed out in the shop when she first moved here, but was quite sure she had never spoken to him.

Even if she had been wearing her usual clothes (which she hated), or been home in California (was it home anymore?), Elizabeth would not have been prepared for this date. It had been twenty years since she had been on a date, and frankly she had been bad at it then. Usually she made it to the second date or even the third, but it would fizzle long before becoming anything like a relationship. That's why she had married Tyler. He was the first one to make it that far, and she couldn't be sure it would ever happen again.

It probably shouldn't have happened the first time.

"Hi."

Standing on the steps was a man with chestnut brown hair and a warm, slightly crooked smile. He was looking directly at her.

"I believe I'm supposed to buy you a slice."

***

All in all, thought Elizabeth as she drove home, it hadn't been half bad. She had apologized for her nervousness and rusty social skills for the first fifteen minutes, at which point Mitch had gently taken her hand, looked sincerely into her eyes to say that it didn't bother him one bit — he was happy for any kind of company. The usual "tell me about yourself" had revealed that he had married young to a woman who had always wanted to live in the city, and how his ten years in Boston had proved to him that he could never stay. They had parted ways amicably enough, and he had focused on his art as a way of healing and accepting this new life path. Time rolled on and Mitch's work appeared in galleries and gift shops all through the Berkshires, giving him a great deal of pride and satisfaction. He forgot about relationships, preferring to dedicate himself to creating the home he had longed for during his time away. It sounded like a beautifully quiet and fulfilling life to Elizabeth, and she said so.

"I love my life," said Mitch. "But I know there are experiences I'm missing, and it's time I left my comfort zone just a little bit to see if I can enjoy them."

He had hesitated here, meeting her eyes over the top of his pint glass, as her chest and cheeks turned their preferred sunburn red.

"Good pizza here," she responded.

By the end of dinner she had agreed to see him again, a walk by the river on Sunday evening. He worked often with fallen wood, and spent some of his days wandering the forests looking for likely pieces. This had struck her as a low-stakes date, and she wondered if he had offered it for that purpose. Mitch's eyes had searched hers as they said their goodnight.

"I'm really glad you joined me tonight, Elizabeth."

"Me too," she said. "It's good to get out more...and now I know where the best takeout in town is." Her glib smile covered the fact that she was stepping backwards as she spoke. Mitch continued to watch her carefully. He took one step forward and Elizabeth began to search her pockets for her keys.

"Thanks so much for dinner, Mitch, I had a really good time. I have to get home...the kids and all..." The distance between them expanded rapidly as she spoke, eagerly moving towards her car. Mitch stopped, and nodded his understanding.

"Good night, then, Elizabeth." He raised a hand in farewell as she wrenched open the car door, and she called "Good night!" as she pulled into the road at full speed. Only when she had regained the darkness of the highway did she begin to breathe normally again.

By the time she pulled into The Sanctuary, Elizabeth had calmed. She tiptoed up the stairs and began her bedtime routine. What she was supposed to be feeling, she wondered. Were there meant to be butterflies? When would she start acting like a woman in love? How long did this sort of thing go before it became...something?

At last she soothed herself by saying it would probably be nothing, and she turned out the light and fell fast asleep.

In the middle of the night, Elizabeth heard voices. At first she was sure she was dreaming, rolled over to empty her head and begin a new REM cycle, but the voices grew louder and louder until she sat bolt upright in bed. Someone in the house? No, because they weren't coming from downstairs. They were coming from the window.

Tremulously, she crossed the room and opened the sash. She felt a hot wind pulsing into the room carrying vibrations, deep feminine voices speaking words she could not understand. Syllables were gar-bled but insistent, making demands of her. Sounds pulled at her body, reeling her closer and closer to the window. Trancelike, she removed the screen, and stepped onto the roof of the house. They applauded, softened into a whispering hiss that swirled around her body. How sweet, Elizabeth thought dreamily. How kind of them to hold me here, between the earth and the stars. She felt as though she was being born on the wind of their words. As though she could fly. Stretching out her arms, she felt the air support her as the song became frenzied and wailing, egging her on, begging her to come, come, come closer.

She woke safe in her own bed when the sun came up. The screen had been removed from her window.

Chapter Ten

Denny, emboldened by what she considered her unequivocal success at match-making, had now started pushing Elizabeth to make friends of the female persuasion as well. "You need community," she said matter-of-factly. "You can't just be on your own out here. It's too hard. Plus people will think you're crazy." This finality came with a sharp look that made it very clear that Elizabeth did not want the people of Solace Spring to find her crazy. She had to admit that being a hermit and a business owner was a bad combination. To do what she wanted to do here, she would have to get out more.

The problem was that getting out more would mean taking time from two all-consuming areas of her life — home repairs, and raising her kids. Lily, she knew, would be fine. The Inn and Cory, however, both seemed perpetually perched on the precipice of their own undoing, and any moment not spent watching them was a considerable risk.

To be fair, Cory wasn't doing as bad as he could be (and Elizabeth knew how deep that hole went). He was attending his classes, and hadn't created any major chaos so far. She had been emailing his teachers weekly to check on his progress, and though he still wasn't turning in any of the homework she made him do at the kitchen table each evening, he was managing to pass all of his classes. This was part of the problem — he was so bright that he had figured out he could get by without doing any work. Elizabeth had brought this up with the principal, the counselor, and the district mental health coordinator, but just as in California, no one had any ideas for her.

"He's still adjusting."

"He'll make new friends."

"Once he's been here awhile, these behaviors will decrease. We've seen it before, and you really don't need to worry so much."

The problem was that she knew her son, and she knew his cycles. This wasn't new behavior, borne of a cross country move or a dead dad. This was how he had always functioned. Every school he had ever attended had handed them to the experts, the administrators, the assessors and the specialists. No one knew what to do with Cory. He was neurodivergent, but not enough so to explain his apparent need for destruction. He was brilliant, but other than lording that over classmates, he didn't seem inclined to use his skills. He was handsome and charismatic, but he never made friends. Elizabeth had tried gentle parenting, strong routine, disciplined consequences, letting him lead. She had moved through every parenting dogma she could find, and still nothing helped her son to feel at home. He was simply always one step from disaster. So she lived her life waiting for the fallout.

In the meantime, the house had been rid of pests and broken appliances, and was now onto more aesthetic repairs. After another nasty surprise conversation from Lisa, this time about peeling paint on the house's exterior, it became clear that The Sanctuary was, after all, looking a bit ragged. She was less concerned with the outside, however, than the in. Outside, the gardens and vistas distracted the eye; inside, there were only flickering lights and mismatched color palettes. Elizabeth walked the interior of the property with a roll of red stickers, marking each bowed step, broken plank, missing baseboard, broken plaster. By the time she was done, the house looked like it had chicken pox. She divided the chores into a list of what she could handle, and what she needed expert help with. Joe had said he would return to do more of these odd jobs, but Elizabeth had realized belatedly that she had no way to contact him. It seemed rude to hunt him down at his car/home and ask him to work, so she made a mental note to keep her eyes open for him at the coffee house. There were likely others who could handle the job, but something in her was reluctant to find someone else. Just thinking of Joe made her smile, and if she remembered the way her hand felt in his ... *another week wouldn't hurt,* she thought. *He'll be back.*

In the meantime, it looked like she had a rare opening in her social calendar.

The notice board at Eyes Up was always full of various handwritten notes or poorly designed flyers, papers that added small town charm but that Elizabeth had never reviewed properly. On her next trip downtown, she stood in front of its multicolored chaos. Traditionally she had sought out groups that focused on some sort of activity, giving her an exit from any unnecessary social interaction. In fact she excelled so much at this type of work that she had received several awards from various groups for the productivity she showed while avoiding conversation. She just needed to find that space here.

"Quilting circle." Surely she wasn't that old. "Toddler Playgroup." Nor that young. "Bible fellowship meeting." Nope. Yoga class. Study sessions. Tea ceremonies. Where were all the middle-aged women? Had the moms been erased? Did they simply go into their homes and lock out the world, as she wanted to? Perhaps the burdens of midlife were simply too heavy to share. Or maybe everyone else was as tired as she was.

But she had made a promise, so she scooted down to the modest town hall across the square, which was never open but perhaps had its own board of activities posted some place. The white washed building stood lazily across from the library, stern columns slightly bent with age, the red door outshining the hazy windows and concrete steps. It looked distracted, as though perhaps it had been so long since its last use that it had forgotten how to be a building. By contrast, doors suddenly flung open next door, and the ABC song echoed briefly from within its recesses.

The library.

Suddenly Elizabeth remembered a hallway of cork board covered with neon papers, just past the checkout desk. She switched direction, grasping the library's heavy door and opening it to a sudden applause from tiny hands. Apparently, she had made the right choice.

Bobbing gentle nod at the librarian, she quickened her pace, looking for the small yellow note she had seen weeks ago on her first visit. There it was, beside a full color poster for the annual Fall Festival, tacked on with a small flowered thumbtack. Book Club. Third Wednesday of each month. Three days away.

She took note of the title and tried to remember the last time she had read a book in under four months. College? Surely not. Before kids, for certain. Somehow she just never found the time for reading anymore. But fast reading was a better prospect than quick sewing. Feeling self-conscious of the late inquiry, she shuffled back to the desk to ask the librarian if, by chance, any copies remained.

"Excuse me?"

A braided crown of red hair bent back, revealing a pale face and blue eyes so light they seemed to vanish behind her glasses. Thin lips gave a careful smile, the same almost friendliness Elizabeth recognized in her own voice.

"How can I help you?" the librarian whispered.

Elizabeth would not have been surprised to find this woman floating on the breeze, so insubstantial was her manner. Everything so soft, so thin. A paper person. Perhaps that was the best temperament for a book tender.

"I know it's late," she apologized, "but I'm new in town and I'm just starting to get...comfortable." A lie, but a white one...no one needed to know how uncomfortable she was. "You wouldn't by any chance have any copies of this week's book club selection, would you?"

A smile shone across that pearlescent face, revealing perfectly white teeth. Her eyes sparkled. "You're Elizabeth!"

Perplexed but flattered, Elizabeth compromised by nodding and blushing furiously.

"Denny told me all about you. I don't go to the coffee house often — too noisy for me — but I'm so glad you've come in! We're all so happy to have another woman in town." Her whisper dropped in pitch a bit. "Sometimes it seems like it's all old men around here." She grinned.

An image of the coffee house popped into Elizabeth's head, and with a shock she realized that this was true — she had been surrounding herself with men without realizing it. "It does, doesn't it?"

"I'm Tiffany." A tiny hand extended over the counter. "We'd love to have you join us for book club. I don't have any library copies available right now, but here, take my copy."

"Oh, I couldn't!" Elizabeth protested.

"I insist! I've finished it anyway. And you don't need to worry if you don't. I would say at most half of us ever do." She paused, looking cheeky. "Usually me, but I have an advantage in that I have no children and a job that lets me read all day long." A bright orange cover slid over the aged granite. "Please, take it."

Elizabeth hesitated. Maybe this was too soon. Too fast. "How many people are in the club?"

"Oh maybe a couple of dozen, but it's rare we have more than fifteen at a meeting. We meet right here at the library, and we love folks to bring a snack to share but it's not mandatory — we know life happens. Really it's just a space for us to gather and share and sometimes remember that there are other stories in the world, too." Tiffany beamed up at Elizabeth, her red hair somehow brightening, too. "I promise to introduce you to everyone and not to make you do any talking at all. Sound good?"

It sounded perfect. Sadly, too perfect to refuse.

"I guess I'll see you Wednesday," Elizabeth said shyly. Good gracious, even this simple conversation had her feeling out of place. But it was too late now. And Tiffany seemed truly kind. Elizabeth had lived enough to know that a kind heart was not a gift you took for granted.

"Can't wait," Tiffany said warmly, handing her a copy of the yellow flyer. "Don't forget!"

Tucking the note inside of her book, Elizabeth waved awkwardly and left in as much a hurry as civility allowed.

***

It wasn't a bad book. The story revolved around a grown woman retracing the roots of her family, pulling up ugly truths and buried happinesses, placing the puzzle pieces over the empty spots in her own life. Elizabeth followed her down the rabbit hole, observing the character's deep emotional purging. What must that be like, she wondered idly, to feel all of that stuck space loosen and emerge? How it must have pained her throat before she screamed. Parts of her began to echo the main character, asking for that same release. For the scream. She put the book down, raw from its intensity. Maybe it was better to focus on the snack she would bring.

Elizabeth had once been much sought-after for her baking, usually in the same groups that rewarded her for most mailers folded or greatest number of donations processed. She was a gentle workhorse, always handling everyone's needs, even those they hadn't yet acknowledged. Bringing baked goods to meetings was her calling card, often getting her out of contributing with her voice. That was what she needed now. Meeting Muffins. No one could ever resist a warm muffin.

Somewhere in the recesses of her mind was Tiffany's kind assurance that she needn't bring anything, nor finish the book. She ignored it. A glance at the clock told her it was a little past 1:00 a.m. She was tired, and her body felt sluggish, but she told herself a good first impression was worth it. A business needed customers, and reviews, and people who would put her name out there. Her family needed her to make this happen. Raggedly, she returned to the couch, determined to make it to the last page. All thoughts of friendship dissipated as she pushed herself to the task at hand — being ready for whatever they threw at her.

***

"Cory?" Elizabeth cautiously opened the door to his room, strewn with metallic findings and what appeared to be the entire contents of his laundry hamper. No reply.

"Lily?" The crystalline purple room was empty as well, not counting the half finished paintings, crochet projects, sculptures, and music sheafs. Her floor was littered with golden leaves she was pressing between books, and birch branches she was "collecting" for some unnamed task.

Elizabeth trudged downstairs, calling as she went. "Children! Kids! Teenagers! Olly Olly Oxen Free!" But apparently there was no one to tell her this was lame and uncool. The house was still.

Peering out the window, she saw signs of movement down at the pond. Lily was likely to be found there, sketchbook in hand, staring at geese and beavers. She had befriended the local wildlife, and they would now let her come close enough to draw their funny faces. Her newest project was carefully preserved dragonfly skeletons, which she pushed into mossy backboards and framed. Both kids had always been drawn to the spaces where life and death converged. The newly autumnal days of New England were everything they wanted.

Cory could not be found at all. This was a new habit, disappearing entirely. There was no way to tell how far he wandered from home every day, and though Elizabeth worried about predators and lack of maps, he always returned by sundown. His forced presence at the kitchen table became a nightly bickering, as mother chided son toward homework while his eyes traveled over and over to the window that watched the forest.

"What is out there that you need to go back to?" she had asked. "Haven't you seen enough trees?"

A crease formed between his square eyebrows while he chose his words. He was mostly hers, with her prominent cheekbones and long arms, and perpetual need to squint even when they could see just fine. That look, however, was his father's. Tyler acquired it when he was stuck on a question he couldn't answer, always a blow to his pride. Cory was the same. Sometimes she wondered if that big brain wasn't more trouble than it was worth.

"It's not the trees," he said suddenly, eyes still fixed on the blackness. Something was lower in his voice, a glimpse into his grown man self who was not yet constructed. "There's something else out there. Not a creature. More a feeling. Something to understand."

Yes. With Cory, there was always something he needed to understand. Yet she knew the feeling. It was what had drawn them here, year after year, the gentle rumble of something in the air, beneath the feet. A presence.

"I feel it, too," Lily chimed in. "It's like something is trying to speak to me, in a language I don't understand."

"Yes." Cory ripped his eyes from the window to meet his sister's. "That's exactly it."

For the briefest moment Elizabeth saw a gleam of light connecting her two children, a revelation shared between them. Then Lily left the table and walked out the door, and her brother followed.

This was the kind of thing they had always done. Simply removed themselves from the world of what was to move into a shadow space of lost time. Elizabeth had never stopped them, feeling that they were safe and tended to and needed to explore such things for themselves. In California, it had seemed a small blip, a silly game, something to set them apart from their peers. Here, however ... here the Otherworld felt real. She remembered the muddled voices, the glowing path ... her window. A darkness pressed in closer upon her, permeating her skin, pulsing within her, and she fought to come back to her empty kitchen table with the door standing ajar. She yanked it open.

"Bedtime!"

***

A lazy wind wound through the kitchen as Elizabeth took out her oldest gray ceramic bowl and dumped in the floury mixture. The bowl had been her mother's, the ubiquitous everything bowl that came out for each birthday cake, Christmas cookie, and loaf of sourdough. It was the touchstone of her childhood, which had been populated by more books than people. Nevertheless, her mother had tried again and again to make friends for her, and what Elizabeth had lacked in social skills she made up for with a warm home full of delicious smells and tastes. As she took down Matty's old muffin tin, she realized that this was something they had shared all of these years, a quirk of connection that eschewed vocabulary in favor of flavor. Cooking was their invitation to come closer. This was her first chance to continue his work. Magic muffins.

She cracked an egg, marveling at its fragility, how something sturdy enough to carry a life was so brittle to the touch. Like her. Carrying so much but always on the brink of losing it all, and making a mess of everything around her. She could not remember a time when she had held less. Absentmindedly, she spun a wooden spoon around the bowl, this tool her grandmother's, as she saw her own life swirling in the batter. Around and around, this vacuous mass of ingredients was always looking for something to cling to, to make everything sturdy. Through the flames and out again, transformed from oozing mess to sweet treat.

On a whim, she threw in a handful of dried apricots and a spoonful of honey. The bright golden river streaked the batter, releasing a galaxy of tiny orange stars. Elizabeth let out a slow breath, and made a wish. Perhaps this time, she would find what she had been searching for.

***

An hour later, Elizabeth found herself walking up the steps to the library with a lined basket of warm muffins and a pleasing smile plastered on her face. There was a foreboding inside of her, as she had always had at PTA meetings, ladies' luncheons, every place where women gathered. The urge to get back in her car and drive back to her little sanctuary in the woods was overwhelming. She had tried so many evenings like this. Sometimes, she was left out; other times, she just left. The ending was the same either way. For a moment she hesitated, unwilling to open the door, to start again the cycle of unbelonging, when suddenly it opened of its own accord to reveal Tiffany standing in a pool of light.

"You made it!" she smiled. "I wanted to make sure you found your way. Come on back." And she turned and walked away, leaving Elizabeth no choice but to follow.

Every room they passed was dark, the yellow lamps overhead just illuminating the hallway and leaving the cavernous spaces beyond to lap at the light. They went by the back service desk and into an employee's hall, past a steep staircase, and up to an unmarked door near the emergency exit. A low buzz emanated from the room. Wildly, Elizabeth wondered if the library kept bees on the premises, but Tiffany pressed open the door to reveal a group of perhaps ten women, all speaking in low tones to their seat mates. They looked up as one, examining the newcomer with interest.

"Everyone, this is Elizabeth," Tiffany announced. "She'll be joining us today, and hopefully beyond." And she sat, with nothing further to say.

Silence rang as Elizabeth looked for an empty seat. The room was crowded with a hodgepodge of sofas, soft with decades of use and a bit threadbare on the arms. An assortment of oversized cushions lay on the ground, gathered around a large ornate coffee table. A teapot sat in the middle, a box of tea bags beside it, and around this centerpiece were various offerings to snack on — trail mix, ripe peaches, cheese and crackers, some cookies Elizabeth recognized from the counter at Denny's. Nothing homemade yet, she noticed.

"I brought muffins."

As always, this announcement transmuted suspicion to welcome, and multiple faces turned to smile at her as they reached beneath the sky blue napkin to grab a treat.

She settled herself on a cushion as Tiffany opened the book and asked, "So what did we think?"

A woman with thin brown hair piped up. "I really related to it. There's so much I would go back and find out about my family if I could. I feel like it would help me understand why I carry so much stuff that doesn't feel like mine."

Elizabeth's head snapped up. Her inner egg. A muffin was cradled in the woman's hand, one bite missing.

"I think for me, it was the loneliness," came a voice from the corner. Elizabeth turned to see a well tanned woman with long blonde hair lean forward, her book in one hand and a half-eaten muffin in the other. "She spent so much time searching for connection, even with people who could no longer meet her. It's like she just wanted someone to help her up, but she never found anyone."

Oh dear.

They were speaking of her. Her life, her patterns. Rigid with shock, she turned wonderingly to the voice behind her, afraid to trust her own ears.

"I agree," Tiffany nodded. "There was so much I felt for her, that I feel for me. That longing for a matriarchal line, for a support system. We have so little of that. I admired her for seeking it out, but I wished she would look beyond her family. Sometimes friends are the family you choose."

And so it went. Elizabeth's heart was slowly sliced open as she sat mute upon the cushions. One by one, each mouth opened, bit through the baked honey, and spoke the words that had burdened her heart. Some had tears in their eyes. All nodded together in agreement.

"Elizabeth? I know you didn't have much time with the book, but any thoughts on the theme? On life?"

Elizabeth looked up, surprised to find her eyes wet. "I think more women should have spaces like this one."

***

That night as she got into bed, Elizabeth considered the dozen new numbers she had stored in her phone, the hands that had grasped hers as the evening ended, the eyes that met hers without reserve. Real women. Real women who had welcomed her, spoken their hearts to her. Never in her life had she felt like this, so...held. Viscerally, she feared being asked to bare her soul in turn, to reciprocate with a vulnerability she was not sure she possessed. In this brand new world, she did not know who to be. She turned off the light and felt a buzzing in her chest, and suddenly she was overwhelmed with exhaustion.

Powerless to stop it, she succumbed to sleep, letting the sound of the bees carry her to a new reality entirely.

Fall

Chapter Eleven

"**S**o can I go?"

Elizabeth deliberated as she kneaded the dough. "I thought we'd go as a family. I think everyone else will be with theirs."

"Obviously not, or they wouldn't have asked me." Lily flipped a long braid over her shoulder. "Come on Mom, please? I just want to hang with my friends. It's perfectly safe, there's nothing illegal going on, we just want to go to the festival together."

"No, I get it," she sighed. After all, it was what teenagers did, and she was happy that Lily had found friends to include her. She glanced at Cory, who was doing an excellent job of looking like he wasn't listening. She knew better. "I'll tell you what, why don't you meet them there? Then you can 'go' with us, but you'll hop over to join them when they arrive. We can get there a little early. Does that work?"

Lily screwed up one eye but seemed to decide that this was close enough to what she wanted. "I guess that's OK. But no being weird, Mom. No asking a million questions or trying to meet their parents or anything."

"Wouldn't dream of it." Her eyes skated back to her son, ostensibly focused on his book. "Cory, you won't leave me alone at the Fall Festival, will you?"

"Do I get a choice?"

"Not really." The satiny round ball slid into its pan and shot into the warmest corner of the kitchen. "It will be fun, it's the biggest event the town has."

"That's not saying much."

She rolled her eyes. "Well as you don't like big events, that should work perfectly." Icy water ran over her hands. "I think it will be a great time."

"Is Mitch coming?" Lily asked slyly, a devilish grin sliding over her face.

Elizabeth made rather a meal of picking the dough off her fingers. She had seen Mitch twice now, and their walk along the river had been pleasant and light. He was easy to talk to and had lots of wonderful stories to share, both from his time in the city and his life as an artist here. But he had leaned towards her meaningfully at the end of their last date, and she had, predictably, panicked once again. Leaving him with a jovial handshake, Elizabeth had brushed it off, and sent him a quick message later that night telling him what fun she had had, kicking the can down the road. The question now was how far it would go, and whether she really wanted to chase after it.

It would be easy to simply tell him it was too soon, to try her again in a few months, that she was too overwhelmed for a relationship right now. Truthfully, though, she wasn't sure if that was the answer. Her response to him, or lack thereof, wasn't part of the mourning process. She didn't mind Mitch, and enjoyed his company, but the thought of going further was disturbing, almost frightening, like moving back into a house that she had moved away from. Like being married again. Yet she didn't want to spend her whole life alone.

She shook the water from her fingers and grabbed a towel. "I'm sure everyone we know will be there, but the only man I am going with is right here." And she grabbed Cory for a big bear hug and kiss.

The Fall Festival was Solace Spring's annual harvest celebration, a glorious day of tradition and gaiety that had continued in the same format for decades. Gourds featured prominently. The flyer that Elizabeth had liberated from the library listed a pumpkin carrying contest, pumpkin catapult competition, and musical pumpkin games for the little ones. Local organizations ran fundraising booths, selling popcorn and candy apples or plates of smoked brisket. For one afternoon, the town gathered to watch the games and hear the music, to share their abundance with neighbors, before winter came to drive them apart. This idyllic autumn evening culminated with the main event — a bonfire.

Denny had explained that the bonfire was the town's official call to coziness. "Lovers of all ages find the flames alluring," she had told them, with euphemistic undertones. Lily looked dazzled, but Elizabeth had no intention of being baited by the flames. She would be watching her daughter like a hawk, while ensuring her pyromaniac son didn't get any ideas.

She had wondered briefly if the inn should have a presence, get the word out about her plans to renovate and rebrand, but as these plans were still evading her, she had nothing to share but a blank slate website and a still-broken sink. Joe had not resurfaced, and Elizabeth had refused to ask Denny for his number. Something told her her interest would not go unnoticed. So she had straightened out what she could herself, with occasional help from Cory, who enjoyed taking things apart and could usually be cajoled into putting them back together.

The space was now clean, working, and free of vermin. An empty canvas. If only she knew what she wanted to create.

Elizabeth had thought that would be the easy part, choosing paint colors and potted plants, but the place that had held so much meaning to her for these past several years had suddenly gone silent. No matter how many times she walked in and out of its door, it remained stubbornly asleep. Frustrated, she would walk away, looking for something else that needed fixing.

Perhaps a little traditional levity was exactly what she needed to clear her head.

The day of the festival dawned white, a hazy mix of mist and sunlight. Earth hovered on the equinox line between sunlight and darkness, waiting to begin the slow march towards rest. Lily was up with the indecisive sun, playing indie music in her room while she tried on the entire contents of her closet. Cory slept. Elizabeth took her coffee to the back porch and stirred it three times clockwise with a cinnamon stick. It was something her grandmother used to do, and on days when Elizabeth felt particularly unmoored, she found it a comfort to repeat the old routine. Her need for sameness was strong today.

By midday, the traffic along their usually empty road was moving at a brisk pace. Parked on the side porch with their sandwiches and iced tea, they saw cars full of kids, trucks full of pumpkins, trailers with oversized grills and generators. Lily kept up a running commentary until Cory called her a boring country gossip, at which point she stomped up to her room and slammed the door. Elizabeth thought vaguely that a family event might be the last thing she needed, distantly behind a day to herself or a visit to a very good spa. But as neither option was forthcoming, at two o'clock she announced it was time to go, and loaded the picnic basket into the back of the car with one surly and one euphoric teenager.

It was hard for Elizabeth to be upset at the traffic as the car line wound around the tiny town. Solace Spring took autumn seriously, and it was clear that everyone had gone all out for the festival. Hay bales stood at attention in the fields they passed, where some cornstalks remained upright and others were bundled around fence posts and gateways. Cheerful flags painted with sunflowers whipped in the gentle wind. Here and there scarecrows stood beside farmstand doors, wide open and filled with loaves of bread and fresh eggs, or bushels of apples in wooden crates. Pumpkins graced the step of every house they passed as they inched closer to the village green, where the store fronts overflowed with rusty mums and crackling branches of goldenrod. In the background were hills beginning to show their dappled colors, long swaths of yellow and orange broken up by bright red patches. The colors reflected in Solace Lake as they passed, the iron-gray water making the foliage into flame.

After the expected parking nightmare and a long walk to the field, they arrived in time for the first event — pumpkin carrying. Dads of various ages, and a few broad-shouldered teens, would load themselves up with gourds on one end of the field and walk them the entire length across. The winner of each heat made it into the finals, where a local farmer won with a record sixteen pumpkins in his arms (and on his shoulders, and one between his legs). It was so ridiculous to watch that even Cory cracked a smile.

Thus corralled, these pumpkins became fodder for the next event — pumpkin catapulting. Time was allowed between competitions so that each team could set up their home crafted weapon. Ever the engineer, Cory wordlessly wandered over, looking critically at each machine. He spent a long time at the final entry, until one of the men on the team came up to him with a smile and began to chat. Elizabeth was too far away to hear what they were saying, but she was grateful that someone had engaged her curious son. The two spent ten minutes looking the construction over, and when Cory returned he explained the mechanics in intricate detail.

"They're using a pulley system but the way they balance the weight is much more reliable than any of the others," he said knowledgeably. "They should have a much more accurate shot, and it will go a lot further. I don't know why the other teams didn't do it that way. They're going to lose badly." And while Elizabeth admonished him to be kinder when he spoke, he was right. The final competitor sailed their pumpkin a good 80 feet, handily winning the trophy and making a huge mess of the field. A petting zoo was set up around the remnants of the vegetables, and sticky toddlers ran across to touch the animals as they feasted.

For their part, Elizabeth had packed a buffet of snacks to last them through the evening. Smoothing the picnic blanket over, she unpacked a snap pea and bacon salad, cheddar biscuits, cold roasted chicken and miniature blackberry lavender pies. Everyone ate hungrily, except for Lily, whose eyes raked over the field every few minutes. She looked as though she was waiting to begin an all-out attack on the enemy.

"Lily!"

Finally the call echoed from someplace behind them, where Main Street emptied onto the grass. Lily's feet hit the ground so fast she appeared to fly. She ran to a group of three girls and two boys, all roughly her age, dressed in ripped jeans and loose sweaters. Lily's outfit of a sage green off the shoulder sweater and black broomstick skirt, despite taking three hours to put together, blended in with the casual crew.

Her abandoned plate sat untouched. "Don't you want anything to eat?" Elizabeth called after her. Lily's eyes went round as saucers as she stared her mother dead in the eyes. Clearly, this had been the wrong thing to say. She put her hands up — *mea culpa* — and turned away from her daughter's friends, only to hear, "Awesome, you've got food? I'm starving."

"Oh, we can go buy something, you guys don't need to meet my mom—"

"Nah, this food is here now, and it's free!" A shaggy haired boy jogged up to them. "Hey, Ms. Whit, I'm Dylan. Don't suppose you have any extras?"

"Sure do," said Elizabeth, who had packed far more than necessary for that very reason. "Biscuit?"

The look Lily gave her could have started the bonfire.

Dylan, either uncaring or oblivious, settled himself down to feast, and the rest of the crew joined him. Cory surveyed them with a mix of distaste and fear, then pulled out his book and his headphones and mentally left the scene. The platter of chicken was passed around next, girls politely declining while the teenage boys were already on second helpings. It never failed to amaze her how much and how fast these teenage boys ate. Between swallows, she managed to ask Dylan, "So what's the best thing to do at this festival? We've seen lots of exploding pumpkins so far."

"Yeah, that's always fun," he nodded, cleaning the meat from a drumstick. "Mostly it's the baking contests, the chili cookoff, that kind of thing. People around here get real competitive about their food." He smiled, and Elizabeth noticed how Lily's face lit up when his did. "But the bonfire is the best part. It's just really cool, you know? Just...big and fiery and stuff."

Behind him, Cory rolled his eyes, but no one noticed.

"Well, hopefully we'll stay long enough to see it," Elizabeth answered, passing him a miniature pie.

"Oh, you've got to! But I get it, it's a long day. I'm happy to take Lily home if that's easier for you."

"What a kind offer. But I'm sure she won't stay out too late." She ignored her daughter's furious expression. "We'll be able to stick it out."

"Suit yourself!" He bit into dessert, eyes rolling back in his head. "Ms. W.! You've gotta enter these in the contest!"

"Oh?"

"For sure! The pie contest is the big one, and these are AWESOME! You just need to give them three, one for each judge. Do you have some extra?"

"I do," she said bemusedly.

"You've gotta enter," Dylan said, polishing off the last of his helping. "Promise me." Bright eyes appealed to her, and Elizabeth saw begrudgingly how her daughter might become lost in them.

She chanced a look at Lily, who flicked her hands as if to say "go". "I guess I could do that. Cory, want to walk over there with me, stretch our legs?" Her daughter's gratitude washed over her, relieved to be rid of the omnipresent parent.

Cory removed one headphone, looked around, and shrugged. Together the two of them waved goodbye to the group and sauntered off with a plate of pies, in search of judges.

"They're idiots," he said once they were out of earshot.

"They're teenage boys, of course they're idiots," she replied, letting the implication hit him. "But they were kind and friendly, and that goes a long way." Cory's shoulders rolled down, and he crossed his arms over his books. Too hard. Too mean. She put a hand on his back. "Come on, let's go see if we can bag ourselves a participation trophy."

Booths were arranged around the outer edges of the field, loosely organized according to type. They gave the churches a wide berth but stopped to buy an iced coffee from the high school drama club, where one of the girls tried and failed to meet Cory's eye. Past the corn on the cob, the bratwurst with all the fixings, and the hot chocolate, they saw a large wooden sign that read "Judge's Table". Elizabeth walked up.

"Excuse me, could you tell me what I need to do to enter the pie contest?"

A woman with a thick bun of gray hair and a heavy frame hoisted herself out of her seat to retrieve a piece of paper. "Just fill this out, hand me five dollars, and put your entry with all the others." She waved carelessly to her right.

Astounded, Elizabeth let her eyes linger over what had to be at least fifty pies of every kind. Crumb toppings, lattice crusts, smooth pumpkin custards and more than a dozen apple pies. Cory whistled. "Well, it's good you tried, Mom." She glared at him over her shoulder. A moment later her form was stapled to a paper plate and they walked away from the table, Cory still snickering lightly.

Both kids had disappeared by the time Elizabeth returned, Lily presumably to a shadowy picnic blanket with Dylan, Cory drifting off to a nearby tree to read in silence. Stretching out on her stomach, she watched the population of Solace Spring move back and forth across the field, tiny caricatures dancing through a static scene. A sense of calm came over her. Watching the town felt like observing time from a distance. She saw the babies on their mothers' shoulders, with toddlers and school children running behind. Teens stood in awkward groups along the edges, and newlyweds walked hand in hand. The elders sat in folding chairs with knitting needles and wide-brimmed hats. And her midlife colleagues? They made the festival run. Each stand was being captained by a middle-aged woman, calling out to strangers and stacking cash while their partners manned grills and coolers. Women like her were the backbone of the community. She wondered where they found the energy.

"You look beautiful."

Startled, Elizabeth turned her head so fast her neck cricked. Mitch was standing behind her. Soft eyes stared at her as people moved back and forth behind him — he was caught in her moment. His heart was worn clearly on his sleeve, and he seemed not to care who else noticed his affection. It was intoxicating, even for her. For a moment the world was fuzzy and warm, and she grew dizzy. Something pulled her down, like a slide that would go on and on. A voice inside of her began to scream. *Too close, too close.* A body was coming towards her that she was not prepared for, wasn't ready to receive, and in the black hole she was falling down there was no escape. She realized that she was not breathing. Gasping, Elizabeth scrambled to her feet, popping the bubble and rejoining the busy world of the festival, smile wide and trembling.

***

The bonfire was lit, to great applause, as the moon rose over the lake. Great tongues of flame licked the inky sky while small children stared transfixed into the alchemical weapon born of twigs and sparks. The fire could be used for anything, yet the only purpose of this one was ritual hypnosis. Old folks and babies alike nodded off. Adults smiled at the warmth, stretching out their fingers to ease the cold. A single woman, adorned in a red shawl over black dress and boots, stood with the lake behind her, face in shadow and eyes lost in the fire, seeing who knew what at its heart. The seminal witch. And of course, teenagers hid in the half light, arms slyly sneaking around waists, heads leaning back against shoulders still soft with baby fat. Elizabeth envied them. What must it be like, to fall into the arms of another without fear, without suspicion? She could not recall it. Perhaps she had never felt that safe.

A hand rested on her back, and she jumped.

"Whoa, calm down, just me," Mitch smiled easily. She had forgotten he was there. Somehow in the haze of smoke and fairy lights, her mind had wandered too far from this reality. Even now, she drifted off with the scent of the popcorn, the notes of the band, the stars. Her eyes closed, and she felt woozy, drunk on bonfires and pumpkin spice. "Hey, you OK?" His smile faded to concern. Carefully, he spread one arm around her, scooping her up and keeping her on her feet. "Did Jake give you one of his special ciders?"

Elizabeth smiled at her shoes. "No, I think I just got ... overstimulated". She meant agitated. She meant frightened. She meant lonely. "Maybe I just need to head home."

"I think they're about ready to give out awards ... want to wait another few minutes?"

Her feeble protest was drowned out by raucous applause as the judges filed onto the stage, a basket of ribbons spilling rainbows over the side. The crowd moved as one organism, bending and stretching into an arc around the stage, all faces turned together towards the light. Elizabeth melted back as the crowd moved in, letting the congratulatory speech wash over her like a tide as she faded towards the blackness. Chili, 3, 2, 1. Cookies, 3, 2, 1. A song of predictable lyrics, each recipient ready in their turn, each announcement punctuated by the slapping of many hands together, hurrah, hurrah. With each ribbon the snowglobe was shaken again, and the performance was repeated with only the smallest of changes. Steadying in its sameness. Until her name broke the spell.

Suddenly heads were turning to find her, this chaotic element introduced to the fixed routine. An anomaly. In the mass she saw Mitch turning this way and that, looking for someone he no doubt thought was at his side, while Lily emerged from nowhere grinning ear to ear. Elizabeth allowed herself to be dragged onstage where she took her red ribbon, looking down at a sea of surprised faces. She was unprepared. Try as she might, she could not hoist her winning grin onto her face. Instead her instinct took over, tried to pull her further back, into the trees, where all of these eyes would release her. Unbelonging was heavy on her chest. Quickly, she hid her head as another woman thudded up the steps to cheers and wolf whistles, a practiced wave and bow as the blue ribbon was triumphantly thrust into the air. Behind it, Elizabeth could see Cory, under his tree in the dark, watching her with an expression of disdain, betrayal written all over his face.

***

Elizabeth, still punch drunk from the lights and sound, focused all of her energy on the road during the drive home, willing herself to make it to terra firma once more. Cory sat beside her, quietly staring out of the window. Neither of them spoke. As the gravel settled under her tires, Elizabeth let exhaustion seep into her body. Home. No need to perform, or smile, or speak. Just rest. Gratefully exiting the car, she dragged in the picnic basket and was just dumping the linens in the laundry when she heard a knock. Curious, she pulled open the door, expecting Denny or yet another complaint from her annoyed neighbor.

"Mitch."

They hadn't really said much of a goodbye, as every festival attendee congratulated her during her harried car pack up. She had thanked him, she was sure. Probably said something about seeing him soon. Not this soon.

"You forgot this." He held out something bright red.

Her ribbon. Second place.

"You handed it to me while you were stowing the basket, and before I knew it you were gone." The words were gentle, but she heard the hurt behind them. He had hoped for more. Without meaning to, she had inflicted her rejection upon a man who had showed her nothing but kindness.

Mutely, she extended a hand. Gold typeface marked the center of the circle with a large, shiny numeral, bestowing upon her the rank of almost. Almost the winner. Almost good enough.

She placed it on the entry table and uttered a short word of thanks. Embarrassment flushed her cheeks as she realized the damage she had done without noticing.

"Would you have a minute to walk with me?"

Elizabeth glanced upstairs, at the dark hallway where her son had clearly retreated to bed. Cory's lazy snores trickled down the stairway, her last excuse shattering as they hit the ground.

"Sure."

He led the way towards the pond, a glittery black expanse in the moonlight. With every step her body grew stiff and cold. She didn't want to be here, in the open air. She wanted to be home, in her warm bed, where no one could see her. She was so tired of being seen.

Mitch looked at her.

"Elizabeth, I want you to know how special this is to me," he said softly. "I haven't felt like this about someone since my wife left." No.

"You make me feel…" No. "So happy. So joyful. When I look at you, I just want…" And his face was coming closer, and his lips were too close, and he was too close, and suddenly the world was collapsing around her and she could not breathe and her body was frozen and somewhere inside her she felt a small voice screaming.

"Too much!" The words escaped like a convulsion, involuntary and jagged. She could barely make out his eyes, receding from her into the shadow where she had fallen. Gently, his hand smoothed her hair. She inhaled. He still smelled of smoke. Scents of bracken and dirt mingled with his cologne. Her face was wet.

"Oh Elizabeth." He pulled her into the softest hug, barely a breath on her back. "Sweetie, I'm so sorry. I didn't know."

Slowly, the pieces of herself began to coalesce. Here at the epicenter, she felt the explosion belatedly, a returning shock wave of fear. Usually she had more warning. Usually she could stop the upheaval that emerged from her core like lava, the tightening in her throat tamping down the screams until they were whispers, and then gone. Usually.

Suddenly the full impact of the scene hit her, and she pulled Mitch into a deeper hug. "Oh my gosh. I'm so sorry, Mitch. I don't know what happened. Sometimes my system just…" Dies. Fights. Can't handle it. "I don't know. I'm sorry."

Arms still twined around her back, Mitch stroked her hair. "It's OK, Elizabeth. You don't have to apologize." He kissed her forehead. "You never have to feel bad for that."

This was somehow worse, being held in the midst of her panic, which at this first sign of weakness shot back up her throat and burned the back of her tongue. Tears leaked from her eyes, angry at being shed, angry at being held. She felt trapped, forced to be vulnerable, forced to be too close. Rapid breaths constricted her chest as she folded her arms around herself. Just her. Just her.

Breathe.

The panic subsided as she gently pressed Mitch away.

For a moment his face registered the confusion she knew he must feel. Then his shoulders rounded as he slowly realized what she had wordlessly said. His smile was sad as he nodded. "I understand." With a nod, he turned and headed back up the path. Elizabeth stood there shaking until his truck drove away.

That night she dreamt of neverending darkness, calling to her and pulling her forward, into a void where she saw nothing, until she moved through an unseen doorway and everything was light.

Chapter Twelve

"Well there's our big winner!"

Denny's voice rang across the shop as Elizabeth stepped into the clean warmth of the shop; the October air was sharp and brittle. Cinnamon wreaths were arranged in the window, and the spicy scent caught the draft. Winter was on its way already.

In contrast, Denny's grin looked like a summer morning. "Look at you, stepping up and winning prizes! I didn't even know you were entering."

"I wasn't." Elizabeth explained Dylan's pleading. "I wasn't trying to win, I just thought it was the thing to do." Just trying to fit in, she thought.

The scarlet prize had not left the table where she had laid it during Mitch's short but impactful visit. Somehow the panic by the pond, as she had come to think of it, had drowned whatever shallow joy she would have taken from it. It should have been her badge of honor, really. Proof that she belonged here, that she had something to offer. But she couldn't look at it without reliving the moment of disassociation, the freezing sensation in her body, the pity in his eyes. No contact had occurred since then, nor did she expect any. She knew the end of a road when she saw it.

Denny measured her with a glance. "Well, from what I hear, you have one hell of a gift. You should be sharing it." She wiped down the espresso machine as it gave a loud hiss. "What about making some for the cafe? The holidays are coming up, and they're perfect for some homemade sweet stuff. You can even get a little extra markup out of folks during the season." Those dark eyes swept over her again. "I bet a little extra income wouldn't hurt, all the work that place needs."

Bullseye. Denny certainly knew how to get to her. Elizabeth had to admit that the coffers were getting low, and were likely to get lower. Winter would bring new headaches and repairs, and no new guests. Extra cash would go a long way.

Denny seemed to sense that the matter was decided. "Tell you what, you bake 'em when you've got 'em, figure out a fair price point, bring 'em in when you can. If they sell, we can talk about scaling up. No pressure, no risk." Her eyebrows danced as she walked over to the steaming machine. "Except maybe to my waistline." And for good measure she grabbed a handful of flesh and shook it.

Elizabeth gave a grudging giggle, agreed to the terms with a word of thanks, and ordered the cinnamon spice latte with extra cinnamon. A little warmth to light a fire in her.

Set up at a table with her spreadsheets, her bank statements, a very long to-do list, and a large mug of sugar and caffeine, she plummeted into the pile of work that seemed to grow larger every time she tackled it. She had gotten as far as prioritizing the projects and was starting to budget when her phone rang.

School.

She knew that call was coming.

***

"Is there any point in asking why?"

"No."

"Would you like me to remind you that your sister and I are here for you, that your teachers want to be there for you, that lots of people would like to be your friends if you weren't so committed to this life path?"

"No."

"Anything I can say that will make any impact at all?"

"No."

They drove the rest of the way home in silence, Cory staring moodily out of the back window, Elizabeth willing herself not to scream. It was frustrating beyond all reason to have completely rearranged their lives only to have this come back to center stage. The angry outbursts of a teenage boy.

It could have been worse, she reminded herself. A one-day suspension was a warning, not a life sentence. The language he had thrown at his French teacher in first period was heinous, but not violent, and she could already see the contrition forming on his face. It was hell to watch him come down, out of his temper. Once he was back in control, he would see his actions in the rearview mirror, the debris scattered across the highway of his life, sometimes irreparable. He would escape to his room, she knew, to ponder the lonely existence that was all he could see in front of him. Beneath his armor was a sweet, empathetic, charismatic kid ... but it didn't matter at all when he couldn't find that man in the mirror.

She got out of the car and enveloped him in a hug. His hair smelled like smoke and pine sap, mixed with the gentle detergent she had used since he was a baby. A child and a man in one. Her lips reached his cheek, so that was what she kissed as she murmured, "It's OK to make mistakes. Change takes time."

Cory's head rested on her shoulder, a warm blanket in the freezing air. She did not know how long they stood there before she realized they were not alone.

Relinquishing her son, she told him to go inside and put on a kettle so they could work together at the table. He managed a small smile as he trooped in, blessedly unaware of Mitch's presence on the other side of the house.

"I just wanted to check in on you," he said as he ambled towards her.

"And say goodbye," she finished for him.

He didn't deny it — just looked at her, as though she wasn't who he thought she had been, was instead some sort of trick. An '89 Toyota pretending to be a Ferrari.

"It's fine," she assured him curtly. "I get it. I'm too much work. I have a failing business, and a half-delinquent son, and so much emotional baggage it wouldn't all fit on the plane." She smiled wryly. "I'm a bad investment. You deserve better." And she meant it. Mitch was a wonderful guy, and he was ready. Ready for a real relationship where he would receive the love he had to give. And that wouldn't happen with her. Tears stung at her eyes as she turned to leave.

"Elizabeth, it's not like that —"

"Sure it is," she spat, now reaching the limits of her patience. "You want someone to make a home with. Someone easy. Someone who can be there for you and your emotional pain, but ask nothing in return.

Someone who's unblemished. Someone who's whole." And now her temper was reaching a crescendo. "You don't want me."

"I do," he protested, looking stung. "Elizabeth, I do want you. I just want..." But here he stopped, apparently unable to articulate his desire. There was no map to take him where he wanted to go. And she surely didn't have directions.

"You want what all men want," she breathed, as icy tears cut into her cheeks. "You want to use us for your comfort and discard us when you're done." It wasn't true, she knew. That man was real, but he wasn't the one standing before her. Her feet began to drag her backwards, away and home and safe. "And this time, I'm done first." Wiping her face with her hand, she slammed the front door behind her, and had already started formulating her December budget when the tires crunched the gravel in the drive and faded away down the road.

***

By the time Lily got home, Cory had gone from angry to nervous in the wake of Elizabeth's bitter silence. Though she went through the good mother motions, asking about her daughter's day and setting out dull apples and cheddar as a snack, her eyes were unfocused and her responses were snappish. Lily looked troubled, meeting her brother's eyes with a question mark stare. He shrugged, looking embarrassed. Closing her eyes, Elizabeth breathed deeply. Her outburst wasn't her children's fault. She shouldn't be taking it out on them. They were the reason, after all, that she was unwilling to get into relationships again. So much loss, so much grief. There was no reason to put them through it. Through this. The endless repeating cycle that always dropped her at an exit.

Right now, an exit was what she needed more than anything.

"I'm going for a drive."

The suggestion was so unlike her that both teens asked her to repeat herself.

"The leaves will be falling soon, and we haven't taken enough time to enjoy them while they're here." In her mind's eye she saw the crisp colors dancing on the branches, another local flame, another riot of chaos and heat. She closed the image and focused on the steely skies outside. "I just want to see the fall."

A wordless conversation seemed to ensue between the siblings, with the general sentiment that whatever was up with Mom, she should be mollified. Coat thrown unceremoniously in the back of the car, she was off, ambling down a spider's web of twisting one lane highways that crossed over the Berkshires, zigzagging back and forth between irrelevant state lines.

Anger fell off of her in chunks the further she drove. Cory did not do this on purpose, she knew. His mind simply worked the way it worked, and when he saw no options open to him, he reacted accordingly. He panicked. Shut down. It was behavior she well understood, and as the rage fell back to a low tide, Mitch's crumpled face materialized in her mind. He hadn't deserved the tirade she threw in his face, had not committed any of the crimes she spat at him. Those had belonged to someone else, yet she was the one carrying them on her back and plastering them on someone new. True, she could not have stayed with him, not in the condition she was in. Her outburst proved that. But as she kept trying to teach her son, the world was not divided into saints and demons, friends and liars. Everyone fell someplace in between, and Mitch was definitely on the sweeter side. It was she who had brought the darkness in.

Vermont looked like New Hampshire looked like Massachusetts, a network of farmhouses and fields, barns and bogs, all broken up by miles of maples, beeches, birches, oaks. Walls of trees formed a sort of impenetrable boundary, disguising the realities of human existence and seeking to slowly reclaim their lost territory. Only a few rows were enough to blot whole neighborhoods from the eye, swallow them up into the forest's dark shadow. Canopies of gold and red were beginning to rain to the ground, leaving behind black limbs that stabbed at the sky. They had been green when they arrived, Elizabeth remembered. Everything had been alive then. It felt like it had all turned in a second, from sun-dappled light to this hazy frost, gripping each fragile leaf and tearing it from its companions. Were these riotous colors flags of surrender? Were they a last gasp of life, begging to be seen, to be beheld in their greatest beauty, to express every passionate cell of of their existence before they decayed on the forest floor?

Did trees feel passion?

Eventually all of the roads looped her back towards home again, and Elizabeth began to feel tired. She pulled over at one of the many faded red roadside stands, a chalkboard by the road advertising maple cotton candy and fresh coffee. Local custom clung to the honor system — a sign taped to the window invited her to help herself and leave her money in the ragged cigar box on the counter. Finding that she couldn't resist the sweetness, Elizabeth took her treat and a warm cup from the stand, deposited a five dollar bill, and emerged into the cold air again. A lone picnic table sat by the running water, one of the plethora of river veins she could not name, and Elizabeth let the steam of her coffee form mystical swirls in the air as the water bubbled along.

Even for the water, time grew short. One good storm was enough to freeze it over. And storms were coming.

"I thought that was you."

For a moment she was sure the river had spoken to her, before she felt the human presence somewhere behind her. She craned her neck to see Joe standing a few feet away, his ubiquitous coffee cup in hand. He was wrapped in a thick coat and work boots, but his head was bare and his hair was being whipped about by the wind. It was the only part of him that moved. Elizabeth was struck again by his intermittent stillness — he was a mountain that simply appeared in front of her, then disappeared when she turned around. Yet here he was again, appearing at a moment when she would much rather have been alone.

Perhaps he sensed it. "I can leave you be."

"No, it's OK," she heard herself say. "You're quiet."

And he was. They sat next to each other, taking sips of rapidly cooling coffee, and watched the water. She felt a wave of his energy move around her, but this time her vision remained clear. He lapped around her ankles without engulfing her. Heaviness weighed her down, and though Joe's hand still haunted her daydreams, in this moment he could not drag her from her seat. This was where she needed to be. No other cars were near, nor was there any sign of human habitation past the river's edge. Nothing but maple trees and silence. Their cups were drained before the last sips went cold. A mother's luxury.

"Walk with me."

She didn't feel like walking, she felt like moping. A cutting retort sat behind her teeth, daring her to speak. Somewhere in the back of her mind, a small drop of wisdom stopped her. Movement would be good for her, it wheedled. A walk would let her anger and frustration exist someplace other than her body. And Joe was the last person who would press her for more. So she nodded and stood up.

Joe led her down a side path, following the riverbank. Idly, Elizabeth wondered if somehow this was the same river she had found him at last time, just a different bend, another current. Perhaps he melted into it between meetings, a god of the infinite water. She looked around for his van but saw nothing beyond the red stand of maples, towering over her with their vivid roof. He turned to glance at her, and she was struck by his eyes, like the darkness of the ocean at night, like the clouds before the rain.

"You should know your maple."

"Pardon?"

He turned again, enunciating more clearly. "If you're going to live here, you need to know your maple." The path veered upwards, and he climbed the steep hill with ease while her feet grappled with the uneven terrain. He did not slow down.

"Sugar maples are the backbone of our community." Joe gestured to the trunks around him. "Maple syrup runs like blood here. It attracts tourism, it creates wealth, it's passed down in families. The trees' roots are our roots as well." Joe thrust his hands into his pockets as he stomped on, and for a moment she saw the stubborn little boy in him. She wondered where his roots were, and what had been passed down into this man. Once more she felt her heart softening to him, without knowing why. Mitch had been perfectly willing, yet it was this taciturn stranger that opened her.

Abruptly, he stopped, and she walked into him. He caught her hip to steady her on the incline, and the touch burned with awareness. Her surprised inhale drew his eyes to her lips, the exhale swirling and warm in the space between them. Joe's hand was still on her, firmly grasping the curve of her body, pulling her towards him. It was an anchor. For a moment she was leaning in, their eyes were locked, and the earth felt as though it was pulsing beneath her feet. Silence roared in her ears.

Then his hand was gone, and her hip was cold, and her breathing was shallow and dry.

"I told you a little about the process, but it's different when you can see it. It's about knowing the trees. We tap the maples in the space between winter and spring. But it takes time to prepare everything, and that process will begin just after the holidays. You have to be ready, because each winter is different, and you never know when the ground will freeze, or when it will thaw. The air changes, the water changes, the trees change." He paused at the peak of the hill, his eyes roving the trunks judiciously, attention beyond her and in the timeless future of snow covered branches and dripping icicles. She could see him assessing, measuring, examining the possibilities of each maple. "Right now we're getting equipment ordered, looking at how many gallons we are likely to get from each tree, planning for storage and restoration. There's only so much we can do until the weather starts to warm up, and the sap rises through the tree again." How many buckets, taps, kettles, hours, cups of coffee. Enough, not enough. Like her spreadsheets, the raw data unrolled in his head.

He placed a hand on the bark of a nearby maple. "In the winter, they reserve everything, right? Just like humans would do. Carefully stockpile what you have, because you don't know how long the cold will last." He took a small metal piece from his pocket. "But eventually, everything warms up again, and the tree eases. It takes down its defenses and lets its blood start moving again. It comes back to life." She may have imagined it, but it felt like he paused a little too long, looked at her a little too closely. "When that happens, we take what we can. Like I told you, a tree that gives too much will die before it can replenish itself. It's a delicate balance — we want the tree to thrive, so that we can use it every season. Planting new maples takes decades...we have to preserve what's here as well as plant more."

One hand fitted the metal to the wood. "Once we insert this spout, we place a bucket beneath to catch what the tree can give us, and then come back in a day and collect it. The sap is mostly water, so inside all of the sugaring facilities are enormous kettles that boil out the water and isolate the sugar. Different grades and colors come from the strength of flavor, different boiling times. It's a matter of preference, so most people will do a little of each." The spout disappeared into Joe's pocket and he straightened up again, resuming the falling path that now led back down to the river.

"There are contests and local favorites from the community, and some folks swear they can taste the difference between groves. If you're here long enough, you get to know the taste of the trees. But mostly it's about who can get their syrup and butter and candy in the best gift shops. One good deal will take care of all of your inventory, and let you keep your land another year." Without asking he placed his hands on her waist and lifted her down the last drop of the hill, then resolutely turned around and kept walking. "It's part of the rhythm of life here. The dairies have one, the farms have one... Hell, even construction has one." He turned to her as they regained the empty picnic table. "But the maple trees are special, and like I said, if you're going to be here, you need to know them."

Elizabeth turned to examine the fiery horizon she had just exited. How old those trees must be. How many generations they had sheltered, watched, bled for. They were the heart of this place, she realized. Joe was right.

"Can my maples be tapped?"

Joe examined her critically, and Elizabeth wondered whether she had failed a test just by asking.

"Matty never bothered. Said those trees like to be left alone. You don't have the equipment to do a big batch."

"Just for me, I mean. A pot in my kitchen. Just to understand."

He smiled. It was such a rare occurrence that she smiled back, a schoolgirl grin gracing her face.

"Yeah. Yeah, I could help you with that."

"When the trees wake."

"When the trees wake."

***

Cory was waiting on the front steps when she got home. Blindsided and bleary-eyed from her walk amongst the maples, Elizabeth sat down beside him and simply waited.

"Sorry," he mumbled.

She nodded to the empty space in front of her. "Aren't you getting tired of it, Cory?" The question hung there in the cold, crystallizing into sharp angles and clear facets. He looked at it.

"Yeah." His voice was neither sad nor angry, just factual. "I don't like being this way. I just don't...know how else to be."

Elizabeth put her arms around her baby, now taller than she was and with the shadows of uneven stubble on his cheeks. He had the chubbiest cheeks as a baby. Even then he was serious, and hyper focused on whatever he did, but Elizabeth remembered the sweet milky smile he always reserved for her. She hoped some part of that child remained within him someplace. Someplace where he'd be able to find it.

"Maybe you don't need to know, Cory. Maybe you just have to try different things until you find what works for you." She stretched to kiss the top of his head. "This isn't working. And now that you know that, you can move on to the next chapter. Next experiment." Mother raised the face of her son, and met his eyes with all the love she didn't know how to give him. "Time for something new."

***

That evening, Elizabeth walked out to the copse of trees behind the house and stood in their center, contemplating them. Before today she had never considered the veins of the trees, the blood that pulsed through them. Where was their heart, she wondered? Her eyes fell from the leaves to the roots, burrowing deep into the earth. The faintest pulse seemed to echo through her feet. Was that what she had been feeling? The heartbeat of the trees? Closing her eyes, Elizabeth stretched her energy into her feet, willing them to grow roots, to reach into the ground until they found life. A dull beat tingled her toes. Someplace between a tattoo and a throbbing. She flexed her toes and let the pulsing move up through her, quaking her blood, climbing her arteries. As the rhythm reached her throat, she felt her mouth fall open, her airways choke, some burgeoning feeling bubbling behind her tongue. Her breath quickened. Suddenly she boiled over, dropping to her knees and spitting yellowish liquid from her mouth. More and more came up as she retched on the ground, expelling the unknown goo that seemed to gather from all over her body, leaching from her organs. Panic overcame her as it spewed from her lips until finally, blessedly, the flood halted. For a moment she simply breathed, savoring the air in her lungs. Sweet residue clung to her lips, and as she slowly sat back on her heels, she recognized the taste.

Maple.

Chapter Thirteen

Mornings were cold now. Elizabeth had to wrench herself out of bed, her body begging for the cozy hideaway of the thread-bare sheets. Their furnace alternated between a blazing inferno and a well-insulated igloo, so her sleepy nest was lined with linen and fleece, discarded scrunchies and fuzzy socks, and several memory foam pillows. Each night she built herself a fortress, trying to maintain her warmth by blocking out everything else. If only she could keep herself in stasis. Just for a little while. Just through the winter.

Of course, the first signs of winter had yet to truly make an appearance. Mild flurries of late night snow had not yet stuck to the ground, though a thick layer of frost clung to every window and bush. It became the hot town gossip: snow. When it would strike, how it would lie upon the earth. What sacrifice would the wintry drops require? Heads bent together in the street, arms stretched towards the endless gray mass of sky, begging for a sign of what was to come.

The undercurrent of stoic foreboding stretched into the houses and buildings through town, sending covered heads into Eyes Up for faith and sustenance. Elizabeth began to treasure her time there less for her productivity rate, which in any case was slowing with the lack of funds, and more for the ability to sit in a silent communal with her fellows, a vigil of warmed hands and sweetened tongues, all taking refuge together. Despite her reservations, she had started baking miniature pies and bringing a tray or two a week, and had been pleased with her early success. The small payoff gave her an excuse to hang out more often in town, learning the language and lore of the valley. As she idly rearranged columns on her spreadsheet, Elizabeth listened to the surrounding conversation, gleaning bits of knowledge from the less cautious voices at neighboring tables.

She learned that now was the time to get her greenhouse up and running, a feat she felt unequal to but nevertheless hammered out with help from Lily and Cory. A temporary structure was erected with a carefully modulated heating source and solar generator. It had been a large investment, but as the gardens around the property began to fail, she saw the necessity of saving what she could and growing more. Part of her plan for the space was to grow more organic food, both for her family and for any interested guests to purchase, and this would quickly become impossible if she had no plan for inclement weather. Talk of warming trays, seed starting schedules, and sales of fertilizer and mulch also wafted her way. Elizabeth hoped she had used enough of this intel to save the parts of the landscaping that could not be safely rehomed. She cleared space for snow ploughs and bought bulk salts for the driveway and pathways. The basement was now home to several twenty pound bags of flour and more of sugar, as well as a sizeable portion of canned goods and powdered milk in case of a blizzard. So Elizabeth was proud of her local learning. Until the whispers landed a little too close to home.

As a rule, she steered clear of Grover, having no wish to draw his sanctimonious ire. He seemed to invariably find something to complain about, from the weather to the food to the local political scene. So she wasn't altogether surprised to find him launching into a tirade about teenagers about a week after Cory's suspension.

"Worthless," he spat into his coffee cup, as his table mate nodded to his phone. "The whole generation. Not a single brain cell to share among them, and a total lack of respect." This rant was so similar to his prior speeches on mail carriers, dog walkers, and people from Vermont that she was about to put in ear plugs to drown him out when he said "And that Cory is the WORST."

Elizabeth's hand paused en route to her purse. Cory. Of course Cory, but also, why should he hate her son? Why should he be singled out?

Handily, Grover slammed on. "You hear he got kicked out of school again last week? Probably messing with chemicals in the labs. Kid could have blown the whole school up because he thinks he's better than us, thinks he's too smart for this place. Some California attitude problem. But I would bet good money he was a pain in the ass out there, too."

Shaking with rage, Elizabeth turned around. A terrified voice inside her begged her to stay quiet, reminded her that this was not her town, not her place, not yet home. She silenced it. Instead a different voice said, "Fuck you."

Instantly, the coffee shop fell silent.

"Who do you think you are, going on about my son? You don't know anything about him. You don't know his dad ignored him every day of his life, while he did project after project trying to get his attention. You don't know that he couldn't speak until he was six years old because his mouth wouldn't form the sounds. You don't know that he was pushed around by every kid who thought he was too smart, too weird, too strange to be included." It felt like every parent teacher conference, every failed birthday party, every new therapist for the past ten years. "You don't get how hard he tried, or how many times he failed, or how much every thoughtless prick like you breaks his heart by giving up on him and calling him a bad kid." Elizabeth stood up, slammed her laptop shut with a cord whip, and shoved her purse under her arm. "He's not a bad kid. He's a kid who sees so much more of the world than you ever will, and I don't blame him one bit for being terrified of what he sees."

She was ready to storm out, tears burning trails onto her chapped cheeks, when another voice rang out: "He's a great kid."

Elizabeth turned, and saw the pinched face of her neighbor, Lisa, glaring openly at Grover, whose mouth hung slightly open. They were friends, and she had often wondered if they might be more, both so sour and set in their ways. Often they shared a table together, and she had never seen them disagree. Yet here was Lisa, who had been quick to complain about every out of place trashcan and errant tree branch on her property, crossing her arms at her partner in crime.

"I'm sorry, Grover, but you haven't taken the time to so much as meet that boy. He's been over at my place every week since they moved in, helping me clean out my gutters and seal up my side door and Lord knows what else. Wouldn't take a penny in payment. Sits and has tea with me, talks about star nebulas and comet tails and exotic particles and who knows what else. Brilliant mind." She nodded at Elizabeth. "You've done a great job with him."

Shock sat upon her tongue while tears flooded her cheeks, her neck, her thick gray sweater. Her whole world was rearranging itself, her conceptions smashed and stretched. Cory had been helping someone, unasked. He had a friend, if an unlikely one. Lisa liked something. Someone. Her son.

And she had people standing up for her.

Whispery words found her again. Her eyes met Lisa's. "Thank you." It was impossible to convey her gratitude in such stinted verbiage but she hoped the sentiment reached its intended target. Softness pushed the fiery temper from her body, and she took a step back. One of her own cinnamon cookies, thrown in for Denny with her batch of pies, was sitting on a bright green plate at her spot. She picked it up, and placed it in front of Grover. Their eyes met.

"I hope you decide to try it, Grover. Maybe you'll find that sometimes, things are sweeter than you'd expect."

Bells tinkled behind her as she stepped out into the cold weather, feeling as warm as if she were beside a cozy fireplace. As if she were home.

***

While Cory seemed pleasant enough after school, Elizabeth decided not to give him the third degree about this newly discovered altruism. Instead, she watched him. She noticed the way he grabbed his laundry from the dryer, made himself a snack. She watched him read his books and make notes in his journals, contemplating concepts she barely understood. He had come a long way. She had not seen the signs under her nose, but it was true...her babies were nearly grown up.

After the burning emotional highs of her day, it was a relief to go to book club that night. She left her children in front of the television arguing companionably about cartoon styles while reaching in blind turns for mini pizzas and apple slices. The toddlers within them were alive and well, emerging in giggles and goodwill once the teens in power had surrendered for the day. They barely noticed the kisses atop their heads before she shut the door behind her.

This time she walked confidently through the dark library, her route to the tiny room memorized, her heart full of anticipation rather than anxiety. The hallways were frigid, furnace clearly off to defray added costs. Yet when she walked through the door, a wall of hot air assaulted her. Three space heaters were lazily swaying to and fro, and a pile of assorted outerwear had collected as a doorstop. Elizabeth gaily defrocked, stripping down to her red bamboo t-shirt and jeans. Still boiling in her boots, she snagged a rickety chair with a battered goldenrod cushion and started waving her hellos.

"Well!" said Annie, a glass of wine in her hand. "It's time to get started, I guess."

Elizabeth launched in. "I actually loved this book! I thought —"

"Not the BOOK," Sarah protested. "We can't talk about the book when you told Grover off in the coffeehouse this morning!"

Elizabeth blanched, but the room applauded, with two women even standing.

"Can we have a toast?" asked Ava. "A toast to our newest member, Elizabeth, for putting that old crybaby in his place for once."

All around her, glasses raised and women's voices cried laughingly "To Elizabeth!" She didn't know whether to be ecstatic or ashamed, and decided the middle road of self-effacing would be best.

"I really didn't mean to, and I should NOT have lost my temper."

"He came for your kid!" cried Tiffany. "No one can be mad at a mama for protecting her kid, even in this town. Besides, I heard Lisa had your back, and others would have done the same."

Pink tinged her cheeks as Elizabeth smiled ruefully at the floor. "I admit, it was nice to have someone stand up for me, and REALLY nice to hear someone say nice things about Cory. It's been such a long road." She willed herself not to begin crying again. Tina, who worked part time in the general store, took her hand and squeezed it. Gratitude flowed through her again. Her shoulders lowered, her neck released. One deep breath to steady herself. "But I still shouldn't have shouted. I'll apologize to Grover next time I see him."

"Don't be in a hurry," admonished Keisha, who taught at the elementary school and was never without her crochet hook. "That man has been a sour old curmudgeon for a long time. It won't hurt him to sit with the weight of his words for once."

There was a general murmur of agreement, and Elizabeth let it settle on her. The support of these women was a form of protection, and she took it gladly. Automatically she reached for a cookie, swallowing her waves of emotion with the molasses and ginger.

"Hey, and next time," Tiffany waggled a finger at her, "we're signing you up for snacks to get some of those pies! Do you do special orders? I won't lie, I love a good pie at the holidays but I am hopeless with them. Mine are always soggy."

"Same," called Tina. "I will happily pay for some for the store's annual Christmas potluck." The group seemed to think this was a fine idea, because a few started shouting out orders and reaching into wallets.

"Oh wow, I hadn't even thought about it," Elizabeth admitted. "Denny is just kind of selling them as a favor."

"Well then do us a favor," said Keisha with a laugh, "and sell them to us, too!"

Elizabeth hesitated. Yes, the pies were time consuming, but she was rapidly accumulating free time, and losing a fair amount of money. A little bump might help her get through the winter season and maybe even purchase some goodwill in the community. Now that she thought about it, this could be a good way to advertise the inn's new identity, assuming she could figure out what that was.

"OK!" she agreed. "Just shoot me an email," she laid out her old business card, "and I will get you set up. Just give me a day or two to figure out tables and turnaround."

As they enthusiastically copied down her information, Tina's brow furrowed. "Hey," she whispered to Elizabeth. "That looks out of date. If you need some new graphic design work for the inn, I'd be happy to trade sweets for skills. I'd love to save the cash."

"You're on!" Elizabeth agreed with a grin. Another item off her to do list, without any effort on her part. Who knew a book club could be so productive?

"And now," Tiffany chided, with her slightly more stern librarian tone, "about this book…"

***

By the time she arrived home, all of the windows were dark. Lily was generally a stickler for an early bedtime. Elizabeth walked slowly, the emotional weight hampering her pace. She felt like her world had been inexorably altered again and again that day, realities broken and rewoven and amplified. There was a fullness to her, as though she had consumed an unexpected feast. The sweet notes battled the bitter. So rather than move inside, she stopped on the path and let the cold wind hit her full in the face, waking her senses, cooling her belly. Through the darkness she could just make out the grove of trees, looking barer each day as their lives succumbed to the coming winter. She followed their trunks down to the ground, where there seemed to be some form of light.

That was strange. She walked past the flower beds and the breakfast table, and into the standing stone circle. As her foot fell next to the first monolith, she saw it. There in the ground was a light, a dim thread of glowing white that extended towards the trees. She removed her foot from the ground, and all went dark again. Cautiously, she placed it back on the same spot, and sure enough, the light returned as her boot met the earth. Was it some sort of magnetism? Some strange effect the cold had on roots or weeds? With another step forward, the path lit in front of her, a second long trail criss-crossing the first. Both undulated towards the trees, just under a thin layer of frozen dirt. A glance up confirmed that the light from the trees was of similar color and quantity, though brighter, as though many such trails had gathered at that spot.

For a moment, Elizabeth panicked. Did that mean there were other people there? Perhaps animals? But no noise reached her, and there was no sign of anything amiss. Slowly, she continued towards the light, illumination spreading in front of her as though she were on stepping stones through dark water. As she grew closer, she saw other pathways extending out in other directions, towards the pond, the wood, the road. But none went terribly far, and no one seemed to be initiating them. In fact, some disappeared as she watched them, while others flared in new locations. The effect was something like Christmas lights, twinkling in a coordinated rhythm.

When she reached the grove, the light was so bright that it might have been day, though it only extended a few feet up. The trees persevered past the glow and into the darkness of the night sky, a haunting void ranging above her head. Elizabeth bent to examine the pathways here, now spiraling and tangling amongst each other, brightest where she stood and running a deliberate pattern towards a cloven oak tree. It was difficult to tell which direction the illumination went — to it, or from it. Yet it was clearly the epicenter, the source, the recipient. She tried to take in the fractal patterns, sure this must be some sort of natural phenomenon, but at a loss as to why it had appeared now. It was strangely beautiful. To think that this hard packed, dusty, and apparently fruitless dirt had all this time been holding a secret network of … life. Beauty where it was least expected. Her curiosity overcame her fear, and for a moment, she stretched out her hand to touch the spiral in front of her.

Instantly her skin felt tingly, energized, alive. Her body had all the symptoms of a plunge in cold water, but remained warm. A jolt to her system, without the shivers and fear. She felt as though she could do anything — a marathon, a business plan, a kiss. Laughter spilled from her lips as she caressed this brilliant earth, running her fingers over the light and letting it run along her limbs in turn. When she finally removed her hand, she found that she was breathing heavily, as though she had run a few blocks. And suddenly she was tired, and perhaps the lights looked a bit dimmer than before.

Resolved to figure out this mystery another time, Elizabeth followed the waning trails of light back to the standing circle, where they bid her farewell at the final stones. She hauled herself up to bed and fell asleep in her clothes, feeling so warm and at ease that her barricade of pillows lay forgotten on the floor.

Chapter Fourteen

As the tide turned more decisively towards winter, Elizabeth's mood grew increasingly festive. Holidays in California had felt forced and performative, a string of parties populated by perfectly toned blondes in expensive outfits. She had loathed Tyler's annual office holiday party, where she felt frumpy and boring in a room filled with millionaire businessmen and their appropriately accomplished (but not too accomplished) wives. In early years she had made jokes and conversation, trying to win approval, but over time she simply became exhausted trying to fit in. Mysterious "illnesses" would take her, and if possible, they would keep her away from her in-laws as well.

In Solace Spring, however, the holiday season took on new meaning. Halloween seemed to exist solely for the joy of the traditional pumpkin patches, which backed up the highway on weekends but were so adorable that Elizabeth couldn't find fault with them. She bought several fat orange gourds for the inn, and spent an enjoyable evening on the porch with the kids, carefully whittling away the hard flesh to reveal butterflies and cats and ghoulish faces. Elizabeth carefully collected the seeds, toasting most of them but drying the rest to plant next summer. The prospect of growing these massive wheels of vegetation for soups and pies, as well as entertainment, brought her more joy than she would have thought possible for such a small seed.

Pies were certainly already on the mind of consumers, as little Thanksgiving touches emerged in between witch flags and burlap sacks of candy corn. Local farmers sold homemade waxed leaf wreaths and bright jewel jars of jam by the side of the road. Tiny billboards appeared outside houses, advertising homemade ceramic mugs or take and bake cinnamon rolls. Elizabeth's own offerings continued to be a hit at Denny's coffee shop, and she already had so many private orders for November and December that she had started turning people away. Her oven was at capacity and she was working through the school hours each day. While there was a certain amount of guilt about leaving her plans for the inn so unfinished, Elizabeth had to admit it felt good to forget them for a time. Losing herself in the measuring and mixing and pinching somehow cleared her mind, and lowered her stress levels. Each perfectly baked pie yielded a much-needed dopamine hit, and if one didn't turn out, she got to enjoy the sweetness of her failure.

While the aura of the holidays settled over the town, however, Elizabeth found herself considering the season closer to home. This would be their first Thanksgiving, Christmas, New Year without Tyler. The move had distracted them for awhile, but with the advent of family-related Hallmark cards and television commercials, they were likely to start feeling his absence again. Grief was tricky like that. It snuck into the spaces intended for joy. It huddled at the edge of her vision, and as she lay in bed at night she wondered how to stop its incursion.

What could replace a lost father?

It was while idly flipping through a magazine at the library that Elizabeth caught the word "Friendsgiving". Of course. Friends. The family we choose. This would be perfect, a homey banquet to remind the kids that even here, even without him, they were loved. They had been here long enough to accumulate a handful of friends each, and it was time to celebrate that small win.

"Can I invite Dylan?" was Lily's first question when Elizabeth proposed the idea over dinner that night.

"Sure," she smiled, ignoring Cory's eye roll. "And any other friends you want. Maybe keep the number reasonable...under ten?" Lily nodded enthusiastically and immediately began to peruse her contacts list.

"Cory, is there anyone you'd like..." This was tricky. Cory didn't have friends.

"Luke and Trent."

Elizabeth blinked. She had never heard of these boys.

"Sure!" she exclaimed, to cover her surprise. "Um...do I know...?"

"Met Luke at the festival, and his buddy Trent. We hang out at school sometimes. They're cool." Apparently this was a sufficient amount of detail, because he returned to his potatoes with vigor.

"That's great, Cor," Elizabeth said softly. "I'm glad you've found some of your people."

He shrugged, but the ghost of a smile played on his lips. On a whim, she decided to push a little further into his secret life.

"What about Lisa, from next door? I thought it would be nice to include her." She glanced at him while cutting her chicken. "She told me you've been doing some work for her around the house."

"That's because you yelled at Grover," Cory said dismissively.

Shock must have overrun her face, because he gave a low chuckle before saying, "It's not a big town, Mom."

Abandoning pretense, she turned to him. "Why didn't you tell me?"

"Because it's none of your business, and you would have fussed." He stood up with his plate. "Are we done here?"

She sighed. "Sure. I'll figure out the date and let you know. And hey," she smiled at him. "I'm proud of you."

***

The first Sunday of November was chosen as the proper time, and Elizabeth made up little invitations to hand out as they felt called. Lily, in her usual spirit, needed more printed after the first day. Cory reported two yes RSVPs and mumbled something about another maybe before closing his door and turning up his music. As for Elizabeth, she secured half of the book club, Denny, and even a sharp nod from Lisa. The last invitation burned a hole in her pocket, as she waited for Joe to stop by the coffee house.

Joe's invitation felt different, and Elizabeth knew why. Much as she hated to admit it, her feelings for him were becoming clearer all the time. His voice whispered in her ear as she rolled out sheets of pastry, and a ghost of his hand held her waist as she stirred the last fruits of the season into swirls of sugar and starch. His eyes watched her lay down each night, and when she woke shaking, his hand held her own. But these were figments of her imagination, of course. Nothing in her physical reality indicated any sort of connection between them. He was a helpful neighbor, no more, and there was no reason she should be grasping for his presence or searching the hills simply to hand him a slip of paper he would likely ignore completely.

She had tried walking down by the river, with the intention of "accidentally" bumping into him, but the spot where they had almost danced was abandoned. The maple grove down the road was likewise empty. So she sat in the coffeehouse a little longer than she should each morning for three consecutive days, checking the door every minute, until Denny slid into the seat across from her and said in a low voice, "You know if you tell me who you're waiting for, I may be able to help."

Blushing furiously, Elizabeth shook her head. "Oh I was just going to invite Joe to our little party ... he was such a help in those early repairs. I thought it would be nice to include him." She did not mention the way his touch burned her skin, nor the sensation of falling that she felt when she looked into those deep eyes. Just speaking his name brought a warmth to her that felt unfamiliar and imposing, like standing in the grove of trees at night, their darkness closing over her.

Denny was unfooled.

"Well, if it's just a little professional courtesy," she said mockingly, "You'll likely find him down the street at the mechanic. They sometimes give him space for his van in the winter, and he runs the tow truck and snow plough to keep busy. When he's not, ya know ... handling your business." The grin she flashed at Elizabeth left no doubt that Denny understood exactly how Joe affected her.

Throwing caution to the wind, Elizabeth decided to ask the questions she had been avoiding. "So is that his deal? He wanders the countryside doing odd jobs, semi-homeless, no family?"

Denny nodded. "Yup. He's a local, born a few towns away and been here since he finished high school. He did a few years at the college part-time, but if he finished we never heard about it." Denny shifted in her seat, leaned heavily onto her elbows and looked Elizabeth directly in the eyes. "You should know, he's got a past. Once upon a time, our

Joe was a happy guy. Married. Owned a little house, nice garden, a motorcycle he worked on to no end. Everyone's favorite bar buddy. He sang a mean karaoke, let me tell you."

She couldn't imagine it. "What happened?"

Denny sighed, and swallowed. "She left. Left him for his best friend. Apparently the things she screamed on her way out were ..." Denny sighed again, and shook her head. "It destroyed him. Everything he felt good about was one more reason she left, so he stopped feeling good about everything. Got mean. Got quiet. Got isolated. He sold everything and took off for months in that van. We thought he was dead. Then on a spring day, he came rolling back into town looking for work wherever he could get it, and folks loved him enough to give him some without asking questions. So he stayed. That was years ago. Sometimes I still see flashes of who he used to be, but ..." her voice trailed off, "I don't know what it would take for him to live again. He died when she broke his heart."

Elizabeth felt worse knowing than wondering. She had never felt that deep connection with someone, that kind of comfort and satisfaction. A lifetime of chasing love had rendered the possibility a mystic treasure, found and held by a lucky few who lived off its goodness for a lifetime. What a tragedy, to have found such a haven, only to lose it all. For a moment she tried to picture Joe laughing, singing, enjoying life, but the vision came haunted by the man she knew. Somewhere in the background had been this spectre of things to come, poisoning him with happiness that would inevitably be his destruction. An unimaginable heartbreak.

What did this mean for her now? She had chalked her idle daydreams up to hormones or curiosity, but learning more about the man made her wonder if, perhaps, her heart was showing her something real.

Denny seemed to read her thoughts, and she took Elizabeth's small white hand in hers. "Hey, that's a nice thing you're doing," she opined. "Some part of him will appreciate being asked. Just don't have any expectations. He probably won't say much, and I'd be shocked if he turned up. But —" she spread her hands and shrugged, "you never know. Cycles end. Maybe it's finally time." She walked behind the counter and poured a large cup of black coffee. "Here. You go tell him I haven't seen his ass in a bit, and I said to get it in here so I don't worry." Denny winked. "Good luck, sis."

Elizabeth's mental map of Solace Spring did not yet include the mechanic, though she had to admit it was probably a good place to know. Like everything else in town, it was small, an operation that would not have survived California's suburban sprawl. The low brick building was on the edge of town closest to the highway, with space for perhaps three or four cars altogether and walls stacked with tires, engine parts, hoses, and a host of other things Elizabeth could not identify. There was no waiting room and no door beyond the yawning open garage, where a large red doorbell instructed you to push for assistance. She heard an insistent clanging inside, and walked in without waiting.

Joe walked out with his usual slow, rhythmic gait, wearing faded blue coveralls and his hair pulled back tightly in a ponytail. His face registered no reaction to her presence. "Car trouble?" he asked in a sedate tone.

"Nope," Elizabeth answered. "A message from Denny." *Bless her.* "She says she hasn't seen you in a bit, and she wanted to check on you, so she sent me over with an offering." She extended her arm with the steaming cup of coffee, and Joe grinned. It altered his whole face, and for a moment Elizabeth could make out the man he once was. There was light in his expression, and his tongue pressed into his teeth as though he was about to crack a joke. Then his eyes met hers and the smile slowly faded, though hers remained intact, trying to join him in the brief moment of mirth. His fingers traced his beard, a new mannerism she recorded in her mind. A sign of reflection.

"Tell her thanks for me. She's right, I've been holed up here. Takes me some time to adjust to living indoors again. This," he held up the cup, "is a good reminder that I need to get out more. I'm working on it."

What a perfect segue.

"Well, would you want to join us for dinner?"

Joe's face blanked completely. "Excuse me?"

"I mean Denny and me. And my kids and a bunch of other folks. I'm doing a Friendsgiving thing," she hurriedly extracted the invite from her pocket, "and we'd love to have you there. If it would help you remember." Her breathing was too fast, and her words were jumbled, but it didn't matter. She had put it out there. The invitation had been made. It was on the table. In her hand. Waiting for him to take it.

She was holding her breath again. Anticipating the curving of reality.

He raised his hand, and carefully took the paper without looking at it. His eyes fell to the floor. For a moment he said nothing, then he turned his back and said, "Let me think about it," before walking back to the empty garage office space without saying goodbye.

Elizabeth turned away and walked out of the shop, wondering how she could be so sad and so angry at the same time.

Chapter Fifteen

An unexpected upside of hosting people in their home for the first time was that they would finally have to make their home … homey. While they had slowly unpacked the ephemera of their daily life, there were still a fair number of boxes that had been deferred to hidden corners, a sizable amount of blank spaces on various surfaces, and a general lack of coziness. The house looked lived in, but not on purpose. Anyone who looked in would think they were still just visiting. Messily.

So Elizabeth decided to splurge a little of their pie money and take Lily into the big town for a girls' day of shopping. Lily loved decorating, and Elizabeth got so little time with her daughter. It hurt to admit, but Cory's struggles with the system meant that Lily perpetually got the short end of the stick, and none of her mother's energy. No matter how good Elizabeth's intentions were, some new chaos was always brewing, and her sweet little girl had become accustomed to stepping aside. She had promised herself that Massachusetts would be different, that she would start teaching Lily to be an intentional woman, the woman she herself had not yet become but that she desperately wanted her daughter to be. Someone happy.

And happy Lily was, at least to the untrained eye, at least. She spent the ride into the next big town talking happily about her new friends, Dylan, her school project, Dylan, trying out for the spring musical, and Dylan. Elizabeth heard the gossip, but also sensed the untold stories beneath. Directly asking would get her nowhere. So she let Lily prattle on, hoping that at some point she would exhaust current events and let herself speak the truth.

Their first stop was the used bookstore, where Lily eagerly raided the teen vampire section while Elizabeth hunted for coffee table books on wellness, history, and local tourist scenes for the house and inn. Then they made their way past the expensive galleries and into the fair trade shops to get catch-alls and vases. As Elizabeth examined some teak photo frames, she thought of an idea. "Hey, Lil ... we need artwork. For the house and the inn." She turned to her daughter, who was already bored with this task and sneaking a glance at the pages of her book. "Would you be interested in drawing something?"

"Oh ..." Lily looked uncertain. "I don't know, Mom. That's not really my thing."

"Drawing isn't your thing? Weird, I could have sworn your room was full of sketch pads and art supplies and —"

"No, I mean art is my thing, but it's MY thing. I don't do it for other people."

Elizabeth frowned. "Well I get that, and you shouldn't, but just because you don't do it for other people doesn't mean other people shouldn't see it."

Lily shrugged. "I don't want them to judge my work. And it's not really mainstream. My style is kind of dark. I don't know that other people would get it, or enjoy it."

A smile stretched her mother's lips. Somehow, by the grace of whatever powers existed, Lily had a better sense of self at fifteen than her mother did at forty. Overwhelmed by love, she put down the shopping basket and wrapped her daughter in her arms.

"I am so lucky to have you," she said. "What an incredible woman you are already."

Lily softened into the mother love she desperately craved and so rarely enjoyed. Her body crumpled over, too used to holding itself up without help, without supervision, without softness. Still just a little girl, waiting for mommy to hug her. For this moment, it was enough. Elizabeth kissed her forehead as she spoke again.

"But I think you should have more faith in people. And in yourself. Tell you what." She took her daughter's hand and secured it in her elbow as she pulled a range of matching frames from the clearance section. "What if I commission some things from you? I'll pay you a fair amount for a beginning artist, and tell you what I want, and you can put your spin on the subject matter." Ruefully she pulled out her credit card, and looked at Lily while the cashier tallied the total. "I really just want pictures of the property, and maybe a little bit from the rest of the valley. Nature. The trees, the leaves, the —"

"MUSHROOMS!" Lily exclaimed. "Mom can I do a series on the mushrooms? Maybe with snails and salamanders around them?"

"Yeah, that sounds awesome!" It wouldn't have occurred to her, but after months of pondering decor she still had no concrete ideas. And Lily's instincts were good. Elizabeth took her purchases and they stepped out into the busy main street. "I haven't taken the time to look at the mushrooms, I guess. What kind do we have?"

Lily launched into a long explanation of the different varieties in the area, how big they got and where they grew, which ones were poisonous and which were edible. By the time they sat down in the cafe for lunch, she had asked for a pen and was sketching each of her favorites on napkins.

"I didn't realize you knew so much about them," Elizabeth said with amusement. Clearly there were whole worlds that had escaped her notice, but not her daughter's. Leave it to Lily to see everything, and say nothing. Just filing away the information, and the beauty, for her own little creations.

"Well," Lily said, "I did a lot of research. But..." she hesitated, rolling her chopsticks between her fingers and staring at the tablecloth. "There's one...mushroom? I don't even know if that's what it is. But this one *something* in our grove. And I can't find anything like it, anywhere." Her eyes met her mother's. "It glows."

For a moment, Elizabeth froze with the sushi menu in her hand. Lily had seen it. With her readiness for unknown worlds, her daughter had seen the strange lights in the oak grove. She was not crazy. Understanding passed between them. "You've seen it, too."

Lily nodded. "When I came home late from the festival, I saw a light out in the grove, so I went to check it out. And I found these lines in the ground, pulsing, moving towards that big oak tree. They were almost electric." Her voice trembled. "But I've gone out a few times since then, and haven't seen them again. Which is pretty weird. Maybe they have some sort of cycle? They light up in a certain phase of the moon? I don't know." She leaned across the table. "I spent days researching online. I can't find anything like it."

Elizabeth nodded. Her own search had yielded the same — nothing. Hesitantly, she formed her next question, trying to validate her own suspicions without terrifying her child. "Have you noticed anything else weird?" she asked. "Since we moved in."

Lily nodded. "Funny dreams, very vivid, almost like seeing the future. Or a future. And whispers." Her eyes narrowed a little at this confession. "Sometimes I hear whispers." The server arrived, and immediately her happy girl mask appeared on her face. She thanked the waitress profusely and deftly picked up a piece of sushi as she insisted defensively, "And I'm not crazy." The sushi began to disappear, as Lily ate with her usual haste. Always on the run, always moving, so she would never have to face what she had been storing within.

Pouring them each a cup of tea, Elizabeth smiled at her. "I know. I've heard them, too." Jasmine scented steam rose from the tiny cup, and she took a cleansing sip. "But I don't think they're bad. Or evil, or whatever. They're just ..." Her mind searched for a word that would encompass the enormity of the disembodied voices of the night.

"Old." Lily was staring into space, a salmon roll halfway to her mouth.

"Yeah. Old."

They chewed in silence. Finally, Elizabeth reached over to her daughter's plate and extracted a tender pink morsel, saying "Well, at least you can't say it's boring here."

Lily heaved an exaggerated sigh. Despite the teenage expression of drama, it was clear that she was truly exhausted. "Mom, I don't know how to say this, but I wish it was boring. I'd love some boring. Between Dad dying and your depression and Cory's CONSTANT chaos...boring would be great." She rolled her eyes as she gulped down her glass of water.

There it was. The cold hard truth of her daughter's life. That she could never relax because someone else was always bringing stress into the life she worked so hard to make calm. Someone was always stealing her peace.

"It's wrong that you have to deal with that, Lil." No point in denying the reality. "It sucks, and it's wrong, and I wish I could make it different." She sighed. "I'm trying to make it different. And all I can say is that these things take time." The words felt incredibly insufficient, yet they were all she had to offer. "I'm with you. Boring would be … amazing." She met her daughter's meadow green eyes, and saw the brightness welling there. How strong Lily was. Her own armor was reflected in the sparkling unshed droplets. "Maybe the voices will teach us how."

"Yeah," Lily scoffed, staring at the last cylinder on her plate. "Maybe." She sounded resigned and hopeless. Elizabeth couldn't blame her.

"And even if they don't … maybe you and I can find some peace on our own. Not always. But if we give ourselves the time to just … be." An insane idea, just being. She had never managed it. "Maybe changing us will change everything else."

Lily looked at her, and just for a moment, her body softened again, a little girl once more. "Yeah. Maybe."

Elizabeth reached across the table and took her daughter's hand. At least they weren't alone. They had each other.

"Excuse me, server? Two green tea ice creams, please."

***

Cold air rendered the world sharp and still on Friendsgiving day. Windows filtered gray light into the living room, now tastefully outfitted with vases full of dried Chinese lanterns and drawings of red salamanders curled around long, lacy fungi. A tray of used coffee table books covered topics from sacred geometry to traditional tattoo methods, and a bowl of local apples graced the kitchen table. Even the new candles from the big box store exuded an earthy sage musk into the room, and for the first time since they had arrived, Elizabeth felt proud of where she lived.

Food would be served inside, with couches available for the frailest guests and folding chairs on the porch for everyone else. They had put together a menu of traditional favorites mixed with their own specialties. Lily insisted on making sweet potatoes with marshmallows, her annual delight, and Cory had been bullied into making biscuits — he had a surprisingly deft hand with the dough. These would accompany a garlic roasted turkey, a pot of Mexican chicken mole, handheld pumpkin pasties, a salad of late kale from their garden and persimmons from a local farm, and fresh-pressed cider, along with a massive cheese plate and a variety of desserts. Dishes, one of the first big investments she had made, sat upon the table expectantly, with thick mugs special-ordered from the local ceramicist (conveniently also a book club member). Everything was prepared.

Except for Elizabeth. She lay in bed, wishing she had never thought of this party.

In her old life, she had been a great entertainer. It took years for her to notice how much she anxiously monitored every reaction to every dish, worried over her look and her conversations, whether people were bored or overstimulated. No matter how many rave reviews she received, it was never good enough to meet whatever ridiculous standard she had set herself. Each gathering was another chance to prove herself wrong, yet even with her high rate of success, she never enjoyed it. Parties were, after all, for other people. She was there to serve them. To make it all look effortless.

So what made this any different?

It's different, said a voice inside of her, *because these are your friends. Not your husband's. Not your family's. Yours. They came because they care about you. They came to support you. You asked them here to show the kids they were not alone...and neither are you.*

She had something different to prove this time. This time, she needed to prove that she could have fun.

So she dragged herself out of bed, and splashed water on her face. Staring down the woman in the mirror, Elizabeth determinedly met her own eyes. Fun. What felt like fun? It had been a long time since she had been silly, or funny, or loud. And then it came to her.

Donning her ancient hot pink sweatshirt, short shorts and knee socks, she marched down to the kitchen and cranked up the best of 90s pop music on their new speaker. As she began preheating the oven and laying out the ingredients, Elizabeth channeled what she remembered of the choreography she had always idolized. Hours spent in front of the television learning each move were clearly well spent. Both children looked at her in frank amazement. Lily spoke for both when she said, "Wow, Mom, I've never seen you have so much fun before a party. Or ever."

Elizabeth grinned proudly. "I am trying a new attitude!"

Cory stared deadpan at her. As she returned to stirring and rolling and mixing, he sat in a chair and simply watched her. He said nothing, but she could see the gears turning in his head. Was it really possible that his mother could change? And if she could change, could he?

Abruptly he stood, and went upstairs. He returned a half hour later, smelling unusually of soap and cologne, wearing a deep cherry red sweater she was quite certain her gothic-minded son did not have in his wardrobe. He looked ... different.

"Cor, that's a new sweater!"

His eyes didn't quite meet hers as he shrugged. "It's dad's." He glanced up but shuffled his feet. A choking sound broke his voice. "I thought it would be OK."

Elizabeth came to a stop, then stretched out her arms. "Oh, Cor," she said, grabbing him. "Of course it's OK. It's always OK to remember your dad." His breath was hot on her shoulder. The sweater still smelled vaguely of Tyler, and she wondered if Cory had hoarded away his father's belongings in order to preserve him eternally. When the scent disappeared, and the yarn faded, would his dad truly be gone?

Tucking him closer in, she whispered "Cory, I'm sorry if I haven't given you enough space to remember him. I was trying to start us over, create something new, so you wouldn't have to drag him with you ... but of course, you wanted to keep him close." She looked her son in the eye. "If you need to go back to California, we can do that. We can take it all back." And her heart cried and her body shuddered but she would have done anything to given him the happiness he had never known.

"He's not there," Cory said, and tears fell from his eyes. "It makes sense, coming here. I don't feel him being gone so much, because he was never here." Elizabeth nodded. "But I miss him." He started to cry in earnest, years of age falling away with each teardrop. "I miss him all the time." Trembling from head to toe, Cory broke down completely, shaking and moaning in his mother's arms. With horror she realized that he had not cried since Tyler's passing. He had been stoic through the rushed memorial, and while she had tried to nudge him to release his emotions when they were in California, since arriving here she had been too full of her own plans and anxieties to notice that he was still holding it in. Of course nothing had improved. He had harbored all of his grief within him.

They sank onto the sofa, and she held him, his back still spasming with random breaths, body flat and exhausted. Laying him down, Elizabeth stroked his hair and hummed a little tune, as though putting her baby down for a nap. Within minutes he was asleep, and she covered him with a cozy blanket from the cupboard. Lily materialized beside her, leaning on her shoulder and accepting her share of hugs. Elizabeth knew her daughter hated to cry, but nevertheless, she held the space. Lily would move through her grief in her own way, and her own time. She would be here when it happened. Mothers were always there.

Eventually Lily dozed off against the soft cushions as well, and Elizabeth set to work again. Taking the roasted pumpkin from the oven, she let her mind wander while she scraped and squished and mixed. Honey, cinnamon, ginger. All the sweetness of the life she had imagined when she was Cory's age. She and Tyler had been together since high school, a match everyone approved. It was easy. It was safe. And if they struggled to connect sometimes, well, wasn't that part of being married? Part of growing up?

But they had never grown back together. All of the sweetness she had planned was too saccharine for him, too emotional and strange. He needed it to be easy. Nothing extra, nothing required, just a heated-through dinner and several hours of television while he stared at his phone and did "work". She was never sure it was work, but the reality of it was indifferent. As was he. So she held her babies tight, created more magical outings and special trips and delicious cookies. She bought them gifts and invited their friends over and read them stories until they fell asleep each night, long beyond the age when they might have been called "too old". She poured all of the love she could into their childhood, hoping they wouldn't notice how little their father had to give.

In the end, though, she could see that it had not been enough. Silly of her to think she could make up for a father who, having been emotionally absent their whole lives, had now become completely absent. Perhaps it was better that way. Perhaps the memory of a father could give Cory the love he had not received when his dad was alive.

For a moment, she felt the old anger rising through her. The responsibility she had been forced to shoulder, the weight she had to drag along, always doing the work of two, or three, or a village. He had sat catatonic in front of a screen and been lavished with love and appreciation while she...she could never do enough. Never enough to make up for his lack, his coldness, his closed heart. Here she was, three thousand miles away from his grave, and still cleaning up his messes. She wanted to *scream*...

Suddenly every light in the house flickered, popped, and went out. Silence followed darkness. Even the birdsong halted. Elizabeth circled very slowly through the kitchen, looking for signs of trouble, but there was nothing. Not a sound, not a movement. As though even the air had frozen. Even the dust particles in the air were still, encased in a ray of sunlight, unmoving.

She exhaled.

Lights glowed on again, the oven resuming its whirring noises, Cory's gentle snores rising from the couch. Her anger dissipated by shock, Elizabeth merely stood, willing herself to breathe calmly, closing her eyes against an overwhelming world.

When Lily woke twenty minutes later, Elizabeth was dosing little circles of pastry with spoons full of dark orange paste, the bounty of the local pumpkin farms. Lily took the roasted shells out to the composter, then began to work next to her mother. Fingers wet, she carefully creased each half moon together, making the crust look braided with the tiny pleats she used to seal them. She sang as she worked in a quiet voice, ancient Celtic melodies rising from her throat. Elizabeth joined when she knew the words, and faded out when she did not.

They stood together, shoulder to shoulder, singing their power and closing each abundant pastry before they placed them in the fire.

Cory awoke of his own volition an hour before the party, bolted down a massive sandwich and assembled the buttery spheres in a minute. He never lingered over the work, like she did, but he had an intuitive understanding of the dough and his creations always turned out well. Piles of fluffy biscuits emerged pale gold from the oven just as she was setting out heaters and candles. Just then, Denny entered without knocking, placed a tray of chickpea salad on the table, and helped herself to some cider and whiskey.

Soon, the house was full of people—some friends, some strangers—all making their way into tiny colonies that formed, broke, and reformed with the passage of time and appetizers. There was laughter and gossip, trivia cards and dancing, shouted praise and requests for recipes. By the time Elizabeth presented the turkey, goodwill ran throughout the small crowd and everyone was feeling well acquainted.

Then Joe walked in.

For a moment, heads turned to see the latecomer, and a momentary hush rippled into whispers and significant looks exchanged between neighbors. Her hostess game wasn't quite fast enough, though at least she didn't drop the turkey. Elizabeth was trying to figure out how to make her way to him and stop him from leaving, when Denny exclaimed, "Well would you LOOK what the cat dragged in! A shut-in!". She laughed raucously and pulled him into a clearly unwanted bear hug, and the rest of the group began lining up to say their hellos. Joe looked both flattered and deeply uncomfortable, so Elizabeth slowly put down the enormous main course and shouted, "All right, come and get it!" before weaving her way through the hungry diners to her newest guest. Joe held out a battered wooden box with a hinge, a flat oak pirate's chest roughly the size of a book. Wonderingly, she opened it.

Inside were little sand-colored sugar jewels, matte pillows of sweetness. Maple candy. Her favorite. Glee spread over her face as he said, "I had some maple left from last year's harvest, so it's not as fresh as I would have liked, but it seemed like the right thing..." His voice trailed off. Joe's usually decisive nature was clearly off kilter. He was out of his element, standing inside with so many bodies.

"Did you *make* these?!?"

"Yeah." Pride shone in his eyes. This was a craft he had honed over time. A true gift of his energy.

"That's amazing. I love maple candy, it's my favorite. Will you teach me to make it?"

He grinned in a way that, in another man, might have been flirtatious. "Then what would I bring to parties?" And he swam away, absorbed by the nearest group into conversation and plate making.

She allowed herself to be pushed and pulled by the tide, making safe and boring inquiries of the teens, sharing recipes with the grandmothers. Even Lisa was surprisingly sociable, regaling them with stories of her wild youth in Bennington. A spectacular sunset blessed their meal on the back porch, orange skies melting into the black spikes of the trees on the horizon. Cory and his friends lit one of the firepits. The teens, both the cool and the defiant, gathered around the smoking beech wood and took turns playing their favorite tunes, which drifted back in one continuous drone to the adults who sat on the porch with mismatched cups of tea, half-eaten pie slices forgotten at their feet. They grew drowsy in the stillness of night. One by one, each guest hoisted themselves up and spoke their thanks, assuring their hostess that they were fine to get home. Finally only the young remained. Elizabeth gave them her blessing to stay until their curfews kicked in and told them to come again soon. Then she headed up the steps, collecting dishes as she went, and strode into the kitchen, stretching her back and groaning.

"Sounds like you hit your limit."

Joe was at the sink, washing dishes carefully by hand. Methodically he circled the sponge over each dish, turned it, circled again, and placed it in the rack. The movement was like clockwork, the small *clink* of each plate's landing jumpstarting the next cycle. He watched her over his shoulder as he worked, taking in her unmasked exhaustion. Feeling she had been caught out of character, Elizabeth tried to straighten her posture and pick up her grin, but all she could manage was a shuffle.

"It's been awhile since I was on my feet all day, I suppose."

"I meant the people." Another dish clicked into the drying rack. "Sounds like you hit your limit on people."

She pulled up next to him at the counter. A part of her was tempted to sit on it, but she couldn't muster the jump. "I do love having people over. Truly. I love feeding them and taking care of them and listening to them. It usually means I don't have to talk about me." Her attention fell to the running water, falling in rivulets into the antique sink. "But yes, I do better with short spurts. This is as many hours as I can manage with a group." Looking up, she found him staring at her, and her breath quickened. Full of whiskey-fueled confidence, she tilted her head and said, "I prefer people one-on-one."

Clink. Joe turned off the sink and turned to look at her. "Do you?" he said quietly. He stepped closer, and she felt his presence rolling over her, leaving her skin hot and her pulse racing. Now she was stranded, frozen to the spot and out of clever replies. So she said the only word she could locate, the one her body was broadcasting in a haze of pheromones:

"Yes."

Chin raised, she met his eyes as he stood just above her. They had never been this close. He seemed to consider her, wet hands on his jeans, eyes boring into her soul. Every fiber on his flannel shirt was magnified, the crease between his eyebrows evident under a streak of silver hair she hadn't noticed before. For a fraction of a second, his hand seemed to reach towards her waist as she leaned back onto the counter. It paused in midair.

"I don't like most people one-on-one," he said quietly. "But maybe it's worth a try sometimes." He looked at her again and this time his hand reached for her hair before stopping at her shoulder, where his gears ground to a halt. His eyes dropped to her waist. "Thanks for having me over tonight."

"My pleasure." She smiled. "We should do it again sometime." Elizabeth felt like a lovesick school girl dropping hints for the prom, but whatever stretched between them in this moment, she definitely wanted more of it. Even if she needed to be the one to ask.

"That's what I was thinking," Joe's voice came softly. The gears gave way, and his hand finally landed on her shoulder and smoothed down her back, coming to rest on her right hip. A shiver migrated in its wake. "What if next time, I cook dinner?"

An offer. Suddenly her nerves evaporated and her hand shot to his hip in return. It was a game her mind had long forgotten, but her body remembered how to play. "Name the night."

Leaning towards her left ear, he whispered, "Next Saturday," before breaking away from her and moving towards the door. He looked back as he let himself out. "Sweet dreams, Elizabeth."

The taste of maple candy was on her tongue when she went to bed, and her dreams were filled with fire.

Chapter Sixteen

Despite her excitement about her impending date, Elizabeth found herself strangely averse to telling anyone about this latest romantic development. After all, she reasoned, perhaps it was not that at all. It was just dinner. And they were friends … or were they? She had to admit that "friendship" was probably straining the truth to breaking point. He was her handy man, and she could count their conversations outside of that construct on one hand. Elizabeth didn't know what they were, but she was certain of one thing.

She wanted to be more.

So she did her best throughout the week to distract herself. The upcoming Thanksgiving holiday, thankfully, occupied a great deal of her attention, both for her nascent pie business and her family. The kids were desperate to be off school, which meant a decent uptick in the number of fights between the siblings. Elizabeth would retreat from their squabbles to Eyes Up, spending her time with the laptop open and her eyes on the door, hoping Joe would walk through it. Her sales copy was, unsurprisingly, flat and hopeless. He never arrived.

Days passed, and Elizabeth heard nothing from him. By Thursday, she had given it up as a passing fancy he had never really meant to entertain. And though she had long ago become accustomed to the back burner, this rejection seemed more personal. She felt ashamed, almost used. It was silly of her, she realized, to think she may have captured his attention. As she broke up yet another shouted disagreement over trivial nonsense, Elizabeth caught a glimpse of herself in the darkened window. Wan, tired, old. The consummate mom. Bones dragging themselves around in service, begging for nothing more than a good night's rest, and perhaps some fuzzy socks. Passion, like beauty, like love, seemed to have passed her by. This woman wouldn't hear from a man like him.

As she walked the property the next morning, noting more landscaping features that were due for replacement, Elizabeth's phone buzzed in her pocket.

"See you tomorrow."

Hand flying to her mouth, Elizabeth doubled over in relief. Not a rejection, then. Not a lost hope. Suddenly the sun looked a little bit brighter, and the morning's magic swallowed her. She hummed all the way back to the kitchen.

Something about the prospect of being alone with Joe was tantalizing in a way that Mitch had not been. They had, after all, been thrown together by the waves of fate over and over again, as though Solace Spring wanted them to be together. A sparkling sense of possibility hovered around the pairing. She tried to remind herself that Joe wasn't exactly a romantic, nor someone who seemed ripe for relationship anymore than she was. He was grouchy and uncommunicative and she was ... well, not in the best place emotionally. Yet she couldn't resist savoring the promise of their first date.

Saturday afternoon stretched into another glorious orange sunset, and Elizabeth tried to control her daydream mindset by putting minimal effort into getting ready. This was all the easier because she was meeting him at work. What did one wear to a first date at a mechanic's shop? Joe's follow up text had given no specifics beyond a time and place to meet, so donning wide leg jeans and a tight black sweater, Elizabeth turned to leave her room. As her hand moved to the light switch, she glimpsed a hint of red in her tangle of jewelry. A rose. Long ago, a friend in California — one of the few kindred spirits she had found — had taken up sculpting. An artist and wild woman, she chaotically jumped between mediums and was always fed by a new fire. Lovers materialized before her, and disappeared when their light began to fade. They worshipped her anyway. Elizabeth had always wondered what it would be like, to take so much from another, to let them feed you to the point of gluttony...and then turn to another, and drink them dry, too. It was terrifying and exhilarating. A life she could not fathom, but which fascinated. Her girlfriend, seeing her longing, had made her this necklace, flower and beads sculpted from clay imbued with rose petals and ash, a dark red kiss of blood that settled in the hollow of her throat. It had felt so powerful that Elizabeth had never had the courage to wear it, but now she slipped it from its hiding place and fastened it about her neck, closing the door firmly behind her.

There was no answer when she knocked at the shop, but something smelled delectable and a thin trail of smoke snaked lazily to the sky behind the building. She walked a few doors down until an alley opened up, then cut across the back patios and saw Joe, standing in front of a grill and giving it his complete attention in the early light of the moon.

"Hi."

"Hi." His eyes did not waver from the meat in front of him. "Drinks are in the fridge." His head nodded to the door behind him, where a single fluorescent light winked in the office.

Caught off guard by the casual (and rather unwelcoming) greeting, Elizabeth entered the office. Dates should begin with a hug, a handshake...at the very least, a smile. Her visions of a long, gooey embrace with hints of more to come were fast evaporating. But she was here, and he was here — things could only go up. Nervously, Elizabeth located the mini fridge sandwiched between an ancient wooden desk and a deeply scarred file cabinet, both covered in pink and yellow carbon copies. She grabbed two green glass bottles of mineral water and returned to Joe's side just in time to watch him wrap the steak in foil and place it atop an already full basket.

"Let's go."

Go? "Go where?"

"To dinner." He finally met her eyes and smiled mischievously. "You didn't think I'd take my dates to dinner at the shop?"

My *dates*. Hm.

He opened the passenger door to the van and ushered her in, before placing the basket securely behind her and taking the wheel. As they drove down the highway, Elizabeth asked, "So is this your standard M.O. for your dates?" She didn't like the way she sounded, but if she was one of many, it was best to know up front.

Joe frowned. "Every once in a while." With this unhelpful answer, he seemed to feel the conversation should shift. "Have you been to the lake yet?"

"I've been past the lake." A sparse children's playground, a closed-down diner, and a few docks clearly marked "private" was the sum total Solace Lake had to offer. There was no "there" there. "I didn't really notice any place to go."

"You must not have really looked," he responded, and his head turned to glance at her. It was a fair criticism. The lake held minimal interest for her, not being a particularly tourist-worthy attraction. She hadn't bothered to look any deeper. "But that's OK," Joe resumed. "I'll show you what you missed."

She was thankful for the car's hidden recesses, so he couldn't see the flush in her cheeks.

A few minutes later, they were parked by the end of a dock that had no sign at all. A single lamp post stood at the end of the floating planks of pine, casting a yellow circle over wood and water alike. Joe walked with a slight swagger down the pathway as he hauled the picnic basket to the end of the dock, then spread a large flannel blanket where the light met the dark. Water surrounded them. Kneeling, he extended a hand to Elizabeth, who sat upon the warm brown wool and took in her view.

The downtown windows were lit, tiny golden squares in the black night. Here and there reflections glittered on the water's surface, stretching the squares into wavering lines and back again. Fog had rolled down the hills and rested eerily along the lake's edges, as though the water itself were adrift, occupying a liminal space between earth and sky. And in front of her was Joe, his shining hair tumbling over his shoulders, carefully unpacking each plate and putting it just so and looking — a little nervous?

"Cory does that." He looked up at her. "The plates," she explained, haltingly. "The plates have to be even before the food goes on them. Which also has to be even." It struck her suddenly that there were other habits she had noticed in Joe that Cory shared, a particular order in their work, their movement, a cadence to their life. She wondered if he, too, had struggled as her son did. Whether he mishandled assignments and connections. But he smiled, and she pushed the thought away for another time.

"He's a good kid," Joe said, putting exact portions of steak, baked potatoes, and grilled broccoli on each plate. "I'm glad people around here are getting to know him." He softened as he handed her her dinner. "I know the good residents of Solace Spring don't always come off as welcoming. Myself included."

"What? You? The life of the party?" she teased. She took a bite of steak that melted in her mouth, and for a moment she could do nothing but let it dissolve on her tongue. "Joe, this is amazing." She swallowed. "I love having someone cook for me," she confessed.

He shrugged. "Single mom. Probably doesn't happen much." Her eyes dropped as he searched her, looking for a reaction. "It's my pleasure," he said quietly. She trembled. Such a simple phrase, yet it brought a flood of emotions to the surface. If she looked at him, she would be undone. Whether she would cry, rage, or throw herself at him, she wasn't sure, but she could not sustain the moment.

"So why the lake?" Safe territory. Literally. What kind of hot date talked geography?

Joe looked out at the serene mirror before them before turning back to his dinner. "No one comes here," he said matter-of-factly. "Like the maples. People want to do things the new way, the removed way, where they aren't on the land. Or the water. When I was a kid, people swam here, drove toy boats here, fished for supper. Now ... it's abandoned. Not gone, just unnoticed." Elizabeth watched him now, mesmerized as she mindlessly swallowed her potatoes. "I just think the water deserves to be recognized. Seen." He shrugged.

He was like the lake, she realized. Known but not invited. Seen but not beloved. Joe was an integral part of the community, but it did not — could not — fully embrace him. She wondered if anyone did.

"You're a caretaker."

Their eyes met again. He considered the word, head rocking back and forth, equivocating as his fingers traced his beard unconsciously. "Yeah, I suppose I am." For a moment he became lost in his thoughts, processing the word slowly, turning it over in his head. She saw the wheels turning, the decision being made. Then he reached for a tin of cookies, offering her one as he added, "You are, too, unless Matty chose the wrong woman."

Her chin raised slightly. "Do you think he did?"

Joe considered her, then slowly shook his head. "No. If the forest has let you stay this long, there must be a link there."

Confused, she asked, "A link? What do you mean?"

"Between you and the land. That forest is conscious. Something about it ... " he paused, as if he was searching for the right words to describe the innocent stand of trees that guarded her home. "It chooses who comes there."

Elizabeth raised her eyebrows. It was the same revelation she had experienced weeks ago, but had pushed away. Hearing it from another made it true. "Really?"

He shrugged. "You know the story of Solace Spring? How the town was founded around the miracle water?" She nodded. "Matty used to tell me another story." Joe's growl was quiet, almost reverent. "He said the trees there are older than the rest of the forest. Much older. The Native Americans who lived here centuries ago believed that oak grove was sacred. It's where they brought their elders to die at the end of life, and where babies were taken to be named. If someone grew ill, truly sick, they would be brought to those trees and left there. Most of the time, they would walk back into the village a few days later, completely cured." He looked at her. "That's why he called the place Sanctuary. He believed the spring was someplace beneath those trees, waiting to offer healing again. He used to say the trees whispered to him." His eyes sparkled and turned dark, like the lake. "Maybe they'll whisper to you, too."

Slack muscles loosened her jaw, her mind racing so far forward and backward that she forgot what was happening in the present. It wasn't in her head, or Lily's. It was a concrete knowledge, held by a select few who were … what? Chosen. Chosen for what purpose? Something strange was happening in their woods. Something special was taking place there. And she … well, what was she?

On a whim, she asked the question that troubled her since she had arrived in Solace Spring.

"Do you think I'm the right person for The Sanctuary?"

It was a bold ask, not least because she knew that Joe, of all people, would say so if she was not. It was also a roundabout way of asking what he thought about her, though why his opinion on this should matter, she did not know. Familiar pangs of overwhelm curled in her stomach, whispering the usual refrain: *"not enough"*.

Joe stabbed at his steak one last time and gazed at the lake. He was quiet for so long that she wondered if he hadn't heard the question, or was ignoring her. Then he said, "Water is tricky. It can look like one thing on the surface, and be something totally different beneath. This lake is calm and still, but the bottom is full of water weeds and fish and rocks … a whole world." He looked back at her. "I think your woods are the same way. A world unseen." He leaned closer to her. "I think you could see it, if you want to. I think you have the ability. But I don't think it will work if you keep trying to do it the way you're doing it."

Her backbone stiffened. Part of her closed off with the criticism, angry at being found wanting. Yet a new aspect of her seemed to peer out through her eyes. It was listening. The sensation was disconcerting.

"What am I doing wrong?"

"You're trying to care for it here," Joe said, brushing her forehead with his fingers. "In the mind. It's not there." Taking her hand, he pressed it into the water lapping the dock, eliciting a sharp gasp from her mouth. Joe swallowed it, his lips seizing the opportunity to enter her own, arms circling her waist as her hand dripped onto his thigh. Shock and pleasure battled in her body, and in response she froze, letting him move around her and on her, a tide upon the land. When they broke apart, he traced a line down her throat and onto her heart. "It's here," he said. Perhaps she imagined the catch in his voice. "You need to feel it."

Yet she remained still as a statue as she quietly admitted, "I don't know how to feel."

He tilted her face to his, looked into her eyes with something that may have been love and may have been sympathy.

"Maybe you're a world unseen, too, Elizabeth."

Then his lips caressed hers again, and she was lost to oblivion, forgetting everything except for the darkness, and the water, and his hand upon her back.

***

She was stumbling a bit when she got out of her car around midnight, the hard angles of The Sanctuary giving way to the ever-shifting shadows of the woods. Joe's kisses lingered in her mouth, smoky and sweet, somehow both familiar and unexpected. They had talked little in their time together, empty plates forgotten while he wrapped her tightly in his embrace. But when the fog had rolled in, they could not see one another. He took her hand, led her back, dropped her off with a casual hug, and walked away.

It had been heaven, until it stopped.

Now, she saw that the fog had seeped up the road and into the forest, slithering between tree trunks like silence. It gave the place an eerie look, but to Elizabeth it felt as though the lake's water had taken to the air and followed her home. Water for the trees, she thought idly. Still unsteady, she traveled towards the curls of white and gray, stopping just outside of the grove. She was unsurprised to see the glowing lines faintly pulsing on the ground, and despite her shivering, she took off her shoes and placed her feet upon the lines. The strange throbbing of the earth began again, more quietly tonight, a sleepier song.

Feel it.

Leaning against the rock for support, Elizabeth allowed her body to go slack (easily done, at the moment), a rag doll upon the sharp boulder. Her feet took in the beat and wound it up her legs. Like Morse code, it seemed to be coming in starts and stops, stretching longer as it reached higher into her body. When the pulses hit her thighs, a hum reverberated through her. Her pelvic bones sang, a lilting tune that answered the earth's rhythm. The songs mixed in a harmonious melody that rang throughout her body, bubbling up through her and onto her tongue, generating heat and movement and words she could not identify as they lifted off her tongue. She writhed on the stone, barely aware of her surroundings. Mist poured into her, filling her with water, only to be exhaled in notes and spells. Spilling over, she came to the earth on all fours, and the drum within her became louder and her song became stronger and the whirling in her womb became faster until with a cry she stopped. Elizabeth's body dropped to the ground while her mind went blank, and when she woke, the mists had blanketed her, and small vermillion flowers had blossomed all around the place she lay.

Chapter Seventeen

Elizabeth's relationship with Joe was different than any other she had experienced. First, it was not clear that there was one. He did not, as Mitch had, ask to see her again, or send flowers, or show any other form of romantic interest. He did not share his day with her, as her husband had done, or ask her to take up any of his burdens. Instead, he would occasionally text her screenshots of newspaper cartoons, or photos of various maple groves at sunset. Vivid shades of tangerine and neon pink clouds seemed language enough for him — there was rarely a caption or even a greeting. She would wonder how best to follow up, but even when she asked a question or tried to begin a conversation, he would disappear. Then in the midst of her frustration, he would show up at her door, saying he was passing and thought he might fix a shelf or a squeaky stair. Lily and Cory loved having him around, as he seemed to find conversation with them infinitely easier than with her. Sometimes he would stay for dinner, making jokes or listening avidly to Cory's latest project, admiring Lily's artwork and catching everyone up on old town gossip. For her part, Elizabeth sat silent, wondering blissfully at his interest in her family.

It wasn't that Tyler hadn't loved the children—he had. But he never really knew what they were doing, who their friends were, or what they were working on. He would mildly agree to anything said to him, and dutifully admire what was thrust in his face. This was the sum total of his parenting, and while Elizabeth had objectively known he wasn't good at it, she also hadn't seen a great deal of better parents. Sure, there were charming stories on the internet, sweet photos on annual Christmas cards, but she had been sure these moments were cherry picked or scripted. It had stopped occurring to her years ago that there may be men out there who excelled at being a dad.

Of course, she would remind herself as she washed the dishes, Joe wasn't here for that. He didn't want to be a dad. He didn't want to be anything, as far as she could tell. They hadn't touched since their night on the lake. Whatever chemistry had existed between them seemed to have evaporated and left her in the dreaded friend zone, no matter how often her eyes followed him around the house. In the chance moments where they were in close proximity, even the simple act of handing around plates, Elizabeth would feel flames rising from the space between her hips and engulfing her body. Longing, she learned quickly, was a painful act. She started to keep to the kitchen when he came by, hoping the physical distance would lessen the pull her body felt towards him, allowing her to pretend she was neither hurt nor confused by his tides. And so they went for the next few weeks, in the purgatorial space between here and there, Elizabeth hating every moment of it but clinging to the hope that, perhaps, if she was patient, he may turn towards her once more.

Meanwhile, she had taken his caretaking advice to heart. For all of her spreadsheets and refurbishment projects, The Sanctuary seemed to be stubbornly opposing her will. She had hoped that by this time she would have a new angle, a way to sell some stays here and turn enough of a profit to keep it open. Yet she had not updated the look of the inn, nor the website that booked it, and there was no real reason neither had been done. Small honey do chores were one thing — putting herself out there was another step altogether. Somehow, when it came to the big stuff, she froze. She didn't feel ready, prepared. She didn't know what she had to offer The Sanctuary. So perhaps Joe was right. Perhaps she needed to ask it.

Despite the continually dropping temperatures, Elizabeth began taking her morning coffee out to the grove each day, simply to be in the woods alone. She would sit upon the crumbling remains of a mossy wall, her back against a tree trunk, and look over the trees in front of her. At first this yielded nothing, except frustration that she was not producing something of value and a strong desire to reach for her phone. But the more she forced herself to sit, the more she felt the vague movements of the earth. She became familiar with the heartbeat that ran an undercurrent through the grove, backing up the scurrying of animals and the buzzing of insects. Wind rushing through the trees lent unexpected choruses, and occasionally the few remaining birds would interject. A symphony of forest. All that was missing was the voices, so clear when she lay in bed at night, so muddy when the sun came up.

One late November morning she arrived at the grove to find Joe already there, the usual black coffee in his hand. Mildly annoyed that he was on her property without permission or announcement, she ran her hands through her bedhead hair and attempted to offer a perky greeting.

He turned to her and, unusually, offered a sweet smile. "I came to see how you're getting along with the land."

"Oh." Was this a test? "Well, we're trying to communicate." Her mouth twisted into half a smile. "I get the feeling we're not speaking the same language, though. I try to say something, but the answer gets lost in translation. She tries to speak, I can't quite hear the words." She shrugged. "But I'm keeping at it, I guess. I don't know what else to do."

"Maybe you need to try listening a different way."

Elizabeth shrugged. "I seem to hear better at night, but I always lose control of the conversation. And the meaning still ..." It would be a lie to say there was none, because she felt the meaning within her. But her body refused to process the information. A runtime error. Does not compute.

He stared at her, sizing her up. Then he walked towards her, placing his coffee on the boulder where scarlet flowers still spilled over the ground, and placed his hands around her waist. Immediately she felt the heartbeat surge through her, and it was all she could do to hold her breath and pretend to feel nothing.

"Can I help?"

His low voice in her ear made her knees tremble. She swallowed. "Help how?" Her heart was pounding, her body was on fire, she felt like screaming in agony or ecstasy or both. Silently she allowed herself to be shattered into a million pieces and put back together, over and over as his fingers caressed her curving flesh.

"Well, I can come down here with you tonight. Maybe I'll have some ideas you haven't tried yet." Breath tickled the hair by her ear, his mouth descending to her neck and stopping just short of her skin. "I've lived on this land a long time ... I know how to talk to her." Their hips brushed together and Elizabeth could take it no longer. She pressed him away but could not break their bond, her body waving towards the grove while remaining tied to this guardian.

Joe's hand caught hers and he pulled her into a bear hug. "It's OK," he said soothingly. "I've got you. You're safe."

And suddenly for no reason at all, she was clinging to him. To safe. Heavy breaths warmed the flannel on his shoulder, making her shaky and weak. He held her until they slowed, became as light as the wind, and the pounding in her head faded to a single birdsong in the trees.

The forest held its breath, too.

"OK," Elizabeth agreed. It felt monumental, allowing him into her evening, her sanctuary, her place of magic. It had been just for her. Her peaceful temple. Yet she knew the grove needed her to go deeper, and she had reached the limit of her knowledge. Joe was right. She needed help. His help.

Gently, he kissed the top of her head, a gesture of such sweetness that her nervous system retreated in submission. Filled with air and light, Elizabeth sighed deeply. The wave of pain had come and gone. Looking her in the eyes, Joe whispered, "I'll be back tonight." Then he bent to kiss her, and again she felt herself moving into his lips and out of his arms at the same time. Embracing him felt necessary but unwise. She needed to know more first. She needed some clarity. And she needed his touch more than she wanted to admit.

Waving timidly, she turned back to the house, silently praying that the children were up to distract her from the whirlwind in her chest.

***

That night, the path glowed white hot, the bluish tinge spilling onto the hard packed earth like lightning. Elizabeth paced back and forth in a frenzy. Hands massaged each other convulsively, staving off the biting wind if not the anxiety. It was insane, having Joe come down here to see her fairy lights, the equivalent of showing him a UFO. With Denny, or Tiffany, it would have been a cute distraction, a conspiracy theory to regale the girls of book club ... but this was Joe. Joe, who was rigid and implacable and serious. Joe, who barely spoke of normal things. Joe, who she wanted so badly, but could not reach.

This point in particular had her pacing. Their relationship seemed to echo the pond, a flat, stagnant space of possibility. She didn't doubt that many things could grow between them, and perhaps already were. His ease with her children was a warm space in her heart, and she watched them together as though she was looking through a snug window on a cold day. A fantasy world of honey smiles and exuberant joy. The father her children should have had. But it was too late for that now, they were beyond the years of replacement and replenishment. He could be her partner, presumably, a lover and a fixture in her life, but he seemed disinclined to move any further down that path. Despite Elizabeth's desire, she could not translate her feelings into an invitation, and for Joe's part, despite the moments of intensity that had erupted between them, he looked right through her. Like she wasn't even there.

It was a familiar feeling.

She had just decided that it was for the best to call him and make a rain check, one that would never be cashed, when there was a scratch of gravel behind her. She turned to see Joe's outline emerging from the formless black garden. His hair was down again, and fell in undulating rivers across his back. Elizabeth restrained herself from reaching out to touch it. Yet she needn't have, because as he reached her, his arms folded around her shoulders, cradling her head beneath his beard. The resulting sigh beside his heart released steam into the night air. Something inside of her began to quiver. Fingers flexed and cramped at her sides, trying to prevent the shaking from expanding. Perhaps she could blame it on the cold, though in Joe's arms she had ceased to feel it. In fact, when she focused on the places where they touched, there was only peace. Protection.

He let go of her, but bent his head so that their foreheads were together, two trees intertwined. Elizabeth felt something bouncing off of the walls in her chest. She willed herself to focus on the imprint of his head upon hers, to dwell in the words that now fell from him in whispers.

"Hi."

"Hi."

"I found you."

Found her, in the darkness. Found her, next to the infinitesimal light half buried in the earth. Found her, shaky and scared and lost. It was nice to be found, she discovered. But though the warmth of his greeting swelled inside of her, the shaking pushed it down, and when she spoke her hands were trembling again.

"What do you think?" she asked, her tone all business. She chanced a glance at him and saw that his eyes were entirely on her, with no attention to spare for the strange tendrils of fungi unfurling on the ground. Clarifying, she stepped back and gestured to the phenomenon.

For a moment, Joe continued to stare at her, eyes bright. Then he dropped his attention to her still-shaking hand and the pathway below it. Neither surprise nor dismay passed on his face, though the slight crease that always sat between his brows deepened. Somewhere in the bright spots of his brain he was rearranging information, looking for what fit, aligning new evidence with old theories. Wordlessly he took her hand in his, kneading the fingers absently as he gazed on the streams of light, and again Elizabeth felt warmth and calm spreading through her body.

Stepping behind her, Joe pulled her to him, wrapping her arms around her midsection and taking each hand in one of his own as he continued to rub her cold fingers. He was silent.

"You seem remarkably unsurprised by glowing ground," she commented.

She felt his grin more than she saw it, like a ray of sun breaking through clouds ... a slow, quiet illumination. His lips nearly brushed her ear as he responded.

"I don't think anything on this land would surprise me. If the flowers sang in winter, I wouldn't do anything but whistle the tune." Now his cheek was directly next to hers, and she grew still hotter, her wool sweater feeling suddenly more confining than cozy. "But it's interesting, that's for sure. It looks almost like a river." It would, to him. The man who was always moving on saw his next current rising, an incoming flood of soil. "Sometimes the river forms rapids around larger stones, and the water will almost bounce over the top because of the rock's shape. This has a similar pattern."

For a moment they watched it pulse, both taking in the brightness, and the dimming, a current that traveled in place. They felt rather than heard its song. Joe's heart beat against Elizabeth's spine, an asynchronous drum enriching the gentle beat.

"Should we follow it?"

The words escaped without her permission. This was an adventure she felt unprepared to extend to him. Follow me, into the dark, into the wild, into The Sanctuary, into the unknown. It felt like a lot to ask. But he unraveled her from his body and with one hand, led her forward.

Though there was no ambient light beyond the tiny flares upon the ground, Joe clearly knew this space enough to navigate his body through the boulders and felled trees. He sauntered forward as though this was his morning walk along the river, an everyday meditation. Elizabeth felt rushed. Surely something like this deserved a more sacred entrance? They should be moving slowly, intentionally, studying the small details, counting the flashes between footsteps. She wanted data collection. She wanted reverence. Neither appeared forthcoming. Joe seemed to find this treasure a simple roadside attraction. Disappointment hunched her shoulders, and suddenly the night was cold again.

As they entered the grove, Joe paused, and Elizabeth, trailing behind, fell into him. Without turning his head, he gathered her to his side, where she wrapped her arms together and buried her hands inside the resulting knot, noticing the numb creeping into her fingertips. Joe's eyes moved in rapid succession through the clearing, noticing the tangled web on the ground and fiery blue glow at the base of the cloven oak.

"Does it respond to touch?"

Elizabeth was frozen in her tangle of limbs, but jerked her head up and down a few times. Was curiosity the same as worship? She wasn't sure. Perhaps for him it was. As Joe bent down and began to stretch his hand towards the mycelium, she was seized with an impulse to bat him away, and protect this magic from being violated by someone who did not understand. But she did not understand either. Perhaps she could not understand without him. Without his touch.

He turned back and grinned, "Promise me if I die by explosive mushroom, you'll put it on my tombstone."

Laughter erupted from her, loosening the knot. Her trembling stopped again.

"I'll inform your next of kin," she smiled. Drawn forward by his humor, Elizabeth knelt beside him. "It felt weird," she confessed. "Like a mild electric shock. But there were no long term consequences." Their eyes met, and she was surprised to see nervousness hovering around him. So he *was* affected by this place. Good. It felt more powerful to have an ally in fear. Like soldiers, they would march into battle together, and woe betide the mycelium that fought them.

She held his free hand, and he closed his eyes as one finger fell to the ground.

He sighed.

Relaxation flowed over his face, as though he had just been submerged in a soothing bath. For a moment Elizabeth watched, fascinated, as all of his muscles loosened and fell, passing immediately into a state of rest. "It feels like water," he whispered.

The river? No energy surge, no sparks? She would never have believed it, would never have even known that Joe could look so peaceful, so well-cared for. His face was entirely open.

And then she lowered her gaze.

"Joe," she breathed. He opened his eyes and followed her gaze. The pulsing lights were no longer the icy blue she had come to know, but a fiery red, lighting all of the trees as though a wildfire surged beneath them. Immediately, Joe withdrew his touch, and the color disappeared, retaking its original hue. He placed a finger upon the earth, and the ruby glow returned.

They looked at each other.

"You do it."

She placed her palm on the line, and felt the surge of energy flowing into her. Her body felt like a radio antennae, electric currents passing through her, a ceaseless flow of crackling energy that ran up her thighs to her chest to her throat. Her head tipped back unconsciously as she breathed, needing to release the sensation from her quivering body. Overwhelmed, she placed her hand on her collarbone, asking her heartbeat to slow, instinctively stretching herself to the sky.

When she opened her eyes, Joe was drinking her with his eyes, as though he had never seen anything so beautiful.

His lips were on her before she could speak.

If she hadn't been caught up in the throes of the glowing earth, Elizabeth knew her body would have shut down. After the avoidance and confusion, the unanswered questions and frigid demeanor, she would have panicked. But the part of her that needed to know it all was mysteriously silent as he gripped her waist, pulling her into his chest with a ferocity she had never seen in him. And she found herself answering his passion with her own. Her arms snaked up his back and held him close as his mouth parted with hers just long enough to nibble on her neck. She gasped. The frenzied kissing resumed, sparks from the tendrils of light now being supercharged within her body, spinning in dizzying circles until she felt both ecstatic and faint. And still he was there, gathering up her weight in his hands.

"I don't understand how you do this to me," he whispered. "Something about you just pulls me back in ... every time ... holds me down ..."

"Joe ... "

Barely conscious, Elizabeth reached for his shirt, moaning as her hand grazed a patch beneath his throat. In answer he moved to hers, massaging the tender skin with his thumb and kissing the slope down to her shoulder. He hit the limits of her sweater, and had to stop. The heat within her was unbearable. She started to fall, but Joe spotted the danger and half-dragged her over to the oak. As he settled her against it, her finger brushed the light, now alternating between red and blue so quickly that to her dazed eyes, it became almost purple. The energy surge was stronger this time, much stronger than anything she had ever experienced. She moaned, until Joe's mouth covered hers again, and he was holding her, and she was imbibing him, and they were melting into themselves and each other and the tree and the earth. He placed a hand on the inside of her thigh, and began sliding it upwards.

Suddenly, her breath stopped. Blind fear flew through her like an arrow, and all around, the lights went black. The night was cold, the wind brittle. Elizabeth found herself shaking, and Joe backed away from her as though she might be contagious.

She was in a dark room, listening to ragged breathing in her ear, staring at the ceiling and wishing it were over. Years of disconnect had dulled the invasion, but every time it began again her body recoiled, retreated, shrank her soul small enough to leave the body entirely. Somewhere, a little girl was asking to be held, to be loved and protected, but her voice was drowned by his need, and she lay in the dark until he pushed himself off of her, and left.

When her breathing slowed, the violent past had evaporated, and Elizabeth was back on the forest floor with Joe. For a moment they sat together in the darkness, fingers lacing them together even as the wind wove its way between their bodies. Elizabeth closed her eyes. What he must think of her. Her shaking intensified, and Joe's deep voice came out of the void.

"You're cold. Come on, let's go in."

Overwhelmed, she allowed herself to be led silently back to her doorstep. She felt foolish beyond belief, which was fast becoming a habit when he was there. He made her feel naked. No matter what she grabbed to try and cover herself, it disappeared beneath his gaze. He saw everything. And ignored it all.

Except for tonight, when he had kissed her.

"Some light show."

She turned to him. "Yeah." It was insufficient. "I'm sorry, I'm not entirely sure ... what happened ... " He stared at her again. Embarrassment shone from her cheeks, blessedly hidden by the night. What an idiot she had been. "I guess there are more questions than answers now." And she met his eyes boldly, daring him to make this anything but a friendly business meeting, a midnight hike between naturalist and student. A look she had seen on his own face.

Joe raised his eyebrows. "I think it answers a lot."

Surprised, she released her aloof posture and quickly asked, "Really? Do you know what it is?"

The look he gave her was knowing, or perhaps patronizing. She wondered if he felt bad for her. "I think you do. Maybe not consciously. But it feels you, and you feel it."

"But you felt it, too," she insisted, "you felt a river."

Kindness rimmed his eyes. For a moment, it was as though he was holding her again, gently and carefully as a dream, though his arms never moved. "I did. But it was separate from me. Something I could witness more than I could experience. With you ..." He reached for her hair, running his fingers through the strands at her temple, and gazed at her. For a moment, she saw a flicker of the desire that had possessed him in the grove, along with something else she couldn't quite place. "It was part of you. And you were part of it. You became the light."

Words failed her. Elizabeth stood with her mouth open, struggling between confusion about this theory and the realization that Joe may, in fact ... admire her?

She chose the former.

"But maybe it would have reacted to you, too. Maybe if you spent more time there, or touched it more, or ... " Her voice trailed off. She wasn't sure what she meant to say. "It could be anything," she finished lamely.

Joe shrugged. "Maybe." He gave her that sweet smile again, letting his hand trail down her neck. "If you ever want to experiment, I'm here for it." He leaned forward and kissed her head slowly, deeply, until her rushing heartbeat became a slow wave. They nuzzled together as he met her eyes. "Thanks for letting me come with you." He held her hands in his own, squeezing them gently. "Good Night, Elizabeth."

She watched him walk away before dragging her body slowly up the stairs and surrendering to sleep.

Chapter Eighteen

Morning arrived at The Sanctuary on golden rays of sunshine, a triumphant revolution against the last rites of fall. Elizabeth blinked lazily at the summery window. Her body felt warm and languid, softly sinuous beneath the sheets. She stretched. The light felt like Joe's hand on her waist, her throat, his lips pulling her into him as her body bent effortlessly into his arms. For a moment she reveled in it, letting her body answer his in the imaginary space of nostalgia, calling back the passion that had coursed through her, the urgency that had been born of the earth, his hand on her thigh.

Then she remembered the dark.

Around her the room grew dim and gray, as though the sun had turned away from her. Elizabeth shivered in the cold, drawing her blankets closer about her. Why had she stopped? Why had she started? She traced the steps that had come before, allowing her body to loosen once more at the memory. There had been no fear, she decided. After touching the spark, everything had been miraculous, easy. Her path was chosen and she was ready for it. Until she came to the tree, and could go no further.

She lay in bed, watching the light brighten and dim on her ceiling as she relived the evening. There was no message from Joe, but she had expected none. It was not his way. Embarrassment and curiosity fought for control in her mind. Had she blown her chance? Or would he, somehow, understand what even she still could only partially grasp? Her thoughts wound into tighter and tighter circles, assuming one premise and then another, until her head was aching. When she could analyze the mystery no further, Elizabeth forced herself to get up, wash her face, don her coziest pajamas, and head downstairs

Cory had made coffee, easily Elizabeth's favorite of his habits, and Lily was sprawled on the living room floor drawing tiny flowers while he was attempting to explain the Ortt Belt to her. She was nodding and affirming at regular intervals, but Elizabeth knew she was employing the same memory gifts she used in class — Lily could recite everything perfectly, even when she hadn't paid attention to a word. Elizabeth could not begrudge her the advantage. Lily bore so much in her heart, she deserved a little ease in the realm of achievement.

She watched them quietly, thinking how old they suddenly appeared, how little time remained with them. Her age seemed to stand just behind her shoulder, a shadow of mortality and wasted chances. So much possibility remained in front of them. So much lay behind her. This house, this inn, represented a last ditch attempt at meaning before, she realized, she would begin to fall into obscurity. Old women were invisible. So many years of giving her precious time to her children to help them grow. What would remain of her after they were gone?

Silently, Elizabeth took her coffee out to the backyard, and walked over the frost-hardened ground. She wandered through the garden and encircled the ring of stones. Finally, when she could avoid it no longer, she cast her eyes down at the place where the path began, and saw nothing. As expected. Following the now-invisible lines, she reached the oak grove, where the ground was likewise clear. She was about to turn back to the house when the oak caught her eye. At the base of the trunk, where her spine had lain against it, was a gaping black crack, burnt and hollowed and crumbling.

She fell to her knees. A constriction formed in her chest, as though the crack was within her. Her body felt cleaved, cold, with air filtering through the void where her heart used to be. Breath came in ragged gulps, and her coffee spilled across the hard ground. What had happened? What had she done? What had been done to her?

Last night played like a film strip across her mind, the darkness, the pathway, the light, the kiss. The touch. And suddenly she was there again, falling into the deep abyss of nothingness, a scream piercing her head as complete panic set over her.

She woke from the cold, after who knew how long. Her cheek felt raw against the frozen dirt, and a mixture of sweat and soil had formed mud in the thin cells of fabric on her stomach. Cautiously, she dragged herself up, disregarding the urge to vomit. Out of the corner of her eye she saw the darkly scarred tree, but she found she could not bear to look at it. Elizabeth half ran all the way back to the house, called to the stairs that she had a migraine, and cast herself into bed before the screaming began again.

***

She stayed that way for days. As the sky remained resolutely gray no matter the hour, she drifted in and out of consciousness with impunity, unable to tell whether she was meant to be doing anything important. Denny appeared at one point to explain that she had a fever, but the kids were being cared for. Sometimes she woke in the middle of the night and went to the window, staring down at the sterile pathway lights that seemed to mock her. When she returned to her bed the dreams always burned, and she would wake soaked and panting before falling asleep again on the shower floor.

One morning, a lone sunbeam came through her window. The clock informed her it was 7:00 a.m., time to get up, and obligingly enough her body felt like doing so. Quietly, she pulled on a robe and shuffled downstairs to discover Cory and Lily eating cereal at the table, full mugs of tea in front of them as they each read separate books.

"Mom!" called Lily, racing to embrace her. Her daughter's hugs, always enthusiastic, took the wind out of her for a moment, and she grasped a chair for support. How beautiful, to be held by her daughter. How wonderful to be loved.

Cory watched with a look of mature concern on his face, and a scared baby boy in his eyes. She held out her hand and Cory wrapped his arms around her neck, his eyes never leaving her face. Her kids were with her, and she was holding them, and that meant she was home, and safe, whatever else had gone wrong.

Lily made her a cup of tea while Cory explained that Lisa, Denny, Tiffany, and Joe had taken shifts being with them over the past week while she had been incapacitated. Each had brought groceries, driven them to and from school, and slept in the inn. Elizabeth was still reeling from walking down the stairs — the news that near strangers had cared for her family was beyond her. A deeply emotional reaction sent warning bells to her chest, and she quickly silenced it to be processed later.

"So you're OK? You didn't starve, or get kicked out of school?" She cast a furtive look at her son, smiling so that it came out as a joke instead of a true inquiry.

Unfooled and annoyed, Cory sighed, "No, Mom." He sipped his tea. "Joe makes good omelets," he informed her.

"But no one's dinners tasted as good as yours," Lily rushed to add, glaring at her brother.

"Guess I better up my breakfast game," Elizabeth joked. "I'll have to thank everyone." Congestion filled her nose and her eyes began to water, but again she forced the tears back as she gingerly stood up. "I think I'll try a slice of toast. What day is it? Do you need to go to school?"

"Friday," Cory intoned. "Joe should be here to pick us up in a few minutes." He jammed the book he was reading into the backpack of crumpled papers at his feet, and crossed the room to look out of the front window. "Yup, there's his van."

Of course it was.

Resigned to unwashed face and unbrushed teeth, Elizabeth did her best to appear solid, if not put together. Lily reluctantly let go her mother's hand as she pulled sandwiches out of the fridge and gathered her various teenage girl accoutrements. The knock came, and Elizabeth found that she could not muster the energy to stand. So she stared at her tea as Cory opened the door and announced "She's awake!"

Joe had crossed the room in a moment and engulfed her in a hug. The soft flannel against her cheek smelled of smoke and coffee and crushed leaves underfoot, and the urge to sob like a baby welled up within her. She kept her eyes shut, and said nothing.

"I've been so worried about you," came his low whisper.

"Thanks," she muttered, embarrassed. "Thanks for taking care of the kids. I can't believe … " Again the stormy tide of sobs pushed forward, and she swallowed the rest of her sentence.

"No problem," he said casually. "They've been great. Probably didn't even need us, but we all enjoyed their company." Tipping her face up, he searched her eyes, which staunchly refused to focus on him. She felt her body go rigid, and his loosen. He dropped her chin. "You should stay still another day or two. Want me to help get you to the couch?"

"I can manage," she assured him, her tone harsher than she intended. "Sorry," she added. "I'm not used to being sick." *Not used to being taken care of*, said a nagging voice in her head. Unbidden, the image of a cracked oak tree came to her, and she began to feel dizzy.

"I get it. But the help is here, may as well take it." He thrust his hands in his pockets, and jutted his chin as he did when his defenses were up. Then he collected himself, exhaled, and he looked her in the eyes. "Let me be here for you." His tone was gentle, the words small. Shocked and defeated, Elizabeth nodded, and he pulled her gently to her feet and guided her towards the couch. Lily put a blanket over her, and kissed her forehead as though she were a child.

"We'll see you after school, Mom."

As the door snapped shut behind them, Elizabeth felt the water pour from her eyes onto the pillowcase, and as the pool beneath her increased, she drifted off to sleep.

***

For the next few days, Elizabeth focused on slowly getting her appetite back, watching movies with the kids, sleeping every few hours.

Life was handled, but only just. She served a small turkey dinner at Thanksgiving and listened to Lily lead their annual dinner time trivia competition without putting her heart into it. It felt flat and unsatisfying after their big party. They could have invited friends again, but Elizabeth found that she didn't have much social power in her. She began to wake at night, presumably because her inner clock had given up entirely and was now merely circling through the hours at random. As her strength increased, she took short walks in the garden, one eye on the pathway, bare feet against the cold ground. It felt good to have something sturdy and icy beneath her feet. Bracing and awake. Reality seemed to have fallen out from beneath her, but the land was still real. The light was still real. By daylight everything felt foggy and intangible, part of a life that wasn't hers. By night, her senses sharpened and her energy flowed. She felt more animal than human, but this suited The Sanctuary, which seemed to welcome her as it welcomed the spiders and the owls, the moths and the mushrooms, and all of the other creatures of the night. In the ring of stones, she could stand still and simply listen, and somehow the world made sense. Only here. Only when she was alone.

She began to get up later, leaving the kids to fend for themselves for breakfast. The daylight irked her, reminding her of the things undone, which in her head were piling up with maniacal speed. The upcoming Christmas season was a heavy anvil on her chest, a test of strength and stamina that she could not bring herself to face. Holidays had been hard enough before, pulling together magical cookie trays and aesthetically wrapped gifts for family members she barely tolerated. Her husband had considered his job done with the purchase of a single gift for her, and the remainder of the Christmas magic had fallen upon her shoulders. The thought of finding new decorations, appropriate gifts, and a reasonable level of holiday cheer made her weak. So she hid beneath her blankets some more, emerging only to take her children to and from school, and waited for some miracle to rescue her.

After several days, Elizabeth realized that there were likely sheets to be laundered and trash to be emptied in the inn, a chore which felt manageable, so after dropping the children at school she forced herself to cross the invisible boundary of the house. It had been weeks since she had ventured over, busy as she had been with pies and parties, and the air smelled stale. Dust lay upon the ground and the window sills, and half-completed projects abounded. Lamp shades were still in their boxes, and replacement floor boards were stacked in the kitchenette. A resonant drip reminded her that she had forgotten to tighten the faucet, and the cold air told her she had not properly seen to the heating controls. Embarrassment flooded her. What her friends must think of her home, her investments, her ability to turn this place around? For a moment she was tempted to go back to bed again, rather than deal with the work she had avoided.

But this was the life she had chosen, so she climbed the stairs and began stripping the beds in the two upstairs rooms. Befuddled though she was, she noticed that yellow post-its were placed around the space, where once her red warning flags had marked work to be done. In cursory script, these new notes read "new switch", "wall patch", "install blinds", etc. She found the same throughout the two downstairs rooms, and in the bathroom and kitchen were copious notes on plumbing, drawer slides, and linoleum replacement. On the kitchen counter, where her own notes on budget and color scheme rested, he had written out a shopping list with dimensions and brands listed, along with the rough cost of each item.

Joe had done her work for her.

Behind the pile of papers sat a small branded basket from Eyes Up, with a coffee press, two mugs, and small individually sealed batches of ground coffee. A tote bag with the library logo included maps and brochures for local attractions, along with "Visitor Cards" for the library and a few popular used titles. An arrangement of dried flowers that she had seen in bloom next door sat in a hand thrown ceramic vase, the gentle grays and blue reminding her of the December skies. A trail of white at the bottom may have been snow, though Elizabeth saw only the mycelial pathway that haunted her dreams.

And now the sobs that she had felt in Joe's arms engulfed her at last. She crumpled on the ancient sofa, emotion wracking her body. Surrounded by mess and mystery, she nevertheless had an anchor. There was love here. There was support. She had forgotten what it felt like to receive without asking, without expecting or begging or pleading. So much time had been spent learning to do it all herself. The years of emptiness showed clearly in contrast to the love in this room. She had been forced to hold it all, to take on more and more despite the aches in her body and the screams in her soul. There was never anyone else to turn to. No matter how heavy each new burden was, she would dutifully add it to her back, because as far as she knew, that's what love meant — doing more for less.

Yet here were these people, practically strangers, returning an investment she had not yet paid to them, giving freely what she had not yet given them. It was a foreign concept, jagged in her chest, a sharp reminder of what could have been if she had only chosen a completely different life. Which, she slowly realized, she had.

Pocketing the shopping list and leaving the notes, she straightened up what she could and threw the windows open to the icy air. The rooms might be cold, but they deserved some new energy, and it was about time she let it in.

*I*t begins

    The descent, the fall, the understanding

The mirror seeks to see within

To Know

What was once unseen.

A quest like this consumes the seeker

And who can blame them?

When the soul is inside out

When the cold air hits the heart

There is nothing else but the pain

The shock

The gradual realization

That all is not as it seems.

We see ourselves so little.

We shield ourselves so much.

She will move faster, now,

The visions will take her,

The truth will unfold,

And after the hurt wears off, she will be

Reborn.

Chapter Nineteen

Despite her improved health and her gratitude to her friends, Elizabeth still felt out of sorts. She made pies for each of them and dropped them on their doorsteps in the dead of night with a note of thanks. Midnight was still her most active time, and she was grateful for the long hours of darkness the season afforded. Wishing the kids goodnight at bedtime, she would move off to the glowing pathways by the forest, examining each swirling light with fascination, drawing them or following their trails with her hand. She had discovered they could not be photographed, and her research online had still yielded nothing. So she simply sat with them, wrapped in coats and blankets, watching the pulsations and listening to the land. It spoke in a choir of voices, a small crowd that interspersed errant notes with unknown language. Elizabeth could neither further her understanding of it nor leave it alone, but sat trapped beneath the trees, just short of the oak grove, where she feared to go. Alone in the darkness.

Her sleep often carried her into the afternoon after her excursions. She tried to make up for the lost time by ordering gifts online, staring at the house and making half-hearted comments about garlands and lights, all of which seemed so pointless and silly. Book club had adjourned until January, and she had heard nothing from Denny or Joe, as presumably both had much to do in this season. In truth, Elizabeth rarely thought of them. She rarely thought of anything except the mycelium.

Lily and Cory were quieter than usual. Whether because of her illness or because of their ages, she could not say. Sometimes she would feel grateful for their silence, and then immediately the guilt would strike her, reminding her that they had no one but her, because she had dragged them from their home. Another repair project that she had tried and failed to complete.

One evening she went out at sunset, eager to see when the lights began to rise from the soil, ignoring the ember skies and staring directly at the ground. She waited until all of the light was gone, the last wisps of pink drained from the sky into the void where life slept. When the night reigned completely, Elizabeth triumphantly spotted the path, and followed it back and forth several times, always stopping just short of the grove. When she returned to the house, she found Cory washing dishes in the sink, and Lily folding laundry.

"What are you guys doing? Elizabeth asked, mystified. Surely it wasn't so late. She had meant to make dinner and had already taken the ingredients from the freezer. She saw them on the counter, a melted pool around them, as Cory cleared the remains of a peanut butter sandwich from his plate. Lily looked up at her, and Elizabeth, aghast, saw her own exhaustion mirrored in her daughter's face.

"You were gone," she said simply. "So we took care of ourselves."

Horror dawned upon her as she realized not only how long she had been gone, but how often. That her children no longer expected her to be there. Despite the warmth inside, Elizabeth felt her body freeze far worse than it had in the frosty December weather. She had forgotten her children, her loves, her purpose.

"I'm about to make brownies."

It was the first thing that popped into her head, her gut reaction to any problem — bake for it. She snapped the oven on and reached frantically inside the fridge, emerging with eggs and butter. Both children watched as she clattered the old saucepan onto the stove and began to melt the chocolate, usually a meditative activity that involved gentle stirring and the smooth, rich scent of unsweetened chocolate perfuming the kitchen. Now she left it to cook while searching for her pan, her sugar, her flour, and the tears were clouding her vision and she could not find the tiny vial of vanilla because her children had been left, left alone like she had been, and she was the villain in her own story.

"Mom." Cory's voice was gentle, and she took a deep breath, willing herself not to lose control. She gave him a watery smile, and he returned it with a nod at the stove. The pan was smoking, and the acrid scent of burning cocoa filled the small kitchen.

"Shit," she swore. Removing the pan, she let water flow over the base, cooling it as fast as she could, and when the smoke stopped she leaned over the sink and breathed deeply, as though perhaps she could take back the past few weeks, or months, or years.

She felt them behind her. Carefully, Lily sprinkled kahlua into the pan, stirring the mixture carefully and removing the burnt bits one by one. Cory added the butter and vanilla, and rubbed her shoulders.

"I'm sorry, you guys," Elizabeth whispered. "I've had so much trouble finding my way here. I keep looking for it, and sometimes I think I find it, and then ..." She spread her hands. She didn't know what happened. She just kept losing her footing. No matter how hard she tried, she could never be what they needed.

"Mom, it's OK," Lily said. "It's taking us time to figure things out, too. And we didn't buy a business."

"Yeah," Cory piped in. "And you were really sick. Maybe your body just needs the rest, Mom. Maybe you don't always need to do everything. Maybe you can just do a little at a time, and that's OK."

Lily hugged her. "We don't need brownies, Mom," she said quietly. "We just need you."

They stood in the kitchen, huddled around the pot of flavor and fat, breathing deeply together until it felt like their world had reformed. Now she could feel it again, Elizabeth realized. This was home.

She finished the brownies after all while the kids did their chores, and they read *The Night Before Christmas* as they ate them hot from the oven.

***

Settling back into a reasonable circadian rhythm allowed Elizabeth to consider the gleeful potential of the formerly daunting holiday season. At the first opportunity, she and the kids headed off to the local tree farm, one of many that were simply regular farms opening up their evergreen borders for a little extra holiday cash. Here they cut down their own tree from the narrow field of sweet-smelling pines, a Christmas luxury Southern California had never afforded them. Elizabeth felt the sap on her fingers as they hoisted it onto the top of the car, the blood of the tree now bonded to her skin. This must be how the maple workers felt, she mused. Entrusted with the careful surgery of giants, the balance of this ecosystem. Caretakers, indeed.

Armed with farmstand wreaths and garlands, Lily collecting branch ends and errant needles from the ground for her artwork, they went home to festoon the inn in seasonal finery. Elizabeth uncovered stacks of burlap coffee sacks in the basement, and used them to create a rustic holiday look that turned out so well that she photographed it for the website she planned to officially launch in the new year. Getting footage from every season would ensure a regular flow of visitors, and she couldn't imagine any place better for the holidays than this little slice of heaven.

She found herself thinking more and more about the inn that she wanted to create. No longer drained by her obsession with the forest lights, her energy searched for a new direction. A new creation at The Sanctuary. Perhaps whatever "magic" existed in the land was a phenomenon meant to be shared with those chosen few. She thought of the legend that Joe had shared with her, how the space belonged to the community, and how her community had returned to that space to care for her during her illness. It seemed as though the land truly did call to those who needed healing.

Having been a straight A science student and a data-driven human being all her life, Elizabeth wasn't truly sure she understood what "healing" meant, but she knew there was a small shop at the end of the street that featured a rainbow of crystals in its window along with the distinct smell of patchouli when she passed, so one day after dropping the kids at school, she stopped in to see what was inside.

Vivid purple walls encased a square room much like Denny's shop, with symbols of lotus flowers and circular trees standing opposite each other. A handful of bells rippled as she entered, and she saw they were tied to the door handle with a white ribbon that had seen better days. White tables held dishes of stones in every color, with detailed explanations of what each of them would do for you. Shelves along the sides of the room displayed decks of cards covered in fantastic images, some bright, some dark, as well as pressed leather journals and books with elegantly scripted titles. And there, lined up perfectly on the long front counter, were candles just like the one she had received, in a variety of sizes and with varying decorative touches upon them.

Elizabeth flew to the display, hungrily reading the handwritten tags that identified candles for abundance, health, clarity, peace, and love. She picked up this last one and smelled the top, where fresh rose petals mingled with a sprinkling of tiny pink gravel. A chalice was artfully carved into the front, and as she held it, she felt her body grow molten. A lazy smile crossed her face.

"That's how women should always look."

A svelte woman with a gray bun and a shawl that looked more like art than clothing had emerged from the back, and was watching her bemusedly.

"You left me one of these."

The woman nodded. "I did. It seemed that a little extra energy would not go amiss. You walked into a bigger project than you understood."

Recognition flashed through Elizabeth's mind. She had seen this woman before. The witch. "You were at the bonfire."

"I pass on many things in this town ... I like my solitude. But a giant fire is always worth attending." Her eyes hadn't left Elizabeth's face. "We all need the gifts of fire."

Something moved within Elizabeth's body. A blaze within her had heard its name and was begging to be let out, to be given its freedom. Its full flame. She felt it licking at the inside of her throat, as though the sparks within were trying to participate in the conversation. She did not know what they wanted to say. Her hand was still on the candle.

"That's why you make these," she realized. "To bring fire closer."

"Sometimes. Sometimes it releases something else...a piece of stubborn earth, like the rosemary atop this one, or water, like the seashells here. Fire is the activation. What it activates is up to the one who ignites it."

Elizabeth stared blankly.

A grin broke out on the elder woman's face, as though she recognized the limits before her, "I'm Tori," she said, walking towards the counter. "And you are Elizabeth, the new hearth tender at The Sanctuary."

"Hearth tender?"

"Indeed. The most venerated position in any society, until fairly recently. The one who kept the fires going, for comfort, for sacred rites, for cooking. Nearly always a woman." Tori looked sideways at her as she ran her fingers along the counter. "One who keeps the hearth for their community provides a vital service, often at the cost of their own energy. Innkeepers of old were hearth keepers as well, providing a safe space for travelers to rest on their journey. Of course, as we are all travelers on the road of life, these hearths are critical to our development as people, our ability to become more. Without rest and food and safety, and the good will of whatever cosmic goodness watched over us, we would all continue to be held back, stuck in old versions of who we were." Again she met Elizabeth's eyes, and smiled gently. "Perhaps you know the feeling."

Elizabeth thought of who she had been a few shorts months ago, before arriving here. How much of her had fallen apart since then. She had thought it a catastrophe. At no point had she considered that it may be a gift.

"So if I burn one of these candles, I'm protected and transformed?"

Tori laughed, a sound like the bells upon her door. "Oh, if only it were so easy. No, a candle can create the space for that work to be done, but it is definitely work, and the one who is ready to change must be the one to do it. They must look at what needs to be burned away, and what needs to be illuminated. Sometimes, that will need a candle ... and sometimes it will need a bonfire. You never know until you are standing in the moment, in the darkness." And now she folded her hands together. "I expect you stand in the darkness sometimes, Elizabeth. Perhaps near the oak grove."

Heart hammering in her chest, Elizabeth clapped her hands together. "You know about the oak grove! What is it? What happens there? What is that pathway made of?" Finally, answers!

Tori chuckled. "Yes, I know of the grove. Matty and I visited it together often. As for what it is, and what the pathway reveals, I am afraid that is specific to each seeker. I cannot answer your questions." Elizabeth's shoulders slumped over, the moment of anticipation immediately quelled by disappointment. Her mystery remained. Moving along the counter, Tori picked up a candle that was half black, half white. "But perhaps this will help you." She handed the candle to Elizabeth, who read the tag: *Light and Darkness — for exploring the duality within*

Elizabeth frowned. "The candle will help me figure out the lights?"

"And the darkness. Never forget to figure out the darkness. That is how people get lost." She wrapped the candle in brown paper, saying "You may want to bring some wood when you light it. In case a bigger fire is needed for you to see." Tori straightened up with a smile, and handed her a bag containing the candle. "On the house."

Elizabeth took the bag, and opened her mouth to say...well, she didn't know what. No words came out. She wanted to ask what to do, how to move, what came next. Tori seemed so sure of everything. And she knew about the lights. Surely, she could lift this strange assignment from Elizabeth's shoulders, let her go back to who she used to be.

"You can't go backwards, Elizabeth."

Eyes wide, Elizabeth asked if she read minds. Tori laughed again.

"No. But I know journeys. I have been where you are, and I have seen others travel their roads as well. There comes a point when you don't know how to proceed, and you really don't want to. You want to be comfortable. You want it to be easy. You want to go back to how it was before everything changed." She leaned in, and put her hands on Elizabeth's arms. "But the path closes behind us, dear. We can never truly go back. And you wouldn't want to." She straightened the slumping shoulders. "You came here for something new. Matty saw in you someone who could do this great work, and I see it, too. You must keep going until you can see it in yourself." Tori released her, and nodded curtly. "Now go find your way."

And she walked Elizabeth to the door, sending her out into the cold again.

The light is coming

Blazing a path through the cold and dark
Bringing warmth, truth, light
For nothing can hide from the fire
And all will be consumed by it.
Long ago,
We too were consumed
Eaten by the petals of the red lotus
As it bloomed all around us
Raining destruction from the heavens
In great black clouds that blocked out the sun
And in this moment of disintegration
We believed ourselves fallen
Finished
Erased from this world
And we wished it
For to be free of the pain was our only thought.
Yet life began again.
We began again.

She will begin again.
After all has burned away.

Chapter Twenty

It was decided that with less than two weeks until Christmas and none of their usual convenience shopping, the Whits would do homemade gifts this year. The mood in the house had become cozy, with everyone sitting in the living room each night with books and craft projects, chatting amicably about their day and remembering holidays past. Elizabeth was ready for snow at any moment, but it was stubbornly refusing to make an appearance. So instead she enjoyed the soothing notes of carols, a constant in this world of change, while she baked tray after tray of spicy, buttery cookies. Lily created dark abstract designs in frosting and sprinkles, while Cory ate them mindlessly in front of feel-good cartoons.

He began disappearing from the house for long periods of time, vaguely remarking he was going for a walk. While he had always enjoyed his isolation, she had thought he was finally spreading his social wings, and was sorry to see him slipping into old ways. Uncharacteristically, though, she decided to let well enough alone. Cory was doing better in school, had made a few friends. Perhaps it was time to let him figure things out by himself.

In his absence, Lily and Elizabeth collaborated on his gift. In the recesses of the basement, they had unearthed a loom, sturdy and timeless and miraculously working. Elizabeth had sourced wool yarn from a farm down the road, which had been dyed a variety of purples and blues. Lily had an intuitive grasp of the technique (which Elizabeth found absurdly complicated), and so they would sneak downstairs after he left and companionably weave away, Elizabeth unwrapping the skeins as her daughter fed them to the primal machine. Elizabeth would think of Cory as the yarn slipped through her fingers, how he would weave his life here with their love to keep him warm. She thought of the stars he watched from his room, and hoped they watched him, too. Perhaps he felt the sky as she felt the land.

For Lily's gift, Elizabeth had found herself stumped. So often, her daughter reminded her of who she used to be, with a soft heart and a dream for every chapter that she lived. It hurt to think of her growing up and turning hard and cold, as her mother had. She could not pinpoint the exact moment when she had lost her joy, but she knew that by the time she had left for college, she had started to live for others, instead of herself. Lily was so much stronger, with such attachment to her identity. What would keep her as she was? Was it possible for her to become a woman without becoming broken? Elizabeth wondered what would have done the trick for her when she was Lily's age.

And so she began to write her a book of poetry. She bought a sketchbook, evergreen leather binding thick pages, and began to rim each one in a different watercolor. The dye seeped into the pages as her blood had once revealed pathways on the earth, and she watched the bright colors create worlds out of nothing. Hills and valleys, rivers and oceans, forests of tiny leaves formed by fate. When the pigment dried, she let words tumble onto the blank remains, searing intensity for the sunsets, quiet hope for the sunrise, divine dreams for the midnights. She sang songs of dizzying evolutions and terrible heartache and the strength to build yourself up again. Everything that she had tried to tell herself, she wrote to Lily. She only hoped it was enough.

And then there was Joe.

She wasn't sure what to get Joe, or if she should get him anything at all. He had kept more distance between them since her illness, or perhaps since their last kiss. In response to her thank-you note, he had turned up with bags of goods from the hardware store, making some of the more difficult repairs while she picked up the kids. He would stay and socialize with them, asking about their lives and interests, but would always leave before dinner. Jocular and pleasant, he nevertheless did not meet her eyes. Nor did he ask to see her again.

She thought of him, though. More and more, he was on her mind, in her body. He felt safe in a way she hadn't experienced before, though she knew that logically, he was far from it. He proved consistently that he wasn't the type for commitment. Yet when she felt him near her, an unexplainable peace filled her. If she didn't know better, Elizabeth would have said his soul was holding hers. If she believed in souls. Or being held.

As for the lights leading to the oak grove, Elizabeth found herself less interested in their provenance, but more drawn to simply walk with them. Whatever they were, they were hers to care for now. She had been delivered to them on purpose. How they got there was less important than where they would take her. She walked them each night, moving into the orbit of the oak tree, pacing around it, sitting in front of it. Still she could not bring herself to touch the blackened space. While the path felt light, the tree itself felt dark, the gaping void glaring at her as though it would swallow her if she came close.

She did not come close.

Instead she began to wander Solace Spring more broadly during daylight hours. Having been focused on her goals for the inn, Elizabeth had spent little time exploring the rest of the town's backwoods and byways. Unlike her Californian suburb, where all neighborhoods were planned and constructed at ruthless right angles with coordinating street names, streets here were randomly spaced and went in strange loops and waves, which had seemed to her too great a challenge in the midst of the move. Now, however, she realized that she had been given this moment to explore the landscape in its wholeness before it slumbered under snow for months at a time. This was her home, too. It was time to see the neighborhood, while she still could.

During the final week of school the winter sun made a special effort to shine, and under the blue sky Elizabeth decided to go further afield. She took a turn past Lisa's property onto a nearby road, and when it yielded little, she turned again. She found herself standing before a wide gravel driveway, leading up to an impeccably kept rustic cabin surrounded by tall pine trees, bright green in their splendor as other species withered around them. A large garage stood to one side with saw horses and tools arranged on a wheeled tool bench out front, and she saw Grover coming out to grab them.

He stared at her blankly, before saying "Don't tell him you saw."

For a moment Elizabeth was merely befuddled, but then she remembered Grover' antagonism towards Cory and panicked. "Saw what?"

Grover looked guilty. "Never you mind."

"Grover, what has my son done? I'm his mother, I have a right to know."

To her surprise, Grover chuckled. She couldn't remember ever seeing him smile. It transformed him into a different person, almost grandfatherly. "He's done a lot, alright, but nothing you'll mind. Alright, come and see, but make sure you act surprised later."

Mystified, Elizabeth walked into the garage, which was outfitted as a full woodshop. Unlike the carefully crafted wood art Mitch had shown her, however, this workshop was all about function. Unfinished crates lined one wall, branded with the names of local orchards and farms. Boxes of various sizes and shingle-style signs were carefully placed on one counter, and on another, an open leather kit revealed small hand tools and knives. Behind these were small items that had clearly been carved by hand…small toys, decorative paperweights, and even some jewelry. And finally, there was a medium box with "Cory" burned onto the side.

She walked forward and peeked in the box. A number of items were in there, in varying states of completion. A model of mushrooms that looked just like the painting Lily had done. A box with inlays that looked as though they moved to form a puzzle. A spinning top that had a gear carved into the circle. And a charm of carved wood in the shape of a flame.

Elizabeth straightened and looked at Grover. "What is this?"

He grinned. "Your son's handiwork. That boy is one hell of a learner. Been over here nearly every day, having me teach him new things, working over and over to make it perfect." He leaned against the counter. "I know some of those are Christmas gifts, so don't go telling him you saw. But it's been real nice to have his company. Not many kids his age who take an interest." He sobered for a moment. "I know I was hard on him, and you, more or less. I'm sorry about that. I judged him too soon … didn't give him a chance to show me who he was. And because of that I almost missed out." Grover met her glance, and there was sadness in his cloudy eyes. "My own grandkids live out in Arizona. Don't see them much, or hear from them. We don't really know each other. I send them little gifts I make, but they don't care. Not part of their world. They'd rather I sent gadgets or computer stuff … or maybe just money." He cleared his throat, and Elizabeth tactfully returned her eyes to her son's projects. "Cory hasn't been here long, but he's becoming a local grandchild to me, and I'm grateful for it."

Now it was her turn to get teary. So this was where he had been going. "How did this happen?" she asked in amazement.

"He was walking just like you, wandering about, and he heard my saw." Grover smiled. "Boy does like his tools. Only had to show him once and he was itching to try. He did such a good job I let him keep going, and now he's on a roll." Grover dusted his hands on his jeans and turned to pick up another tool. "He seems like the type of kid who isn't always interested, but once he is, nothing stops him."

Elizabeth smiled. "You really do know my son." The place in her heart that was always filled with panic over Cory — what he had done, what he might do, what she would have to fight — felt suddenly warm and light. Breathing was easier. Her shoulders relaxed. Finally … someone who would support her son. "I'm really glad he found you, Grover."

"Me, too." Grover turned towards his tool bench again, then looked back and said "You won't tell him?"

"Not a word."

Grover nodded, and went back to his power saw, and Elizabeth walked home, marveling at how a few months here had made a home faster than decades in a place where she never belonged.

***

That night she went out to the lights, heart full of happiness and hope, thinking that perhaps this was the day she could return and touch the oak at last. In imitation of Tori, she wore her red dress and black boots, and let her hair cascade down over her shoulders, hoping to channel in some of that fire energy. On a whim, she rubbed a bit of Lily's rose essential oil over her heart, and some behind each ear, thinking it would help her to hear the voices once again. It worked. They seemed to sing as she walked down the steps, through the garden, and past the standing stone where she found ...

Joe.

She froze.

He stared at her, swathed in his familiar flannel and jeans, hands in his pockets as ever. His hair was loose, too, the unfamiliar softness framing his face. He looked ... open.

"Hi."

"Hi."

They did not move.

"What are you —"

"Waiting for you."

Her breath began to quicken, and her pulse grew loud. Was he finally coming for her? Or was she misunderstanding once again?

Slowly, Joe moved towards her, as though she was an animal that may bolt at the smallest provocation. "I know the last time we were here, something happened. I don't know what it was. But ..." He hesitated, choosing his words carefully, refusing to be rushed into any-thing he did not mean. "I'm losing myself. Somehow I keep coming back here, in my mind. No matter what I'm doing, some part of me is always ... with you." Joe stared intently at his shoes, before throwing his hands up and moving closer. "I feel like I'm supposed to be here, somehow." He was very close now, and he stopped just inches from her face. "So I thought I would wait for you, and see what happened."

Elizabeth exhaled, growing more sensitive while the air around her grew dull and thick. "You want to see what happens?" Involuntarily, she added, "With me?" The soft creature inside of her placed a tremulous foot out of the darkness.

He cupped her face.

"Yeah," Joe said. "I do."

He dipped his head and when his lips fell gently upon her own something broke inside of her. She floated upon this river of sensation, this sinuous feeling that snaked through her stomach and thighs, playfully licking at her neck. Joe seemed in no hurry. His hands were locked on her hips, pulling her closer to him in waves, letting her fall back just enough for him to draw her in again. She let her fingers trail around his waist, tracing circles in the soft fabric of his shirt. How badly she wanted to feel the skin beneath it. For a moment she hesitated, unfamiliar with the etiquette, the flow of a moment. Joe took the opportunity to release her, and cold air settled into the crevices he had warmed.

"Come here," he whispered.

Swinging his body around, he moved towards the edge of the forest. She followed, and now the air was shaming her, reminding her of her age, her commitments, her work. What business had she being out here, kissing a handsome man who might be gone tomorrow? He had been absent more than he had been there, and she had no reason to believe that would change. All of her choices tumbled before her, silly and infantile, and the gladness of her heart was fast being eaten by fear as Joe held out his hand and escorted her into the grove.

Red light emanated from the central circle. Perhaps it felt Joe as strongly as she did. Elizabeth barely had time to take in the rosy hue of the tree trunks before he was kissing her again, no longer sweetly but deeper, searching. Layers of her were being worn away, leaving bits of truth exposed. The river was coming towards her, and she wanted to steel herself from it, from the impact of the water, from being carried away to who knew where — a distant shore she may never return from. And then he spoke, heavy words dripping from his mouth while his arms circled tightly about her.

"I don't know what I'm doing, Elizabeth. You're incredible. Being with you feels so much like ..." His voice trailed away and his body hardened next to her. Again she felt a door closing within him, leaving her firmly on the other side. Apparently, he felt similarly. "I know you have a lot locked up inside. I know what it's like. And I want you to be able to open, you have no idea how much. But you have to help me."

He looked at her, thumbs smoothing her cheeks.

"What do you need, Elizabeth?"

Need. It bothered her, that word. *Nothing,* said the wind as it rushed by her ears. *Nothing, you need nothing, for you do it all yourself. You hold. You build. You never break. You need nothing.*

But the river was stronger, and as his lips lingered by her cheek she reached up and brought him to her, her lips silently begging him to continue, to touch her, to find her. Answering enthusiastically, his body pressed up against her, bending her back onto a nearby tree. Elizabeth felt a jolt to her system, as though the tree had fused with her spine. She felt larger, steadier. Her feet gathered energy from the glowing ground beneath her, now turning a wavering purple. It was delightful, this level of power. Fears melted as Joe cascaded over her, hands running over her neck and breasts and stomach like a waterfall after drought. The desiccated roots of her skin drank him in thirstily, demanding more. She felt her breath come in gasps, her thighs grow wet with need.

Need. He had asked what she needed.

She needed these clothes off. Hands found his waist again and pulled up the cotton to discover luscious coppery brown skin that was hot to the touch. Hungry palms rubbed the surface of him, trying to understand the flow, the mechanics of the current. Elizabeth wound her fingers together at the base of his back and arched into him, willing herself to become the water so that she could swim in his depths forever. Joe moaned as their lips pressed together again and again, and he half carried her away and placed her instead on the ground in front of the oak tree, where he set to kissing her as she stretched long on the earth. The wind could not find her here. Instead she felt the pulsing beat of the drums, the light springing from the ground as Joe reached beneath her dress and clutched gently at the inside of her thigh.

Suddenly a cold gust blew her skirt further upward, exposing the space between her legs to the cold. A panic spread through her body and she gripped Joe's shoulders as a rush of unwanted reactions traveled in upon the tide. Rejection. Abandonment. Pain beyond pain as her heart broke over and over and over. Waves held her down and drowned her until her heart was in so many pieces that she could not put it back together. In an instant, the storm was over, and she could only see the devastation in its wake.

What was she doing?

"Who am I?"

Joe paused in the act of gathering up her dress, his hand still kneading the soft flesh of her thighs. He kissed her again, nuzzling her mouth. "Who are you?" he repeated, puzzled.

"To you." Elizabeth fought to keep the panic out of her voice. "Who am I to you?"

Everything stopped. The pulses, the lights, the warmth, the river. Everything froze, including the man who lay atop her, an inch from her open gate.

"I don't know."

And just like that, the gate closed. Triumphantly, the glacial air settled around them, and Joe shivered. He shook his head a little, then saw the expression on her face, looking up at him from the cold forest floor, now lit softly white.

"I know you're special, Elizabeth. I know you're a wonderful person. I know you're meant to be in my life, and we are meant to be here. But beyond that..."

She closed her eyes, so the drops of water wouldn't show.

"How do you feel about me, Joe?"

His hand disappeared from her thigh, and she felt him carefully replace the dress. Heat evaporated from her skin as the distance between them grew, sprouting a new forest all darkness and thorns. Cautiously, she raised her eyes, to see him facing the pond instead of her, eyes on the ground.

"I don't know."

The darkness was complete and unbroken. There was no path left to follow as Elizabeth rose from the ground and walked away.

Winter

Chapter Twenty-One

Alles schläft; einsam wacht..."

Elizabeth had never been a church goer. Her parents were atheist, her husband the same. Southern California churches had held very little appeal, encased in cement blocks with trendy logos and social media handles tastefully advertising for Jesus. But not here. Churches here were old. Each white steeple represented one town, one village, one meeting place that had harbored tiny communities for centuries. The walls had given shelter during storms, seen births and deaths of several generations, celebrated harvests and sunlight and union. She didn't know what she thought about God. But she knew that this church felt safe.

Vespers was a local tradition. Every year the whole town turned out to hear the choir sing the same time-honored program. Lily had been recruited by friends before Thanksgiving, and Elizabeth beamed as she watched her daughter fill with the music and deliver it flawlessly, radiant in the beauty of the words she barely knew and would not truly understand for many years. The power of night, silence, and calm. The burgeoning hope of joy. The space between.

Afterwards, tables out front served hot cider and baked goods, with donation boxes waiting to receive their gifts of toys and canned food. Elizabeth had spent the week baking dark, treacly spiced snowflakes, dipped in glaze and powdered with silver. They twinkled from their pure white dish beneath a dome of glass, a song turned snow globe. On a whim, she had added a small card reading "From The Sanctuary", with the website carefully written beneath. While the accommodations were not yet ready, she had decided it would be best to add her goodies to the same virtual home, listing pies and cookies she could easily have ready to sell this holiday season. Molasses Snowflakes joined Pecan Pies, Maple Shortbread,and Spiced Apple Muffins on the site's carefully curated menu. She was pleased to see today's allotment already running low.

After congratulating Lily on a beautiful performance and sending Cory and his friends to help move the heavy boxes, Elizabeth walked aimlessly around the lawn in her velvet holiday dress, full skirt swishing across the bare remains of the lawn, admiring the Christmas lights and the view of the town. From this vantage point, she could see the lake and the river, the sprawling forest and the bend in the road that led to The Sanctuary. Slowly, she was becoming able to map out her surroundings, as a compass formed in her own small universe. Grover's house, Denny's shop, the orchard where they picked apples and the maple grove where she had visited with Joe.

She tried not to think of Joe.

"Your girl did a great job up there." Denny was slowly wandering up with a cup of cider in one hand and a cookie in the other. "I'll tell you, a lot of people can sing, but not a lot of people can make you feel something." She bit into her cookie. "She should come sing at the shop!"

Elizabeth smiled. "Honestly, Denny, that would make her Christmas. She has so many lovely songs and a great voice, but I think she keeps them hidden because they don't have a place." She looked sideways at her friend as she sipped her drink. "Are you willing to be her place?

"I absolutely am," Denny nodded emphatically. "I hear your son made himself a second home with Grover; Lily can come be with me."

"You heard about that?"

"It's been a long time since Grover has been in that good a mood, and I'm nosy." Denny chuckled, then studied Elizabeth, who had both arms wrapped around her. However homey Solace Spring felt, she had not yet adjusted to the winter temperature. "And what about their mama? Have you found a place to be?"

Joe's face sprang to her mind, then disappeared.

"I thought maybe I had … but I'm not sure it was real."

Denny pressed her lips together. Then she opened her mouth, hesitated, closed it, and sighed. One of her hands rubbed her forehead absently. Elizabeth turned to face her, surprised by her unusually serious manner.

"Look," Denny finally said. "I know you and Joe have had a little … something … going on. I love Joe. He's a good man, and he was handed some hard things in life. I'd love to see him happy." She stopped and sighed again. "But he's not good at being happy, Elizabeth. That man is forever getting in his own way. There's been some talk about him lately. Folks seem to feel he may be taking advantage of you because you don't know him yet, don't know how he works." Denny took Elizabeth's hand and squeezed it. "It's not you. It's just who he is. He doesn't stay with one place, or … one person. As soon as someone gets real cozy with him, he's off to the next one. And the next. And the next." A grimace settled over her face as she delivered this unpleasant news, as though she was telling Elizabeth to put down her beloved pet while there was still time. "He doesn't mean it, and I don't think he knows that he does it. But he flows in the same circle over and over. And he will wash you out of his life if you get too close. Girls who just want to play do OK. They don't expect anything from him. But you … " And now Denny folded her into a hug, and Elizabeth felt stiff and wooden and far, far away from herself. "You just take care of yourself. You deserve someone who chooses you." Denny gave her shoulders a squeeze, and kissed her on the forehead. Just like Joe had. "Now, let's go see if I can talk Lily into a New Year's Eve debut at Eyes Up."

Elizabeth followed dazedly. So she had made the right choice. Or the wind had, or her body had. Something had known that Joe wasn't safe. He would have left her, just like Tyler had. Just like they all had. It was better this way. Denny was right. She deserved someone who really felt for her, and knew they wanted to stay in her life. The river always flows forward. And she was ready to stay in one place.

***

That night, after the kids went to bed, Elizabeth sat with the candle Tori had given her. Duality. What did that even mean? She thought of the yin yang symbol. In grade school, she had bought a necklace with that symbol in two halves — one for herself, one for her best friend. So they would always be together. She wondered where the necklace was now. She wondered where the friend was, too.

Was that duality? Finding yourself in someone else, then losing them? Or was it finding someone else in you, and keeping them?

She stared at the candle, ash on one side, clear white on the other. The darkness had become so tiring. But the brief glimpses of light she had experienced over the past couple of months had excited her, made her feel that there was more out there than she had anticipated. Maybe this candle would help her find the light within this new life.

Carefully, Elizabeth struck a match, and lit the candle.

At once, all of the lights went out in the house. From the windows came a blinding white glare, and Elizabeth felt her body tingle, all of her hairs standing on end. Grabbing the candle, she rushed outside, looking for the source of the luminescence. All around her was the path, glowing gaily under the black sky and making it bright as daylight. It wove up to the house and through the gardens, past every bed and stone, through every sculpture and walkway and firepit. The glare reflected off of the pond, magnifying the intensity. And there to the east was the oak grove, glowing golden.

As she stepped onto the path, she felt electricity shoot up her feet and into her legs. The next step hit her thighs. The next, her pelvis. She began to run as the jolts hit her whole body, somehow both painful and soothing, as though each muscle was being forced back into its proper shape unwillingly. As she reached the oak grove, her body melted into the warmth that awaited her there, and she realized she was sweating profusely from her short journey, her velvet gown still rustling around her legs. She looked back at her path, but it had disappeared. The night was black again, and no trace of the glowing pathway remained.

"You can't go backwards," whispered Tori's voice in her head.

Elizabeth turned towards the great oak tree, its twin trunks leaning apart from each other even as their boughs were intertwined. The leaves that remained at its roots were crumbly, transparent brown confetti riddled with holes. Now there were only black branches above her, reaching for their fellows, forming a perfect circle around the black moon. Elizabeth stumbled forward, candle still in one hand, and stared into the hole formed by the trunks. It was pitch dark, wide and yawning, big enough to hold a person...but would she be able to get back out? She knew that it could not be more than a few feet in, yet the limit of the space was lost to the gloom, and for all she knew the void could go on forever. She could disappear into the mouth of the tree.

Perhaps all she needed was light.

Duality, she thought. The darkness needs the light. And the light...she looked around at the beautiful, halcyon radiance the mycelium produced. From the ground. From the dark. From the dead.

Elizabeth dropped to her knees, and placed the candle in the hollow of the tree. From deep within it, she heard the sound of rushing water.

Skittering backwards, she barely had enough time to hold her hands before her face as water spurted up from the roots in torrents, hitting her squarely in the chest and slopping over her knees and feet. The force pushed her back into the center of the clearing, landing her hard on her back as the lights gleamed a deep indigo blue that made a sea of the oncoming waves. Water continued to wash over her until a final slap of liquid coasted towards her, bearing the now extinguished candle and depositing it between her legs.

All was quiet. Until she screamed.

She shrieked and screamed and slapped her hands and feet in the muddy water. She dug her nails in the dirt. She raged at the voices and the pathways and the trees and every moment of magic that had led her here and made her believe she could change. She threw the candle at the oak with all of her might, only to have it land unharmed in the network of gnarly roots at its base.

Elizabeth wanted to curse every being upon the planet, none more than herself. What had she expected? Someone to save her? To answer all of her questions? A quiet man to hold her close and tell her all was well, a friend to listen to her weep? It was just a candle, after all. Just a pillar of wax, and a broken tree. She was alone.

Wet and shivering, she laid upon the ground, thinking how nice it would be if the golden light returned again to warm her. It had felt so delicious on her skin, Elizabeth remembered, that melting, gooey feeling, as though she was being bathed in some luxurious bath of honey. As she brought the sensation to mind, the earth turned gold again, and glimmering vines of thick, heated air began to spread over her like a blanket. A warm blanket. Confused, Elizabeth sat up, and the lights immediately faded back. She lay down. Nothing. She imagined the golden grace, and once again felt the cozy glow envelop her, and her clothes were dry, and her weight was lifted, and her skin felt smooth and supple.

Carefully, she sat up again, now holding onto the sensation while still enabling herself to move. It was difficult to hold her imagination and her reality together — the phosphorescence winked on and off, gold and white, cold and hot. Eventually, she managed to both stand and maintain the vision of comfort, and was surprised to find she could walk with it. An amber cloud surrounded her as she slowly moved towards the house. It was, she realized, an act of foreseeing. She had to act as though she was already ahead, already on the next step, and knew what was there. If she could not create the vision ahead of herself, the light would disappear.

As she reached the front stairs, Elizabeth looked at the bare white rose bushes on either side of the staircase, dormant now until the summer temperatures returned. But she was the summer temperatures, she thought to herself. She reached out to touch the thorny black branch, and as her thumb caressed it, a perfect bud formed, then bloomed, leaving a heavy white rose in her hand. Elizabeth was overcome by its beauty, and also by the sudden exhaustion she felt. Supporting herself on the bannister, she managed to make it up the stairs and inside the door before collapsing on the floor.

She was only dimly conscious of Lily's voice, calling for her brother to help. Together they lifted her on the couch, still caked in dry mud, and as if from a great distance she was sure she heard Lily say, "Mom is really ruining it." She wondered if "it" was the couch, or the holidays, or everything, and whether a white rose in winter was enough to fix it all.

*G*ifts are never given

    Not like a sunny day

Or a clear river

Or a rose in winter

No, gifts are earned

For to wield a gift

You must understand the cost

To every light is darkness

To every fire a sea

And to create beauty in this world

We must experience the pain.

You must allow it to throb within you,

A constant reminder

Of what happens when you stray too far from the path

When you get lost in the darkness

And forget how to return.

Only by becoming the night

Can you find your way by the stars.

Dawn will break eventually

But you will only see the sun
If you are ready to open your eyes.

Chapter Twenty-Two

When Elizabeth woke on the couch (miraculously unsullied — was that magic?), she felt nothing. No pain, no anger, but also no joy or sudden urges to cast spells or shoot sparks from her fingertips. She remembered the evening as clear as a bell but the only lingering side effect seemed to be an emptiness. Not a bad emptiness, she realized as she snuck up to her shower. Just a clarity, as though she had new glasses or was finally following a reasonable diet. She simply felt clear, and empty, and open. Like a glass vessel, waiting for its flowers.

As the droplets coursed over her, she thought of the flower she had called into being last night. It had been a product of the oak's aura. That warm, shimmery feeling, not unlike this hot shower, actually. Both felt the same on her body, that delicious feeling of laziness, of waking up from sleeping in with no place to be, of morning coffee sipped in silence on the porch, of the scent of flowers on a summer breeze ...

Around her, the steam formed great flowers in the air, and the scent of roses was heavy when she turned and saw them hanging , crystal clear in the air.

Elizabeth shut off the shower, panicked, and the images fell away. She closed her eyes, and willed herself to enjoy the remaining warm steam, letting the little hairs on her arms soak up the last trickle of water. The flowers reformed.

It seemed that the gift remained.

Tempted though she was to make steam flowers all day, Elizabeth dressed and went downstairs, pondering this new development. Could she just make flowers? Did it happen every time she was happy? A beautiful enchantment, to be sure, but like the path, not terribly useful. Characters in books and movies usually got something like the ability to fly, or make things appear out of nowhere. She tried wishing for an ice cream sundae. Nothing. Calling the sensation of flying into her body, she jumped off the bottom stair. Nothing. She supposed that all would reveal itself in time, and marveled again at this new clear aspect of herself that was somehow unworried about the magic now springing from her body. It made sense, to this new Elizabeth. The tree had made her feel, and now her feelings came true. It was a subtle magic, to be sure, but Elizabeth was sure that she had always been able to do these things ... she had simply never known how.

When the kids came down, she gave them extra large hugs and thanked them for helping her into "bed" after her cold walk. Elizabeth saw them exchange confused glances when she turned her back, but it seemed that neither of them wanted to stir the pot. She placed a plate of pancakes before each of them, warming the maple syrup in a pot and adding a cinnamon stick for good measure. As she inhaled the scent, she imagined her children having a beautiful, fulfilling day, feeling their imagined joy run through the vessel of her own body.

Then she carefully poured the hot syrup onto their shortstacks, saving the dregs and the cinnamon stick for her own morning coffee.

"Dang, Mom, these are really good," said Cory, scooping up half a pancake in one bite and swallowing it whole.

"They really are," said Lily, perplexed. "Did you do something different?"

"Just extra love," Elizabeth smiled. She watched both kids become more animated as they ate, discussing the classroom parties planned for this final week of school and wondering what the two weeks of winter break would hold. Both were eagerly awaiting the snow.

After taking them to school Elizabeth stopped by the coffeehouse, bringing some leftover treats to Denny in aesthetically pleasing bags for her to sell by the register. Looking up at her, Denny did a double take.

"You look good," she said appreciatively. "Spa day?"

"Since yesterday?" Elizabeth laughed.

"Spa evening!" Denny corrected. "I don't know. You're glowing."

For a moment Elizabeth looked down at her hands in a panic, before realizing that Denny meant it in the traditional way. "Thanks," she replied. "Just getting a clearer sense of myself, I guess."

Denny nodded sagely. "I get it. You got too caught up in him. It happens." She shook her head. "Glad I could help you out."

Elizabeth's smile slid. Of course. Joe. Joe who wasn't going to stay. She took her coffee with a tight smile, and was unsurprised to find it ice cold. Bitterness sat on her tongue, and try as she might, she could not find the sweetness within her. When Denny turned back to other customers, she abandoned the cup and sidled out the door.

As she walked to her car, Elizabeth noticed a sign next to the long-empty restaurant by the lake: "For Sale". She knew the building had been abandoned for some time. Once the heart of the community, now it was taking up space, space that someone would no doubt transform into something else. She found that she was sorry to see it. A vacant building was unappealing, but who knew what they would replace it with? Who's to say it wasn't better as it was — a memory?

The road swam before her as she drove, preoccupied. Was this what she was doing, with The Sanctuary? Taking a beloved institution and transforming it so much that the spirit of the place could not survive? How much could something change and still remain the same? She knew some alterations were needed — the cleaning, the fixing. But changing was surely different. Changing was an alteration to the soul.

When she parked in front of the house, intending to finish up the last of Joe's project list at the inn, she was surprised to find Lisa walking down the steps. She hollered a hello, and was rewarded with a jolly wave.

"What's up, neighbor?"

"Just dropping off some dried flowers for Lily. You know when I was here, I brought some over, and she just loved them. So I promised to bring her some more. I told her she's welcome any time, I can teach her how to hang them dry and which ones she should grow and all that good stuff." Lisa's jowls wobbled slightly as she spoke, and Elizabeth recognized that for all her fire, she was quite old to be living alone out here. She looked at the bouquet on the porch.

"I loved the ones you brought over here, and the vase, too. I'd love to have some regular orders for the inn, when it opens."

"Well doesn't that sound nice! Never done it for money, just wanted to use what the land gave me, but I suppose if it's ongoing that would be reasonable." Lisa smiled.

"It's nice that you can use them. Once they're dead, I mean."

"Oh, everything dies," Lisa responded with a wave of her hand. "Matty died, I'll die someday soon, in the end that's always the way of it. No point in fighting an ending. But if you take what you create and make something beautiful and lasting out of it, well...it lives forever." She shrugged. "Well, not forever, but I guess it lives twice. And then goes back into the ground to grow something new." She lowered her head, as if to tell Elizabeth a secret. "When you get to be my age, you notice how everything comes alive again. Sometimes lots of times. Some things never really die, they just go away for awhile. Other things die but come back in new ways. It all balances out in the end."

Balance. Duality. It was chasing her.

Elizabeth took her neighbor's hand and said "I get that. Or at least I'm starting to."

Lisa squeezed her fingers. "You're a good woman, with good kids. Glad to have you as my neighbor."

"You too." Elizabeth pulled out her last bag of cookies, one too many for Denny's basket. "Take these for the road. I'll send Lily over one day during Winter Break."

"You do that!" Lisa gave one final wave, and shuffled back to the main road and her own familiar driveway.

***

She set to work on the list of projects, all of which (she told herself) she could learn to do with video tutorials and a little grace for herself. After a reasonable amount of swearing, she managed to prise up the kitchen linoleum, which was a fantastic mess but felt like a large accomplishment. Thus empowered, she set to work replacing the kitchen faucet, which also turned out to be easier than expected (if a bit wetter). This was, however, the end of her triumphs. Installing the new thermostat felt like some sort of brain surgery, and when the upstairs shower knob wouldn't come off, she whacked it with a wrench and managed to both break the old piece and turn the shower on full throttle.

It was at this point that Joe entered, to find her swearing loudly at the plumbing with a soaking wet backside.

"I see this is going well," she heard from behind her.

Elizabeth turned to see him grinning at her. Unwillingly, she began to laugh, and the magic coursed through her veins again. As Joe moved towards her, toolbox in hand, time became a love song, and she could see his movements slightly before they occurred. One long, languorous stream of him. Like water. Each breath seemed an eternity. Each step fell like a bass drum. Following the future she could only feel, she reached up and pulled him into a kiss.

One hand pressed into her lower back, as he enthusiastically returned the embrace. She answered with increased intensity, taking his tool box with one hand and gently guiding it to the floor. How strange, to be kissing him in here, where there was no supernatural force, no summoning mushrooms. Just them. Wanting each other.

She loved him more for it.

There was a bed not six feet away, and without parting her mouth from his, she slowly backed towards it. Sitting down on the mattress, Elizabeth reached for his shirt, and once again pulled it up to expose the smooth skin beneath. She kissed the space below his heart as his fingers played with her hair. Her lips traveled down to his stomach, and his head dropped back on his neck just a fraction of an inch. And then her lips began to sink lower, and he was pulling her head back gently to crush her mouth beneath his, pulling her up on the mattress as he kneeled over her and put his own hand beneath her shirt.

"He doesn't stay. Anywhere, or with anyone."

Denny's voice shot like an arrow through her.

"Everything comes alive again," whispered Lisa.

Panic rose in her again, and the magic drained from her body. She was cold, and frightened, and when Joe moved her shirt upwards she screamed, "Stop!"

He stopped. Exhaled. Put both hands up, and stood. The frustration was plainly written on his face, etched in anger.

"I don't get it, Elizabeth. What do you want?"

Want. Not need. Want.

"I want you to stay with me."

The words surprised her as much as him. Until that moment, she could not have said with any certainty what she wanted, and would surely have talked herself out of most possibilities for fear of being inconvenient or disliked. But that was the truth. She didn't want a random roll in the hay, or bed, or forest floor. She wanted someone to love her. She wanted someone to stay.

"Stay?" he echoed, as though the word was foreign to his tongue. Both hands met in front of his mouth in a prayer, rolled to the back of his head, spread the fingers wide in confusion. "Elizabeth ... you're great. I think there is a lot of you yet to discover, for sure. I don't know how long that would take. I also don't know how long I want to do it for." He looked at her, sadness in his eyes. "I can't even touch you right now without you running away. How could I stay with that?"

Duality. Elizabeth began to understand. One half of her was angry, wanted to scream, wanted to tell him how awful he was for leading her on and making her think she mattered.

The other half realized that he was right.

Why should he stay with someone who couldn't let him in? She had been cold and distant, had pushed him away, and had revealed almost nothing about herself. That wasn't a path to love. Love stayed because it wanted to, not because it had to. Love stayed because beneath the tender words and earnest looks was a raw, ugly relationship — a death. Something had to die for the love to live.

"He isn't dead."

Joe's eyebrows raised in confusion. "What?"

"My husband." Elizabeth straightened her back, though she couldn't bring herself to look up. "He isn't dead. That's what he wanted me to tell the kids." It was their pain she had locked away inside her. The pain she had shouldered so that they wouldn't have to bear it. "He ran off to Florida with a younger woman, someone from work. He didn't want us." She forced herself to look at Joe, whose arms felt like home and therefore entirely unsafe. "He wrote me a check and told me to tell the kids that the accident incinerated his body. That way they could move on easier. He could move on easier." She cleared her throat and tried to pretend that her face hadn't flooded. "So we came here to start over. But I think I brought his ghost with us, whether he really died or not."

It was all she could manage. She didn't say that she had spent years being ignored, unloved, touched intimately without being cared for. She didn't say that she had tried to be who he wanted her to be, until she couldn't remember who she wanted to be. She didn't say that she had watched her children try, over and over, to seek the affection of a man who had none to give, and learn, as she had, that they were unlovable.

But she saw it. Finally, clear as the daylight through The Sanctuary's window, she saw the darkness she had been running from.

Silently, Joe climbed up next to her on the bed, and placed his arms around her. He held her while she cried, and held her when it stopped, and left her fast asleep on the bare mattress in a rare ray of winter sun.

She's closer than she knows
*   We know*
We feel her move.
I feel them move.
The thickness of my spine
The roots drinking deeply, too deeply
I am not enough
For this.
You are
You have always been
We called you here to remind you
That you are one
One of many
One of few
One of us.
You are never alone, child of earth
And your pains are sharp
But ready to be dulled
Ready to be washed away

By the forces of feeling
And time.

Chapter Twenty-Three

The joy of the morning evaporated almost immediately. She was late to pick up the kids, having no way to wake herself from the unexpected nap she took. Joe had been absent when she came to. She could not blame him. Looking back, she really couldn't blame him for anything. She had been closed to everything she had wanted, and truthfully, she did not know how to open.

The magic, said a voice within her. *Use your magic.*

But misty roses and lazy time seemed like poor compensation for her children, neither of whom spoke on the way home. Elizabeth saw them communicating wordlessly in the backseat. It was clear that this was not their first conversation in this manner. How much had she missed, blinded by her own pain?

As they arrived back at the kitchen table, a meaningful look from Cory seemed to push Lily forward. "Mom ... we need to talk to you."

Of course they did.

Elizabeth sat at the table, feeling for all the world like a little girl ready to be scolded. Oddly, the same warnings that Joe set off seemed to be put into practice now. *Unlovable* they blared, over and over. *Unworthy. Not enough.*

"Mom ... we know how hard you're trying to make a life here. And we understand how difficult it must be to do it alone."

Alone.

"But it's Christmas. And we feel sort of ... left out in the cold."

Elizabeth met her daughter's eyes. How brave she was being, to say this. To call her own mother on her selfishness. She noticed Lily's heavy limbs, the bags under her eyes. The teen had gained a few pounds over the past month, and suddenly she saw the broken version of herself she had dragged to Solace Spring being silently transferred to her daughter's body.

"This is our first holiday season in a new place, with new people, and frankly ... we ... we ..." Lily could not finish.

"We want to go home."

Cory stepped forward, suddenly a much larger and more imposing figure than she remembered. When had he aged so much? How had she missed the turning point between boy and man?

"It's not that we don't like it here, we do," Lily hurried. "But ... you're not really with us anymore, Mom. We don't know who you are. You leave randomly, in the middle of the night. You come home from the trees like you're half drunk. You cry all the time, and you think we don't notice, but we do. We're not little kids." She sighed. "But we need a mom, and you haven't been one lately."

"We need a home," Cory added, with what may have been anger, or pain. "We have no home."

Silently, Elizabeth nodded to the dining room table. Nothing they said was factually inaccurate. Just as with Joe, she had shut her children out. In her attempt to pretend that she was not hurting, she had created a smokescreen version of herself, a fake mom who was there, but not present. She had been outside of herself looking for answers, when the biggest answer had been right in front of her.

"I don't know if I can make a home," Elizabeth admitted quietly. "I think I don't really know what home feels like." She looked up at her kids. "Your dad had a very specific vision of what life should be like, and I did my best to carry it out. But what I want life to look like? What you want life to look like?" She sighed. "I don't know. I think we need to talk about it. What we want our lives together to be about. And then you'll need to help me create it." She reached out her hands, and each child took one. "You're right. You're not little kids. And you can be trusted to build a life, too." Elizabeth felt the magic returning slowly, pushing words off her tongue that she had never expected. "I'm going to be the best mom to you when I am holding less. And you guys have already done such a great job creating friends and mentors and community." She squeezed their hands. "I thought you guys would be lonely, like I was. I worked overtime to make sure everything was perfect, so you would know you were loved." Big sigh. "But that just took away the mom you needed. So from now on, I'll try to do less and let go more, and you guys can help me out. Then we can all learn how to build a life." Final squeezes. "Does that sound OK?"

Lily nodded, and Cory bumped his chin down briefly.

"We love you, Mom," said Lily. "We need you here. We just want you to be happy."

Elizabeth got up and hugged them, noticing as she did that they were nearly taller than she was. "That's what I want, too," she said. "And it's about time I made it happen."

***

Elizabeth felt the turning. Her dark half wasn't gone, but it was making way for a new dawn. Her secret wasn't so heavy on her chest now. It wasn't the ending she had wanted, the fairy tale she had given a life to maintain. Tyler's departure, she realized now, hadn't broken her heart. It had broken her perspective. All of her energy for the past twenty years had gone into ensuring that this story, this timeline, was flawless. She had never allowed herself to consider another path, therefore one had never appeared to her. His "death" had shattered the illusion she had abandoned herself to maintain, and now ... now she had to go another way.

Her life had a new direction. And her heart ... well, she still had to see to that.

As she pulled up to the mechanic the next day, she wondered what to say. Apologize, again. She felt she should explain, but she couldn't. Part of her wanted to tell him that it was fine, that he didn't need to stay, that they could just fool around ... but she knew that would only bring the shadows back faster. To discover who she was, he would need to make it past her past, and to do that would take time and effort. He would need to stay, or risk starting her traumas all over again. So she needed to give him that choice, and accept whatever decision he made. No matter how much it hurt to put herself on the line. He needed to know that she loved him.

But as it turned out, she was spared the trouble.

Joe's van had disappeared from the shop. He could have been making a house call or out on a job, but something told her this wasn't the case. Slowly, she walked down the main road, processing the truth she knew was coming.

Her eyes asked Denny the moment she walked in. Coming out from behind the counter, her friend gave her a soft, gentle hug. The other patrons tactfully looked away, raising the volume of their conversations ever so slightly to preserve her privacy. She was grateful.

"He's gone," Denny whispered. "Left this morning. Jenny Parker went with him...they've been a thing on and off for awhile." Her face collapsed, while Elizabeth's felt strangely rigid. "Oh, Elizabeth, I'm so sorry."

"It's fine," Elizabeth said tonelessly, briefly meeting Denny's eyes before searching her pockets for something, anything. "Really, Den, it's OK. You warned me, and I knew. He is what he is. It's fine." She found her keys, and waved them awkwardly in the air. "Gotta go get those gifts while I can." She turned to the door. "I'll see you later."

And with that Elizabeth walked out of the door, as she had walked out of Tyler's office months before, leaving behind yet another man for whom her love was simply not enough.

She's almost home.

They do not come standing in their power
Full of abundance and joy and hope.
They do not come with visions of triumph
Strength radiating from their bodies
Peace on their brow.
This does not lead them home.
Home is where they arrive broken
Exhausted
Out of options and out of time
Swallowed by the darkness.
And only after arriving
Do they realize
That it is within the darkness
That they are born again.

Chapter Twenty-Four

All official business quietly went to sleep, with the promise not to wake again until the new year. School let out, final marks still hanging in the balance. Even the best of students could not bring themselves to care. Friends went home, went on vacation, went to sleep, swearing to call over the break. The library extended all due dates, the galleries shut their doors, and even Eyes Up was closing early just so Denny could wrap and send her gifts. Overnight, Solace Spring came to a total standstill. And finally, Elizabeth felt she could breathe.

Joe's departure still weighed on her, in stabbing pains that came and went in quiet moments. But in truth, an ending was better than the muddy puddles they had been wading in. Never knowing what they were or weren't ... it would have been too much for her. It had been too much for her. His eyes had held a thousand promises of unlocking something deep inside of her, something primal and beautiful and ancient. Longing for that future still immersed her when his face crossed her mind. The woman she would have become when she joined with his energy would have been magical indeed. A radiant and powerful being, fed a steady diet of passion and safety. Yet they were on two different sides of the grove, and could not find a place to meet in the middle. Elizabeth would go out to the oak with her tea, and think of what it would have been like to let him touch her, to let him know her. She had to admit she would not have known the way. Perhaps the next time a flood came upon her, she would simply have to drown.

In the meantime, she turned back to her family. Now that everyone had dropped a level or two in stress, they found a comfortable rhythm of reading, walking, and creating. They sang in the kitchen as they made dinner together, and eagerly flipped through flower catalogues, planning the spring garden. Glossy green beds rolled across the pages, with closely cropped photos of translucent pink petals and riotous yellow blossoms. As another gray day loomed ahead of them, visions of growing things felt deliciously anticipatory. It turned out Dylan was quite the botanist, and for Christmas had purchased Lily a beautiful book of hand painted flowers with their symbolism and medicinal uses. They read it hungrily, wondering aloud what they might ask The Sanctuary to accomplish. Lily planned a love garden, with roses and lavender and "two-lips" in pink. Cory was ready to construct a celestial garden, with sunflowers to follow the day and moonflowers to greet the night, planted in a galactic elliptical orbit. As for Elizabeth, she wanted rosemary for clarity and sage for wisdom, and bright orange poppies to remind her of the sun.

It was while they were out marking their spaces and watching the angles of the sun that they saw them. Honks echoed from the sky, and they looked up in time to see a great black arrow slowly piercing the setting sun. The geese had far to go, no doubt. They felt storms coming before the air had begun to spin, and their feathers yearned for the journey. Like her, they felt the irresistible urge to move forward, even as they mourned the home they left behind. Elizabeth watched them go, following their progress until the dots on the horizon disappeared. *Spring,* she told herself. *They'll return in the spring. It isn't so long now.* As their flawless lines dissolved into the horizon, she turned back to the patch of earth in front of her, tossing in a handful of lupine seeds that would grow into scalloped purple spires by the time they returned.

Geese were wonderful fortune tellers.

The next morning, they woke to find gentle flakes of snow falling outside of the windows. A soft blanket of white covered The Sanctuary, not so deep that the remaining plants could not be seen, but enough to render them all undulating shapes beneath winter's mantle. Elizabeth pictured a Christmas card, with a cozy little house near a friendly forest, snow drifting over it like powdered sugar. Inside it would say "treasured moments this holiday", or "tidings of comfort and joy". For this is what she had now. She did not have great romance, or piles of money, or a job she held a burning passion for. She had comfort, and joy. And she could grow both.

Her magic led her that day, taking her by the hands and twirling her around. It begged her to dance with her daughter, and she held Lily close, feeling the teenage body soften against her mother's heart in the crystalline wonderland of their garden. It guided her as she traced her name in the snowfall, only to have it erased by a new layer an hour later. Song seemed to emanate faintly from the icy hills and divots, as though the discordant voices that had haunted her through the fall had finally resolved into harmony beneath the barrier. Hugging her children, she swayed to the rhythm that no one else could hear.

They hung their Christmas tree with decorations they had made from found items in their new home ... pinecones wrapped with wire, curls of birch bark tied in ribbon, pieces of fallen wood painted to look like Santa Claus and shooting stars. Elizabeth pulled a scarlet afghan from the closet of blankets and gently tucked it around the trunk. She remembered when her babies were young, and she had treated them just the same, surrounding them with fluffy tokens of her love and trying to keep them as nourished as she could. Maybe it didn't matter what she gave her love to. Maybe the purpose of love was simply to spread it on everything.

The lights of the town were beaming yellow moons onto the snow when they arrived late that afternoon. Denny was standing in the front door of the coffee shop, her own eyes trained up to the sky. Steam from her cup melted a clear space around her, though the flakes were falling thicker and faster as day faded to night. A strange sense of calm wove through the open shops. Even the cars rolled dreamlike through the street. Elizabeth always forgot how the snow muffled footsteps, rendering the whole world quiet and ready for rest.

They gathered enough food to last through Christmas, tea and sugar and cranberries and turkey. Heavy cream for topping cakes and cocoa. Vegetables that would keep on the counter. Remembering her neighbors' advice on snow, she bought loaves of bread she didn't need and gallons of milk she doubted they would drink. On a whim, she picked up the grocer's last jar of honey, from a farm down the road that would not replenish their stores until summer. It could stand on the kitchen table, a golden beacon of better days to come. Cory and Lily cheerfully loaded up the car, planning a late-night dinner of tomato soup, grilled cheese, and eggnog. They weren't the only ones. Solace Spring breathed a gentle jubilation. There was palpable relief that the winter had now begun in earnest, freeing up the energy from wondering and giving it over to holiday cheer. Local kids were selling homemade wreaths at a stand next to Denny's place, and though they had more than enough seasonal decor, Elizabeth bought one anyway. The evergreen boughs were hardy beneath her fingertips, sharp and clean-smelling, an everlasting circle of constancy. She would find a place for it.

Final errands complete, they crowded into Eyes Up for a final communal drink with their neighbors, many of whom were also out restocking before the snow set in. Lily shot into Dylan's arms within seconds of entering the premises, and Cory sat companionably with Lisa and Grover, who were sitting closely at the same table. Tiffany was in animated discussion with a woman who looked like she might be her older sister. Elizabeth pulled up to the counter and sipped her ginger chai while she looked out the window, watching the soft white blanket get tucked in around Solace Spring. And here she was, safe and sound, held by this tiny town. Magic purred within her as she allowed herself to simply be, be loved, be free to be herself. A tender contentment filled her chest, and lifted into the air. She watched it color her field of vision with hazy gold sparkles, slowly extending up to the ceiling. As she turned her head, she saw it pour into everyone sitting in the cafe — her children, her friends, her neighbors. Sweet yellow light flowed from her heart into theirs, and their expressions turned misty and intimate. Elizabeth tactfully averted her gaze as Dylan applied his lips to Lily's neck, though she did not miss Grover's hand on Lisa's knee. Denny seemed to radiate a sunshine aura all by herself. And turning back to the window, Elizabeth caught her own reflection in the growing dark outside. She was glowing, too.

Excusing herself, she walked down the street alone, letting her eyes sweep across this small territory that had become hers. Energy expanded from her chest and across every window and door she passed. When she reached the end of the street, she found herself in front of the mechanic shop. Through the front window, Elizabeth saw the outline of a familiar van. Parked inside the empty shop.

For a moment, the balmy beams vanished. She stood on the street, wet and cold, shaking with grief. Inadequacy flooded her. He was there. Without her. Because he didn't want her. Not enough.

Time stood still as she stared at the aging vehicle. Then she remembered the first time she had seen it. Down by the river. With golden leaves pouring from the sky, and the river bubbling nearby. Joe handing her something hot and sweet and real, while music played, and their eyes danced together. Like falling in love.

Eyes closed, Elizabeth allowed the memories to keep coming, filling her up like a cup. Joe kissing her by the lake, telling her the legend of the oak grove. Joe playing with her kids, and nursing her to health. Joe touching her skin and —

Sparks flew from the "Closed" sign in the window, and all of the lights on the block extinguished completely. Elizabeth caught herself panting — whether from the shock or the memories, she wasn't sure. But as love hung in the air around her, a shiver began in her feet. She looked down, and saw an errant branch of evergreen, probably thrown from a wreath. Small, but strong. A perfect arc, ready and waiting to become part of the circle. She stooped to pick it up, and took the red ribbon from her hair. Carefully, she tied it to the base of the branch. A new force flowed through her as she placed her hand to the door, and found it open. It led her into the vast shadowed cavern of the shop, and the echo of her footsteps was thunderous after the dampening effect of the snow. She walked to the driver side door of the van, and placed her hand affectionately on the hood. His embrace in the grove. His lips on her lips. The way he held her hand.

Slowly, she deposited her offering on the handle, then turned away and left the darkness for the light.

***

Winter Solstice dawned slowly, pale pink rays of sun glittering off the snow-crusted earth. Snowfall had continued overnight, leaving a solid foot of white on The Sanctuary's gardens. Individual plants were no longer discernible, merely vague impressions of something slumbering beneath the ice. The world slept. And so did Elizabeth.

She had found so much joy in rest since she had begun to live according to her enchanted whims. Stretching the full length of the bed, she would roll luxuriously in her new flannel sheets and down comforter, inhaling the scent of the pine candle on her nightstand. Morning's first sun teased at the window, and Elizabeth watched the dust flicker in the air.

This was a day with nothing to do, and for once, she let it stay that way. Lily and Cory both spent the requisite morning in the snow, before heading out to "finish some things up". Elizabeth took advantage of the silence to walk through the inn, which would officially open on the first of the year. She had finally found the balance between new and old, an update she hoped would honor the earth as well as the guest. Each room was furnished according to season. Sunny golden walls complimented green bedding and corn husk artwork in Summer. Vibrant ochre in Autumn was set off by a wheat-colored quilt and Lily's painting of expansive pumpkins and sunflowers. Spring was enclosed in pale green, a pink coverlet embroidered with flowers demurely floating upon the bed. And Winter was a perfectly matched scene of palest blue, a reflection of the world outside the window. The living room and kitchen she had left mostly untouched (though substantially cleaner), a farmhouse decor with glowing warm wood and cast iron touches, with hand-knitted afghans in moss green and gold. Lily's drawings of mushrooms were thoughtfully placed in hidden nooks, letting the wide windows attract the eye while her art rewarded the seekers. The kitchen was stocked with packets of Denny's coffee, calico sacks of pancake mix, squat jars of apple butter, and of course, miniature bottles of maple syrup. Cabinets held stoneware dishes from a local ceramicist, and a cutting board she had ordered from Grover. He had also fashioned the low bookshelf in the living room for the retired library books she had bought from Tiffany. Tori's candle for peace blessed the coffee table. The only person missing from this space, she realized, was Joe.

But he was not missing. He was in the cracks in the walls, the sparks of each light, the space between floorboards ... he was in all of it. Joe was the foundation of what was here. Even though he had left, Joe's energy had set the stage for everything that she had created. The safe space for her soul.

Elizabeth sat on the floor and let the love that had been woven into The Sanctuary fill her up. Like the spokes of a wheel, they beamed into her, and she in turn sent them back into the space. Her magic permeated the house and spread into the gardens, skipping like stones across the pond. In her mind's eye she could see the forest in the wintry landscape, clouds speeding by as day turned to night turned to day. She watched seasons pass, stars move, decades go by. Trees grew inch by inch, and where one fell another grew, and where creatures died new ones were born. Time was circular. And as she saw the immortality of the land, she was brought to the oak grove, and the circle that lay there. Her eyes flew open.

Hurriedly, Elizabeth shoved on her boots and grabbed the wreath she had purchased the night before. With the final moments of the shortest day of the year upon her, she knew she had little time. Racing across the gardens, she felt her way forward along the now-hidden path. The snow gave way under her feet, and the closer she grew to the grove, the more vibration she felt beneath her. There were no lights to see, but she knew they remained, guiding her way. As she arrived at the oak grove, the last streaks of daylight exhaled, and night covered the land once again. Though she could not see the center, she felt it. It felt as The Sanctuary had — a space where all the energy from every direction met, where one compass point anchored the revolutions. She was that anchor. She was The Sanctuary.

Laying the wreath at her feet, Elizabeth took a deep breath. And moved into the void dividing the oak tree.

It was dark, and close. After her initial dive between the trunks, there was only room to crawl. Her logical mind screamed in agony, insisting there could be no more than a few feet of space to turn round in, reminding her that this was only a tree. But the magic within her knew better, knew that each tree was all trees, and all time. Eyes closed, she let the spiraling force unfurl from within her, and lead her on, further in, deeper into darkness.

The pulsing in her fingers became the pulsing of her heart. All around her, Elizabeth felt the mycelium, spinning webs through the passageway, visions of what once was and what was still being created. Fears that held a vice-like grip on her heart surface with terrifying ferocity, insisting that all was lost. She kept moving forward. She saw Tyler, as he had once been, a man who had loved a version of her that had so desperately wanted to belong to someone. She saw Joe, as he could still be, someone who would hold her hand and her heart while she grew. She saw her children, aging faster than she could possibly have imagined, smiling and happy and proud of who they were. And The Sanctuary. Just as she had dreamed it. The forest bent and changed and breathed, but never fell. Its soul was infinite. And so was hers. Brilliant, and beautiful, and overflowing with love. Even through closed eyes, the love lit everything around her with a light that would never go out.

Where she went, Elizabeth would never truly know. When the light retreated, she found herself sitting comfortably in the hollow of the tree, which was somehow just big enough to fit her form. A full moon had just risen over The Sanctuary, where a plume of smoke told her the children had started a fire. She grinned. All around her new pathways were coming to life; she could feel them rising, singing new songs, inspiring new dances. They would unravel in their own time, and she would follow those that chose her, and those that she chose. So many wonderful things were still in front of her. But for now, what awaited was a warm bowl of stew, a fresh loaf of bread, and the company of the people she loved best in the world.

Chapter Twenty-Five

Christmas morning was an exhilarating thing in the sea of snow. Elizabeth would never have guessed the weather would make such a difference, though a lifetime of sunny Yuletides had already taught her that pine trees and palm trees didn't mix. Nevertheless, the presence of ice white blankets outside the window was more powerful than she had anticipated. The arms of The Sanctuary seemed to wrap themselves in the snow and hold the family close, sighing in cinnamon over their small festivities.

Settled on the couch with a deep green afghan covering her legs, Elizabeth watched her children crawl around under the tree as they did every year, dividing gifts into piles despite Santa's excellent efforts at even distribution. They had never been nearly as interested in what was inside the boxes as they were in the process of creating them, wrapping them, handing them around. New clothes and gadgets from magical elves were remarked on, jovially raised for all to see, then put into a pile to be forgotten a week later. On to the next package, and the next. She watched her children move forward without a single attachment to their treasures, and wondered at the purpose of it all.

"Cory, I love them!" Lily turned the carved mushrooms over in her hands, fingers skimming the smooth oiled surface of the wood. "These look just like the drawingI made for my room."

Cory blushed. "Yeah, I made them to match."

His sister gaped at him. "You MADE these?!?"

"Yup."

"What? How did you learn to do that?"

"Grover."

Lily narrowed her eyes at him. "That is such a completely unsatisfactory explanation, Cor."

He shrugged, but smiled, and for once the expression was free of bitterness. He had found something he truly loved. Elizabeth feigned cluelessness as she, too, admired the fragile carving.

"Mom." Cory was handing her a small red box. "This one's for you."

Her fingers ached as she scooted the brown ribbon off the side, and opened the lid. Inside was the whittled flame charm she had seen at Grover's workshop. A little smaller than her thumb, the base of the fire curved like a bowl, holding the tongues that flipped upwards in impossibly delicate tendrils. It hung on a snaky dark copper chain, the reddish hues of metal and wood lending truth to the illusion. The fire was warm in her palm, and as she placed it around her neck, the flames licked the hollow of her throat.

"Cory, this is beautiful. And powerful. You've created something really incredible." She took her son into her arms. "I'm proud of you."

A gruff "Thanks, Mom," came from the muffled folds of her dressing gown, and Cory held on a little longer than usual. When he released her, he stayed by her side, companionably reading over the new book his grandparents had sent.

"This is for you, Lily." Elizabeth handed over the book of poetry, wrapped in a scrap of linen and topped with an evergreen branch. Lily opened the journal and began to read the offerings there, the love of her mother pouring from the pages. Her hand went to her mouth, and the journal to her chest. She held it there, her breathing for once slow and steady, assured of her mother's love.

"Mom, I love it." Lily hugged her mother, then immediately returned to its pages. "Do you think maybe I could use some of these in my songs?"

"Sure, if you want to. It's my gift to you. You can use it however it feels good." Feels good. What would make her feel good? Elizabeth shook her head. Something must have gotten to her last night.

A vision of illumination surrounding her and the smell of the earth after rain. Cozy arms around her. Moving forward into the unknown.

They gave Cory his blanket and watched him feel the fibers as Lily babbled about the weaving process. Elizabeth saw the comparison in his head...they had put as much time into his gift as he had into theirs. It was an offering he understood now. Elizabeth watched him embrace his sister with true love and affection, something that had not happened in...well, she couldn't remember how long. She watched her children holding each other on the floor of their little living room, surrounded by old wood and new furniture, closing another loop in their lives. Together again.

Now what?

The feeling of "now what" continued to follow her around as she griddled the French toast and sorted the ribbons into recycle and trash piles. It sat on her shoulder while she knitted through three Christmas movies, and watched her prepare the roast for dinner. After the children went to bed, and the dishes were cleared, it waited for her, until she sat at the kitchen table and looked it in the eye.

Having emerged from her battle in the oak tree, Elizabeth had been ready for everything to be fixed. Rosy glasses would descend from on high and suddenly she would be able to see her path forward, what she would do next and where she wanted to go. Christmas, of course, had been first priority, and had occupied her full attention, but now ... now what?

Light all around, light piercing her skin, light washing over her closed eyes. In that moment she had felt the possibility that stretched endlessly in all directions, awaiting her as she left her dark hollow at the base of the tree. And here it was, this field of unblemished snow that had settled around the house. It was overwhelming, compared to that tiny pocket of wood that had held her. She had been small for so long, kept in one space, one moment. She had relived the same story hundreds, maybe thousands of times. Of course she wanted something new. Of course she wanted it to be different. But with that massive void outside, how was she to know which way to go?

Curls of steam rose from her nighttime cup of tea, compact and white as they left the mug and then suddenly disseminating into a wide cloud before disappearing entirely. Another flower of vapor to add to her collection. Curious, she applied her energy for a moment, looking to activate her magic. White mist rose in a flat circle, then a labyrinth, and suddenly flowers bloomed around it. Elizabeth studied the path, trying to find the way through to the center, but the fog dissipated and then there was nothing. She tried again, but only received an empty circle for her troubles. Frustrated, Elizabeth drank the tea in one great draught, turned out the lights, and went to bed.

***

Nothing could convince her children to move. They spread themselves out on the living room surfaces as though on their sickbed, surrounded at all times by snacks and distractions, and a hefty amount of Matty's blankets. Despite her occasional feeble remonstrations and insistence that they should get outside and enjoy the snow, Elizabeth was happy enough to leave them to their rest. Their few months here had been bursting with adjustments and creation and destruction and alignment, and perhaps a week of couch rotting was well deserved.

New Year's Eve heralded the end of this lazy enjoyment, however. Denny had talked Lily into singing a set at the coffee shop for what she called the "Stay Awake Celebration". To Denny's credit, Elizabeth mused, there was no way she would make it to midnight without a considerable amount of coffee, so perhaps it was for the best. "Glamorous Attire" was requested, which was an exciting break from the town's casual style. Local bands would take turns playing, a partnership with the pizzeria had been established so that pies and coffees could be purchased at both spots, and a champagne toast would take place in the middle of main street at midnight.

For her part, Elizabeth was bringing small, savory pies full of caramelized onions and melting cheese, and a tray of delicate black and white cookies. She had thought them classy, the correct accompaniment to sparkling glasses and fancy gowns, but as she placed them on a silver tray she mindlessly turned one in her hands. Dark, light, up, down. The duality. The stark white field. On impulse, she bit off the matte black half moon and left the white to eat in the morning.

They arrived at Denny's promptly at seven. Lily's first set began at eight and she wanted time to socialize and get photos. She was swathed in one of Elizabeth's discarded cocktail dresses, a green satin fit and flare that she had purchased for an ill-fated garden party. The dress had stayed in her closet for years, always admired, never worn.

Now Lily's ears were dripping with beveled pink crystals and she had added a pale pink belt, along with knee length brown boots and a large barrette depicting an outstretched luna moth. Ever the fairy, Elizabeth thought. Lily looked just like the flower that shared her name.

Both children dropped their coats and ran, Lily to the stage to check the system, Cory to his teenage friends who were immersed in the pizza menu. Alone, Elizabeth smoothed over her black satin dress and closed her eyes, wishing to be home in her comfortable little inn, without a care in the world. Except how to run it.

"You ready?"

Denny was sitting across from her when she opened her eyes, hand propping up her chin and an order pad on the table before her.

"No." Elizabeth gazed vaguely at her. "I'm not ready."

"To order, to watch your daughter sing, to start a new year?"

"Any of that," Elizabeth agreed. "To open the inn. To start something different. To be on my own." She looked at her friend. "I'm not ready."

"Sure you are," Denny glared at her. "You've been running around doing the work for months. Place looks good. You look good." A note of approval here. "Kids look good. You're all set."

"To do what?"

"Well, that's up to you. What do you want to do?"

Elizabeth sighed. "Honestly, Denny, I have no idea."

Denny nodded. "I get that. Sometimes when you don't know where you're going, best just to take stock of where you are and do the most immediate thing." She picked up her pen. "For you, that means opening that inn. Showing people what you have to offer. Making them feel welcome. Bringing this community into the space, and having them take it back out." Denny looked at her hard. "For right now, that's enough. Don't push it."

"Yes ma'am." Elizabeth began to review the coffee menu for the evening.

"Hey." She looked up to see the older woman's concern. "I wanted to ask you, before the year ends and the moment is gone … why did you choose him?" Elizabeth must have stiffened, because she felt Denny's soft hand covering her own. "I don't mean to bring it up, I know there's still pain there, and there will be for awhile. But I've been thinking about it, the hearth tender and the wanderer, the busy bee and the slow mover." The light and the dark. She hadn't seen it, but the words hit her like a slap. "Just wondering what you two had in common. Why him?"

Slowly, and surprisingly, Elizabeth smiled. Thoughts of Joe filled her heart and slowed her breathing. She could feel him hold her, see his face as he spoke, watch him laugh with her kids.

"He made me feel like more of myself. He made me feel more alive." Her throat caught, just a little. "He made me feel."

And that was it. She had been a greater woman when she was with him. Too much woman for her to embody, too much for him to hold. But wonderful, and powerful, and deeply her. Full and complete. Because that woman could feel absolutely everything without breaking.

Denny squeezed her hand, promised to come back for her order, and walked away, just as Lily returned to go over her set list one last time.

An hour later, Elizabeth was feeling jittery from caffeine and nerves as Lily introduced herself for the crowd. There was no hint of her usual shaking, no carefully scripted sheen over her eyes. This was Lily feeling safe, and comfortable, and ready to present herself to the world exactly as she was. Proud and strong, she opened with a song about a caterpillar that lilted in the air like the promise of a spring day. Whatever worries she may have had about the reception of her art must have cleared quickly — the enthusiastic applause was unmistakable. Lily played a whole hour of songs ranging from moody teenage angst to odes to the dragonfly. There was even a quirky love song she played on ukulele, staring at Dylan the whole way through. As she came to the end, her sparkling eyes surveyed the coffeehouse, packed with friends and neighbors, and announced her last song.

"I want to dedicate this song to my mom, who has been there for me through thick and thin, and I am so grateful to her for ..." Lily paused, and smiled at her knees. "For being her."

The first few notes wavered in the air as Elizabeth watched her brilliant baby, her first born, sing back the notes of her own simple poem.

When the black night comes upon you
And your fear has made you cold
Never forget I'm right behind you
Offering my hand to hold.

Her words. Her words shared by her daughter, her beautiful ethereal princess who used to hand her sticky fistfuls of crayons. Now she had her own little world of creations to call her own. The time had passed too quickly, and she had nearly missed it.

As the song ended, Lily took a final bow and beelined over to her mother, where the embrace elicited further hearty applause. In that moment Elizabeth knew nothing else, not a care in the world. Lily was happy. She has raised a happy child, on the brink of womanhood, who could do more than she ever had. If Lily could sing of salamanders, anything was possible.

"Thank you for inspiring me," she whispered to her daughter.

"Thanks for loving me," came the answer.

Moments later, Lily was torn away to be feted and celebrated by her friends, until she disappeared out the back door with Dylan. Elizabeth stepped outside onto the snowy sidewalk, now covered with tracks from boots and high heels alike. It wouldn't do. She needed it fresh.

Trusting her absence to go unnoticed, Elizabeth got in her car and drove around to the other side of the lake, where a single light shone on an abandoned dock. The space before it was flawlessly white, a serene field of snow.

Elizabeth stomped on it.

She kicked. She scooped. She wrapped her long jacket about her and threw herself backwards into the cold, waving her arms and legs as though she was flying. Lily had sung about a butterfly, a meager worm transformed into something that would rise up into heaven when the wind changed. Her wind had changed. It was time for her to fly.

She stood up carefully, so as not to muss her final project. Giving it a wide berth, she chose one last patch of snow, and using her gloved hand, she wrote a brief epitaph before returning to the party, breathless and rejuvenated.

Elizabeth was here.

She was ready for something new.

Chapter Twenty-Six

With her kids back in school, Elizabeth was finally able to turn back to the inn. And her first order of business was to find a way to make it hers.

So she sat on the floor, in the middle of the living room, and simply waited. She opened up the edges of her magic, settling her body into comfort, allowing that comfort to make her suggestible. The feelings of love she had received in this very space after her illness crept into her. Somewhere in that foundation was Joe, his deep waters, his protective embrace...but she pushed him gently away from her thoughts. He wasn't here. She was here.

Maybe it was her own love she was looking for.

Quietly, she closed her eyes. In a soft voice, she asked herself ... "what does my love feel like?" Immediately, she found herself on the other side of the wall, in her own living room. The door between the two remained closed, and Elizabeth, now short of breath and feeling her body for missing pieces, could not think of how she had materialized here. She had asked only about her love.

But looking around, Elizabeth saw her love here. It was hanging Cory's favorite jacket by the door, so he wouldn't forget it. It was framing Lily's newest drawing, even though she wasn't sure it was good enough. It was putting aside the cookies Denny liked, that book to lend to Tiffany. Her love was in the way she treated people, and in how much she saw of them. The little things. All those details that caused her so much anxiety, the million checkpoints on her interminable lists…those were love. All these years, she had cursed each item as something forced upon her, when in truth, these were seeds that she had not allowed to grow. Forcing them to bend to her will had turned a gift into a nightmare, but now she had a chance to fix that. By slowing way, way down.

Slowing down would give her time to create.

If she sat with each seed, what would it become? She thought of the basket that would collect all of the tiny treasures that no one else saw. Cory's kindness. Lily's fears. The mycelium on the pathway, and the darkness of the grove. How could she give others that gift?

Elizabeth stood, head in hands, a small voice in her head whispering of business plans and financial ruin. None of this made money. None of this was value. She had no place inserting herself … but here she stopped the voice. Coming back to the slow pace, to the sitting, to the noticing, Elizabeth asked herself what she was to all of these people. And as she turned her head, she saw the small mirror Matty had affixed behind the door. They never used it, and had often wondered why he did. In this moment, Elizabeth suddenly understood.

I'm a mirror.

Of course. That's why she could see more of them. *They* could see more of them, with her help. The spaces she created around her gave them a safe place to feel. Like her children, who had felt safe enough to heal the wounds life had set before them. Like Grover, and Lisa, who had let their icy exteriors melt for her. Like each person who had tasted her food and allowed themselves to feel vulnerable.

Like...Joe?

Without stopping to think, she grabbed her car keys, and drove straight to Tori's.

***

"Yes, you are."

Elizabeth stared dumbfounded at Tori's bemused face, wondering how this jolt of information had failed to surprise.

"Not for everyone?"

"Of course for everyone. We all are. And the closer we come to someone, the more we act as their mirrors." She shook her head. "I won't lie to you — it doesn't make you popular. A lot of people will hate to see themselves. It makes them angry, to see what needs their attention, their love." She shrugged. "You cannot journey for others. What you can do is provide a soft space for them to have as they work through what they're working through. You can give them —"

"— Sanctuary." Elizabeth at last understood. Whoever offered their hearth to those seeking to know, and forgive, and love themselves would need to be able to hold that space. As she had done with her children. It was not a business plan, but a calling, a necessity. She remembered her friends in California, vapid and aloof and unkind. Who could they have been with such an experience? How might they have changed? Sanctuary was a simple concept — a place to rest and heal — but in truth it was a portal for those who were ready. And she in turn was the priestess, the vestal maiden charged with strengthening the seekers and guiding their path. The work before her seemed suddenly monumental.

"You can say no." Tori was watching her carefully. There was no judgment in her tone, no condescension in her eyes. She meant it. It was too big a job to be forced upon anyone. The work had to be done willingly, with an open heart.

Elizabeth breathed deeply. "I don't think I'm ready."

"No," Tori agreed. "But that's not the decision, Elizabeth. It is not whether you already know all you need. It is whether you wish to act as a bridge, whether that is the path you choose. *Is* this who you want to be?"

Elizabeth thought of all of her years of mothering. Finally, she muttered, "I worry I will lose myself, and my joys, and my blessings, to the darkness of others."

"A fair concern, for many have." Tori studied her. "I can teach you ways to protect your energy, but it will be up to you to fill your own cup with a life that you love so much that you can allow overflowing. Only then can you begin doing the deep work."

Fill her own cup. With what, she wondered? Books with friends. Hot coffee on her porch. Her children in the garden, and the pond at sunset. Or sunrise.

And love.

Love was what she wanted to fill her cup. She wanted someone to bring out her passions and her thoughts, her comfort and her curiosity. Joe had shown her snippets of what she wanted, but she had been too proud to admit to herself that her deepest desire was for a love that nourished and filled her, that left her energized instead of drained. A love that would allow her to reach that level of overflowing abundance. A love she could trust.

"Teach me."

***

That evening found her once again in the sacred grove, for the first time since she had emerged from its hollow. A warm red glow emanated from the mycelium as she sat before the tree with her powers activated and her thoughts focused.

"Who do I want to be?"

In front of her, the snow formed statues. Sometimes she appeared in a business suit, other times in voluminous harem pants. Sometimes she sat at a computer, while on the opposite side she danced with abandon. Surrounded by her potential identities, Elizabeth was losing patience. Where was her answer? Why couldn't she find it? Her fingers bent into talons, and without warning all of the snow sculptures exploded, as powder rained down upon her head.

She threw herself onto the ground.

Tori had spoken of a void that would occur between the vision and the embodiment. Somewhere along the line, she would know who she wanted to be, and then it would take time for that person to form.

But she was stuck before the first step had even begun. She had no idea who she wanted to be.

In her mind's eye, Elizabeth saw the dancer. Her breathing slowed. In front of her, the discarded snow began to form a flowing skirt, leading to uncovered waist. Elizabeth saw herself weaving through others on a dance floor, hips rocking smoothly from side to side, a physical manifestation of music she could not hear. That one, she thought. That's the woman I want to be.

Sensual. Powerful. Intentional. Moving so, so slowly.

Perhaps she could sit in the void if she could find a way to enjoy it.

Every fiber of her being revolted. *A waste of time*, her mind said. *An insane daydream*, said her body. Her heart was silent, longing for a reality that it did not believe could happen.

Elizabeth called forth her magic, and the mycelium released its song. Slowly, she got to her feet. Legs bent, she allowed her hips to shift from side to side, sliding up and down her body, while she twisted her wrists towards the sky. She closed her eyes. She saw the grove as it was at night, dark and close, lit from below. On the ground she saw flames, like those at the bonfire, moving aside at her steps. Blindly, she began to dance in a circle. The fire shifted around her and within her, letting loose a wild woman. She spun and dropped and swished in the oak circle. Her breathing quickened, her body pulsed. In her ecstasy, she called out, "Joe!" But he was not there.

She had brought the love all by herself.

Exhausted, she collapsed in the middle of the clearing. What to do with this energy? Her fingers itched to build, to create. Sinking them into the snow, Elizabeth pushed her breath through her teeth. This was the overflowing that Tori had spoken of. Now she understood. She needed a channel to send it through.

The Sanctuary.

She rose to her feet again, and started circling more slowly, swaying her neck to an unknown rhythm. The earth answered her with gentle beats, a piano waltz instead of a frantic tango. Her body stretched each moment to its fullest extent, slowly unfurling like the leaves would do in a few short months. She brought her arms up her body, touching her stomach, her chest, her throat, her hair. How could she make her love go further at The Sanctuary? How could the space expand into a deeper experience?

More, her body whispered. *More guidance. More space. More gathering. More.*

Elizabeth raised one finger in the air, and drew a straight line towards the ground.

Instantly, the snow rose up and rearranged itself. A map of The Sanctuary appeared at her feet, as though she was seeing it from the sky. The house remained still, but the paths around the gardens and forest seemed to pulse. Looking closer, Elizabeth saw the movement was to be found in the blooming flowers of each bed, and tiny people walking about and tending them. In the ring of stones, an icy fire was crackling, and a circle of characters moved rhythmically around it. And on the path that led her here, she saw words appearing in the snow. Seek. Find. Know. Live. A figure knelt in the oak grove, and at the entrance to the clearing, a woman in a full skirt placed a tray on the ground. Steam rose from the impossibly tiny snow teapot, and as she watched, it formed a cloud over the map, until all of it melted away.

Elizabeth ran back to the house and grabbed her carefully organized notebook, ripped it open, and began covering the pages in slanting handwriting and drawings of teapots.

Chapter Twenty-Seven

"**G**rover, you can't put that there."

"I know where to put it."

"Grover, it doesn't fit there."

"It will fit."

"No it —"

"Lisa, let me do my job!"

Lisa rolled her eyes, and Elizabeth hid the smile creeping over her face. She still wasn't sure what the relationship was between these two, but they were good entertainment value while they figured it out. Cory was already walking over to help Grover place the edging (hopefully where it did fit), and Lily was pragmatically calling for Lisa's help a few beds over. Both were bundled in their warmest puffy jackets and snow boots, as was everyone else, prepared for a morning of gardening in the snow.

It had seemed a strange start to this new life she was weaving for herself. When she had spread the word that she needed volunteers in the garden, the residents of Solace Spring had looked baffled.

"It's February." They looked at her closely, confused by her upbeat tone. "We can't plant anything for months."

"I know," Elizabeth assured them. "We aren't planting. We're building."

And so they were. Digging into the snow, they unearthed the old flower beds and began to expand them. Sometimes they would join two or three together, using wood from the forest to boundary the new space. Sometimes they would simply take a small square and give it new, rounder edges, letting it spill over onto the path and rerouting the walkway to match.

"Why are we doing this NOW?" Denny said plaintively.

"So we're ready when the snow melts," Elizabeth answered. "We can't start growing yet, but we can create space."

Truthfully, Elizabeth knew she could have waited. And she could have done the work herself. But that was not what The Sanctuary needed. It needed the energy of the town, the injection of intention. It needed to be prepared to hold more. And so she had begun the work of making room, knowing that the physical barriers were far less relevant than the cooperation she saw between her friends.

She had put a note on the Eyes Up bulletin board, asking for volunteers and ashes. Mystified, people had turned up with spent firewood and chunks of charcoal, which she happily tipped into each bed, dying the snow a vivid black. Denny had, as always, supplied coffee, and Elizabeth had made her trademark muffins with the last of the summer's honey. People sat upon the porch, looking out at the white landscape with its black polka dots, the dark skeletons of trees fencing everyone in together. They talked of their own gardens, their hopes for spring, the plans they had made to do one thing or another, the heaviness they hoped to escape in this new year. A regular rotation set in, each person working, then resting, then connecting, then working again.

Elizabeth moved between beds, helping to find fallen tree boughs of just the right length, standing on her trusty step stool to make sure each circle was as round as the moon. As the work wrapped up, she took from her pocket a handful of acorns, collected from beneath the split oak tree. She placed one in the center of each circle, buried it in snow and ashes, and finally decided that, for now, the work was done.

Stragglers continued chatting as she removed her gloves and switched to mittens. It was difficult to socialize in these winter months, she had realized. Everyone went to their own space, letting their body dictate their time. Moments like these were precious. A chance to remember that they were not isolated, after all. The world was simply waiting for them.

"So what will you do with this?" Lisa was frowning at her. "The flowers have always been fine here."

"They're beautiful," Elizabeth agreed. "I just thought there was room for more. The kids and I started planning different garden spaces for different purposes. Some will have flowers around a certain theme, some will have vegetables and fruits the guests can harvest, some will have herbs for teas and scented candles." Here she stole a look at Tori, who had graced them with her presence but had spent the whole of her time on the porch with a mug of tea she brought herself. Her eyes twinkled now as Elizabeth outlined her vision. "I just want guests to have multiple ways to connect to the earth here. Something for everyone, you know?"

Lisa nodded sagely. "I suppose that's true. Not everyone has the space."

"Are you changing anything else?" Grover asked gruffly. His beady eyes squinted sideways at her, and she understood that any and all changes were deeply suspect.

"Not really," Elizabeth said. And it was true. She would change little else in the landscape. But she would also offer direction to those who came. "I'll add a bench and table where the path meets the forest, for people to sit and write or think." A tiny tea table, big enough for her to leave a tray and a candle. "I'm going to create a little guide for the property, explaining some of the history of the place and how people might best explore it." This was already in the works, along with the redesign of the website Tina had helped her to create. "But I am planning on holding more gatherings like this one." Eyes lit up, and tight faces loosened. "I figure during the week there will be fewer guests, so that's my chance to share the space with all of you." Her gift to the community. The gift of space.

"I can build you the table and bench."

"Grover, thank you, that would be amazing."

"As long as Cory helps me."

Cory, just walking up the steps, was caught off guard, but Grover was soon talking measurements and pine versus maple and safe stains for the garden, and they were away with their project as Elizabeth began to pick up plates and mugs. Tori put a hand on her arm, and Elizabeth stopped what she was doing.

"I brought you something," Tori said quietly. "Now that you've taken up your role here. Matty would have wanted you to have it." Reaching into her coat pocket, she pulled out an old-fashioned recipe card, yellowed and creased, and placed it in Elizabeth's hand. "He memorized it long ago, so he left it in my keeping. Although," and here she took a bite of Elizabeth's muffins, "I don't believe you need it." The older woman squeezed her shoulder, and walked away.

Elizabeth took the card and squinted at the cramped handwriting. Muffins. It was Matty's old recipe, served to every guest who arrived.

And Elizabeth could see without reference that it was exactly the same as her own.

Chuckling, she pocketed the card, which she would frame and hang in the inn's tiny kitchenette to be shared with her guests. She went pack to gathering dishes, as Denny heaved herself up to grab the two remaining cups and followed Elizabeth inside.

"Did you hear?"

Elizabeth turned from the kitchen sink.

"Hear what?"

"He's back."

Elizabeth turned back to the water. "He's been back." Joe's van had remained at the mechanic's since New Year's, she knew. She had seen it traveling the road up to the maples. No one mentioned it to her, but she thought her friends had been watching her a little more carefully. There was no need for it, Elizabeth knew. She wasn't angry. Even the sadness didn't hold her for long. As long as she didn't need to see him, or feel his presence near her.

It wasn't that Elizabeth held a grudge. In truth, while she thought of Joe often, he had held a place in her life before she had become herself. He was part of an ending, not a beginning. Had he stayed...well, perhaps she would not have become at all. And what a loss that would have been. But now, if he was back, they would need to start over.

The only question was — as what?

"Nah, he's been hiding," Denny said emphatically. "No one has really seen him since Christmas. Not for groceries, not for work, not even to warm his hands by someone's furnace. But he stopped in for coffee yesterday," Her side eye was pronounced, and Elizabeth pretended to ignore it. Denny softened her voice a little. "He's back."

Joe was the last distraction she needed. She had just started booking guests. She had crafted community fireside evenings to begin at the Spring Equinox. She felt good in her skin.

She couldn't let him take that from her. Or let her take it from herself.

"Look, I know that Joe is beloved around here. I know he's important. He was important to me." She hadn't admitted this aloud before. It was heavy on her tongue. Denny's eyes blinked sympathetically. "I have a lot of work here right now, and by the time I'm done, it will be sugaring season." Joe's lessons had stuck after all. "We'll stay clear of each other for now. When the snow melts ... we'll see."

Cocking her head to one side, Denny seemed to be formulating a question. After a minute, she slowly said, "What's the vision, Elizabeth? You both live in this town. It's not big. You're going to see each other. What do you want it to be?"

A few months before, this question would have sent her spiraling. Now, Elizabeth felt a wave of peace rolling through her chest. She looked out the kitchen window, and Joe's face appeared in the wan sunlight that flowed into her home.

"Love." Elizabeth turned to Denny. "It can't be anything but love. So if he's not ready for that, we'll need to keep clear of each other." She placed the last dish in the drying rack. "But the love will be here if he ever decides he's ready."

Denny set her hands on her hips. "You can't wait on him, Elizabeth. He may never come back."

"I know it. He's stubborn and rigid and I'm not sure I'm what he wants." She shrugged. "But my life is plenty full, Denny. I have you." She hugged her friend. "I have the girls at book club and my awesome kids, and hey, Mitch and I have started taking dance lessons in Northampton!" The erstwhile couple had run into each other weeks ago in the grocery store, and realized that while there was little spark between them, they enjoyed each other's company. Mitch had taken her to a fundraiser ball on Valentine's Day, and the dancing had lifted her spirits so dramatically that she was hooked. Her body melted into the music and allowed her to be carried away in someone else's arms. She was addicted to the movement, despite the long snowy drive on Friday nights. "This space is going to be so incredible, Denny. I'll get to create what I want here. A life I want. An offering I want. All of that is love, too. So if someone shows up and wants to be part of it, that invitation is open. If not," she shrugged, "they don't belong here, and I don't need to give them my energy."

Still looking concerned, Denny hugged her again. "Promise you won't let him hurt you again."

"I won't," Elizabeth promised. "I'm ready this time."

Denny sighed, and held Elizabeth's shoulders in her hands. "Lord knows if anyone could soften that man's heart, it's you." One last hug. "We'll just see what happens."

They walked to the porch, where everyone was collecting their things. Elizabeth stood in her red parka and waved as everyone drove away, shouting her thanks and promises of good things to come. As she turned to head inside, she noticed a van parked just outside of Lisa's driveway. For a moment she simply stared at it. Then she stretched her magic forward, letting The Sanctuary multiply her energy. Bright white tendrils appeared on the ground, racing like a river towards the van, which briefly glowed in the light that surrounded it. Elizabeth sent her embrace into the light, holding him against her while her lips brushed his own. The snow around the van began to melt, leaving a pool of water behind.

Suddenly the ignition started, and the van spun out of the mud to turn around and head back to town. The light chased him down the road as he went.

Spring

Chapter Twenty-Eight

Like the apple trees, Elizabeth had rested this winter. She had stayed in the oak grove and listened to its teachings, and she had studied with Tori to understand them better. The Sanctuary would be offering weekend yoga classes and sound baths in the warmer months, and had already begun to facilitate fireside visualizations in the winter. Many members of her book club had become enthusiastic participants, some even beginning their own studies of earth, and life, and magic. They brought friends and family, and Denny crafted warm beverages to soothe the soul. She and Lisa were now working together on a line of herbal teas, inspired by Lisa's prolific garden. For her part, Elizabeth had slowly learned how to integrate different strains of her energy into the treats she baked, deepening the experience and connecting the hearts of those who broke bread together.

Meanwhile, the inn had begun to receive a steady stream of weekend guests, mostly locals looking for a staycation but occasionally visitors from Boston or even New York. Reviews had so far been good, and Elizabeth was pleased to find that beyond a few extra muffins and an extension of good cheer, the comings and goings of these guests had affected her life little. The Sanctuary chose its visitors carefully. Early plans were in place for a transcendence retreat later that summer, with Tori leading a variety of activities for women wishing to let the space transform them into who they were always meant to be. Sometimes Elizabeth felt that too many things were coming her way, and she would sink back into her old anxieties, but she found that as long as she allowed paths to open for her, rather than forcing them, she never received more than she was meant to hold.

The children had flourished beyond all reason. Cory was creating a local astronomy club, and often spent his evenings on local hilltops with friends and a telescope. Lily's drawings were for sale in Tori's shop, helping her raise money for her own car. Dylan was a regular fixture at dinner now, and a rotating group of teens always seemed to find a place around Elizabeth's table. As much as she loved the community, she was also glad that the children had developed lives away from the house, so that she had time for rest. Lots of well-deserved, and long overdue, rest.

Green buds appeared on the plants before the ice had melted. Strange, the way life and death could coexist. Elizabeth still marveled at the wisdom of the earth, and how well it held its opposites in union. White blossoms would appear within weeks. Firm, red apples would hang from this bough in six months time. The ice made these things possible, allowed the tree to rest, and awaken, knowing where its priorities lay.

Following their hibernation, the maple trees had begun to give up their sweetness. Sugaring season transformed the rural community, calling each family from their homes and welcoming them back into the sunlight. Suddenly each weekend was a new celebration, filled with fried dough carts and fresh maple cotton candy, cheery signs and vats of cider lining the roadside. The Whits took full advantage of the epicurean delights that were the heart of Solace Spring, learning the grades of syrup and choosing their favorite sugar houses. Elizabeth tried every maple candy for twenty miles, but none were as sweet and soft as the gift Joe had once offered her. So she would walk through the groves and touch her fingers to the metal buckets that hung from each tap, slowly gathering the drips of clear sap that would be collected, boiled, transformed, and consumed. She felt the trees, their sacrifice and their growth, the joy they received from the caretaking they did. And she remembered what Joe had told her — that he would teach her this skill when the trees awakened.

One Friday in March, while blossoms were still tightly wound on the tree, mother watched daughter croon sweet songs of fireflies at Eyes Up, where her sets had become a regular feature. Relaxed and content, Elizabeth inhabited her body differently now, letting it settle into space rather than perch on the edges of life, waiting to run at the first sign of discomfort. Her eyes were half closed as the music ran over her, a familiar stream she had heard echoing from down the hallway over the last several weeks. Her tea smelled of lavender and mint, and something she couldn't place. She turned to Denny.

"What's in this one?"

Denny looked sternly suspicious. "Secret herbs."

"I got that. Which ones? I smell the flowers, and the peppermint, but there's something underneath."

"Ohhhhhhh." Denny walked over and took the seat next to her with a delighted look on her face. "That's the surprise ingredient. Wakens the body." She leaned in with a salacious grin and whispered, "Pine needles."

"Pine needles?"

She could taste them now. Astringent, clean, woody. Bright on the taste buds, then slowly warming, comforting. Not a Christmas taste, somehow, but a taste of spring. Evergreen indeed.

Lily finished her set to general applause, bowed deeply, and came to join her mom. After downing Elizabeth's newly refreshed cup of tea, she asked to go to an after party at Dylan's. Cory was attending, too, a gesture Elizabeth deeply appreciated as Cory's social skills were still slow to increase. Every chance he got to be a normal teenager was a gift. Blessings received, they left, and Elizabeth returned home alone, still tasting pine on her tongue and humming lightning bug notes. Twilight lit the sky behind a blaze of fire that spread across the heavens. It was such a glorious sight that Elizabeth decided to take a walk rather than head into the house. After so many months inside, a sunset wander was exactly what she needed.

Down the road she went, inhaling the scent of wet earth and new grass. Patches of snow intermingled with puddles of mud, and bright hillocks of green were beginning to poke through both. No matter how rough the conditions these little blades were determined to make their way through, reaching up again and again, regardless of how many times they were felled. Elizabeth took care not to tread on them, skirting the tiny swaths of seedlings and choosing a path to the right that remained resolutely brown.

At the base of the hill, she realized that this was the glen she had found herself in many months ago, when she had first arrived in Solace Spring. What was then a haven of green and golden leaves was now a dark and damp forest, with bare trees shaking out the first buds of the season. Little fists slowly unfurled to reveal tender leaves, tiny and pale, that she knew would grow exponentially within days. By her next trip, the canopy would be lush and cool, with flowers carpeting the ground.

She smiled to herself as the little grove revealed itself to her, showing her the signs of what was to come.

Then she heard the river.

It was running again. The full gushing symphony that had called to her last summer was still a thing of the future — ice likely still held much of the water in check. But enough had thawed to produce an audible trickle, and she moved towards it eagerly.

When last she had come, the river had been a soundtrack. Now, it was an experience. Elizabeth marched carefully towards its sound, humming Lily's songs under her breath, and choosing her steps carefully in the mud. As it grew louder, she scanned the ground for signs of water, but saw only an assortment of river rocks rubbed by the flow. How many years, she wondered? How long did it take to smooth a stone? The satiny surface meant that it had been tumbled about, turned, pushed, smashed by pebbles and scoured by sand. Surely an uncomfortable experience. Yet over time, earth and water achieved a balance, and the stone was able to sit serenely on the river bed, helping the water move forward, and holding it when it needed to stay put.

A large boulder jutted over the river's edge. Elizabeth scrambled onto it, and sat with her feet dangling, watching the thin stream of water crawl along, getting stuck on great blocks of ice that remained where the bedrock went deeper. It carved beautiful shapes as it traveled. The river pushed tiny inlets into the frozen earth, waves pressing against the silt and clay to make quiet bays where tadpoles and ducklings would jostle for real estate. Ice undulated below the surface, curving first one way and then another, slowly melting back to its primary state. The water had been trapped, just as she had. Something had immobilized them, and even when they were free, it took time to become. To unlearn, and let go. It was painful to see who she had been in that state. Frozen, like the ice. Immobile and rigid. It had cost her so much, so many possibilities, so many people. Or perhaps just one. But once everything fell apart, they were finally able to run forward once more. She only wished they could run together, now that she was free.

Sitting on the boulder, Elizabeth looked out at the black expanse of trees, and the tiny unseen kernels of life they held. She closed her eyes. Silently, she asked to see ahead. Her senses registered the rapid growth of spring leaves, and heard fawns munching on fresh green grass. Bees buzzed around her head, and the sun warmed her face. What had been a trickle grew to a deafening roar, and then slowed to the joyous run she had encountered almost a year ago. She heard music from someplace. Gladness filled her heart, and she swayed to the unknown harmony, feeling held and safe and loved. Beside her, a weight fell into place, and Elizabeth's skin prickled with the warm, steady breath of another. She pulled herself back into the present. Opening her eyes, she saw the world as it was in this moment, black and muddy and waiting. But the scent of coffee and maple remained.

Wordlessly, Joe reached over and took her hand in his. She felt the fear in her throat mingle with hope. Maybe too much had happened. Maybe too much had changed. With the cold rock beneath her and the sun in her eyes, she waited. She breathed. Slowly, Joe pulled her close to him, and snuggled her into his hip. He kissed the top of her head, and gently whispered "I missed you." A dam burst inside of her, the frightened little girl carried away by the flood of relief that wove through her body. Eagerly, she turned her face to him. One delicate finger tucked a strand of hair behind her ear. His eyes were clearer now, the lines around them somehow softened. They reflected the light that beamed onto them. Elizabeth allowed herself to fall into that light, into his arms, and onto his lips once more, as Joe gently pressed his mouth to hers and uttered, over and over, "I'm sorry". She swallowed his apology, and showered him in forgiveness.

Love and joy sprang from a well within her as he gently pushed her back, looked into her eyes and said, "Elizabeth ... I don't know if this will work. I don't know if I am capable of giving you what you want or what you deserve. I don't know if I am going to want to ... or if you will want me to. There are a lot of differences here, and they aren't just going to go away." Sadness creased his forehead as he cupped her cheeks in his hands. "I want you with me. I believe we're supposed to be together. But I don't want to hurt you."

A tsunami built in her chest, and the darkness began to scream. But this time, it felt a long way off, and Elizabeth, with the sun on her face, stepped in front of it. Timelines swelled and melted away, seasons rolled one atop the other, and in every future, she felt him beside her. Her heart overflowed. And as she allowed love to wash through her, her hands found his face, touching the lines that would deepen with age, tendrils of hair that would wane silver and white. Time passed in a heartbeat, yet in this moment, the fear was still written in his eyes. He could not see the future. He could only see what was in front of him.

"Will you stay for today?"

Joe looked at her, sun shining on her soft hair, eyes blue as the spring sky. Mutely, he nodded.

"Then let's be together today."

Beneath them, the river laughed and the earth sang, as that slow smile spread over his face. Elizabeth had just enough time to return it before his lips descended enthusiastically on her own.

"There's no place I would rather be."

He held her against him as they watched the sun set over the hills of Solace Spring.

Epilogue: May Day

The days were unpredictable now. Sometimes spring, sometimes summer, with a dash of winter still thrown in at random. At The Sanctuary, the garden was beginning to grow, well beyond the expected yield. Lettuces erupted from the earth to become healthful salads for hearth tender and guest alike, while tulips kissed the thorns of the rose until they released their blossoms. Tall spires of delphinium bordered the celestial garden of black petunias and white jasmine, which opened its petals at night and suffused the whole garden with its delicate scent. Apple blossoms showered the pathways, their white petals fading to pale pink hearts, releasing the tree as the fruit ripened.

She, too, had ripened in the spring. Carefully balancing her energy between the inn, her children, her life, and her relationship was constant work, but she found that the more she enjoyed each, the more it fed her. Overflowing energy moved between all of her connections. She poured it back into the land, giving her guests encouragement to wander the spaces that called to them. Some sought the peace of the pond, others the grounding abundance of the gardens. A select few were called to the grove, and it would always wake her with its light. She would wait with a cup of Denny's best tea for them to emerge, and give them a place to unburden themselves and find their own path forward. This work, in particular, often drained her energy. So she called upon Joe to help her fill it.

After his return, whispered conversations were held on the river-bank, with hushed apologies reaching through the twilight. No fault was found, no blame assigned. Instead, they honored the great un-known that frightened them both, and decided to take it slow. Joe became a fixture at family dinners once again, and she knew Cory in particular was grateful to have him. While he was not in any way a father, the space at the table no longer felt empty, and the feeling of a missing piece was greatly lessened. Someday, Elizabeth began to think, perhaps she would explain to the kids. That not all people are meant to be parents, that some simply could not do the work of loving. That their father may not have been one, really, but just a man who gave them life, so that others could guide them to where they needed to be. She hoped that one day, they would understand that sometimes leaving is the right choice.

When the kids went to bed, Joe and Elizabeth would sit on the porch, snuggled in Matty's loving blankets, talking of nothing or not talking at all. Elizabeth found she didn't need to fill that space. They could exist happily, just holding hands. Without her fears, she was able to enjoy him as he was, and this in turn lifted the pressure on him. He had not pushed her away, nor made any plans to leave. If anything, he was more consistent now than he had ever been, and Elizabeth knew this had other ramifications as well. He had been asking for steady work around town, rather than relying on seasonal bits and pieces. Now officially a part time mechanic, he could be found heading to the fields and forests in the afternoon, before tinkering on cars in the afternoon. His van, recovered and refurbished after the hard winter, was once again down by the river, where they often spent weekend evenings, watching the water warble by.

Only one thing remained. Joe had not touched her body since his return.

This time, Elizabeth knew it was not a lack of desire, but instead a need to complete each step in order. To find stability on each stone across the water before leaping to the next. But after weeks of simple kisses and tender embraces, Elizabeth began to feel that the time had come.

On the first evening in May, she asked him to walk with her. Leaving the children to their movie, they wandered past the red roses in the garden, and the tiny scarlet posies on the path — they had multiplied since her blood had grazed the earth last fall, and continued to show their brazen hearts to the sky. Hand in hand, they passed the stone circle, the pond, and the tea table. And before they knew it, they stood before the oak tree, with white light pulsing from the ground.

Slowly, she raised her hands to Joe's face, letting her fingers brush over the lush hair, the high cheekbones sliding down to his full beard, the heavy forehead full of worries. She looked into his eyes, and spoke the words that had been piercing her heart since they met.

"I love you."

Silence.

And then he bent his head to her and whispered, "I love you."

Their lips met softly, the first trembling steps of an exploration, but they met no obstacles. Elizabeth readily deepened the kiss, and Joe's surprise showed only in his smile. As he put his hands around her waist, she shuffled her feet closer, only to find her foot striking something hard on the ground. She looked down.

It was a candle. Half black, half white.

Elizabeth grinned. "Do you have a light?"

He pulled a lighter from his pocket and looked at her quizzically. Silently calling upon every energy present — his, hers, The Sanctuary's — she knelt in front of the oak tree and placed the candle on the ground. Joe's hand caressed her neck as she sparked a flame and lit the wick. Within seconds, a ring of low fire had erupted around them, not wildly but in soft flickers like the candle, melting away the last vestiges of snow and giving them just enough light to see each other clearly under the crescent moon.

They came together like a wave crashing upon the shore. Love had opened the flow between them and passion surged on both sides. Elizabeth pulled the ribbon from her hair, letting it fall over her shoulders as she settled onto his lap. Looking him in the eyes, she began to smooth her shirt upwards. His hand stopped her.

"You don't have to, Elizabeth," he whispered softly. "We can go as slow as you need to."

"I know," she whispered back. Gently, she took his hand, and reached up under her skirt to place it upon her thigh. A low moan escaped him as he squeezed the flesh there, and she answered it with a cry of her own. He helped her out of her shirt, and kissed the curves of her stomach as she lay upon the ground. In turn, she pulled his flannel away and let her hand glide under the t-shirt beneath, feeling the liquid-hot skin and letting herself be carried away with the simple touch, the pinnacle of so much longing. They lay there a moment, lips brushing against each other, murmurs of adoration flowing back and forth, each waiting for the next chapter to begin. Elizabeth found that she could not start, but she could utter the first word.

"Please."

Faded jeans were added to the pile, followed by her gathered skirt. Elizabeth let him nudge the silver fastenings of her bra, until her bosom fell from its restraints, only to be covered again by Joe's warm mouth. His finger reached between her legs and found the pool awaiting him, swearing lightly beneath his breath as he began to push forward.

"No." Elizabeth placed a hand on his chest.

Breathing raggedly, Joe stopped, his eyes closed. "We can stop, if you want. Or we can just go that far. Just tell me what feels good to you."

Elizabeth sat up just enough to take his mouth in hers, nibbling the lower lip. "You feel good to me." And she deftly removed his shorts and held the length of him in her hand.

He looked at her, now gleaming from sex and firelight, a primal goddess activated and waiting here for him. She smiled, and kissed him again, allowing one hand to gently pet and pull as the other pulled away her own last scrap of cloth.

Joe held her in his arms, flames reflecting in his bronze skin. "I love you."

"I love you," she answered. And then he was inside of her, in a magic older than time, creating new lands and new pathways from their union. She felt stars burning in the heavens inside of her, and they breathed in rhythm with the land beneath them as it pulsed. Joe pushed deeper, and Elizabeth arched her back to see the oak behind her, exultant in her ecstasy. She was the gateway now. A portal was born between her legs, and she felt Joe enter her so completely that as she surrendered to his love, they became one. She straightened up to hold him close to her heart as the world spun out of control and into place again, and the two of them exploded in harmony, lips sealed and hearts entwined, surrounded by fire and ice.

Years passed. Lifetimes transformed. Pathways rose and fell according to their journey, letting them move from one evolution to another.

But this union would remain, the anchor for all of their wanderings. No matter how far they went, or how much time passed between them, they would always be able to find Sanctuary within each other.

Support Independent Authors!

Love it?

Leave A Review
on Goodreads

Love it?

Leave A Review
on Amazon

About Three Sisters Sanctuary

The Sanctuary is loosely based upon a real place - Three Sisters Sanctuary in Goshen, Massachusetts. Three Sisters Sanctuary is the creation of artist Richard M. Richardson, who began building the sanctuary over 25 years ago. Lying on eight acres of property and surrounded by 3900 acres of state forest, this monumental creation began as a home and evolved into an art project that merged art and nature. Multiple artists have collaborated over the years, contributing sculptures, gardens, and art objects to the sprawling grounds. Visitors are welcome to come and explore, and lucky guests may also stay on property, as I do. I encourage you to visit https://threesisterssanctuary.com to learn more about Richard's work.

Three Sisters Sanctuary invites you to heal the heart, mind and body through the Merging of Art and Nature. This is a space in service to others to receive and disperse Life's gifts and energies.

Shadow Work with Sanctuary

At its heart, *Sanctuary* is a story of shadow work – the inner reflection we do to know, understand, and accept the darkness that lies within each of us. While you may work through these in therapy or other healing containers, this is work that we should each be willing to enter as a regular part of our existence, in flow with the seasons of our life. It is my hope that this story inspires you to do some of your own shadow work, and to this end, I offer the questions below to get you started. After all...

The magic is in the darkness.

Summer

1. What mask do you present to the world? What programming, teaching, or conditioning taught you that this mask was an asset?

2. What roles have you taken on to please others?

3. What emotions do you share with the world? What emotions do you hide?

4. Do you know what your strengths are? Do you share them proudly?

5. When do you feel truly seen? Do you enjoy being seen?

6. Do you believe you are capable of greatness? What is in your way?

7. What is your greatest success?

8. What is your deepest failure?

Fall

1. What are you afraid of?

2. When do you feel most anxious?

3. What obstacles to intimacy lie within you?

4. What do you see when you look in the mirror? What parts of you are vulnerable?

5. Where in your life do you judge yourself most harshly?

6. Who really knows you? What parts of you do you hide from those closest to you?

7. What memories are still painful for you to touch? How do these impact your present moment?

8. When you stand alone in the darkness, what is waiting for you?

Winter

1. What does rest mean to you? When do you truly rest? What stands in the way of your hibernation?

2. How often do you sit in silence? What feelings arise as you sit in quiet solitude?

3. Do you fear death? What endings do you fear?

4. What parts of you do you believe have disappeared forever?

5. What are you refusing to let go of?

6. Where do you hold a "scarcity mindset" – a belief that there is not enough for you? Where do you believe that you are not enough?

7. What are you ready to leave behind? Why have you held it so long?

8. What do you want to say to those you love?

Spring

1. What seeds do you hope to plant in your life?

2. What are you afraid to try again?

3. If you could start a chapter of your life over, which one would you choose, and what would you do differently?

4. How do you treat yourself with tenderness? Or, if this is a challenge, why do you struggle to treat yourself tenderly?

5. What have you created with your whole soul? What stops

you from creating more?

6. How long has it been since you have allowed yourself to be childlike? How can you invite more innocence and play into your life?

7. What shadows have followed you since childhood? How can you protect your inner child now?

8. Who or what do you need to forgive, so that you may move away from that chapter of your past?

Book Club Questions

1. What themes were woven into the narrative? How did each character contribute to those themes?

2. How do we see the eras of a woman's life – maiden, mother, queen, and crone – in the characters of Solace Spring? What does this demonstrate about women?

3. How does Elizabeth represent the modern American woman?

4. Motherhood is central to the plot of *Sanctuary*. How is it portrayed? Is this style of motherhood realistic, or dramatized? Is Elizabeth a good mother? Why?

5. What do the siblings, Lily and Cory, reveal about the differing ways children respond to the same environment?

6. Neurodivergence plays a role in *Sanctuary*, perhaps in several ways. How does the intersection between neurodivergence

and community contribute to the story?

7. Small town America is quickly vanishing. What messages does *Sanctuary* send about small town living? In particular, what role does technology play in Solace Spring?

8. The relationship between Joe and Elizabeth is complex. What is in the way of a healthy love between them? Why does it bother us to see relationships like this? What is our expectation for love?

9. How does the dance between the masculine and feminine energies play out in the book? Which characters embody these energies most strongly?

10. What symbols lie in the physical landscape of The Sanctuary, and the wider space of Solace Spring?

11. How do the seasons function in the narrative? What does each season represent?

12. The magic in *Sanctuary* is very subtle, and sometimes we aren't sure if it is real or imagined. Why is this? What is the role of magic in reality?

13. *Sanctuary* is a story of healing. What does healing look like in this narrative? Did it feel like any healing you have done?

Acknowledgements

This book was a labor of awakening. My deepest gratitude to everyone who helped me wake up from the inauthentic life I was leading, from my friends and family to my healers and gurus. Blessings to the Sisterhood of Avalon, who have held space for me in their hearts and taught me so much about the mysteries of this world. My biggest hug to Richard M. Richardson, creator of magical sanctuaries in the real world. And of course, my enduring love to my partners, who inspired me to such highs and lows of emotion that I could do nothing but write them into fiction in order to move them from my body. Thank you for lighting my way.

About the Author

Ember Markussen weaves a life of soulful storytelling and shadow work. A Sister of Avalon, she holds undergraduate (Smith College) and Master's (UC Irvine) degrees in History, and is certified in Breathwork, Reiki, and End-of-Life Doula Work. Ember is passionate about feminine energy, sacred union, and the creation of a New Earth. She mothers children, cats, and ducks, and devotes herself to tending her hearth. You can find her at TheStoryPriestess.com.